The Diary of a Side Chick 6

A Naptown Hood Drama

Tamicka Higgins

© 2015

Disclaimer

This is a work of fiction. Names, places, characters and events are all fictitious for the reader's pleasure. Any similarities to real people, places, events, living or dead are all coincidental.

This book contains sexually explicit content that is intended for ADULTS ONLY (+18).

Chapter 1

Embarrassment and humiliation can take its toll on just about anyone. However, these two terrible feelings will really affect someone who has already had to deal with hard times. When Desirae ran back into her mother's house, after taking the naked beating in the front yard from Greg's wife, Veronica, her heart pounded. She held her chest all the way up the steps, across the porch, and in through the front door. Once inside of her mother's living room – the very doorway that was next to where she'd been on her knees for Greg – Desirae quickly slammed the door shut. There she was, alone in the house except for her sleeping twins upstairs. Her round ass pushed against the door as she tried to come to grips with what had happened.

"I don't fuckin' believe this!" Desirae said to herself. She looked at her beautiful, thick body. There were cuts and leaves and bits of grass on just about every visible area. The side of her face stung from Veronica's hard slaps, and her head throbbed from having been hurt so badly. Her eyes swelled with the tears from her horrifying experience – tears that would soon roll down the sides of her face and drip off of her jaw, onto her mother's floor.

Desirae buried her face in her hands, shaking her head as she imagined all of the eyes looking at her. There were so many people from up and down the street who came walking up. Nobody did anything to stop it, which was really no surprise to anyone, not even Desirae. She thought about how she'd seen Tron. His eyes were so cold and indifferent toward her when she'd finally gotten up off the ground. There he sat, in his SUV, as if he had simply pulled over on the side of the road to make a phone call or send a text. Within seconds, Desirae's blood boiled.

"Fuck him!" she yelled out loud, thinking that maybe Tron had been the person to tell Veronica where Greg was. Desirae then came to her senses, realizing that all of that happening probably wasn't likely. She shook her head, unable to pull her soul out of the shame. Never in her life had she thought she'd get drug across her mother's front yard, naked.

3

Desirae rushed quickly toward the dining room. She looked back at the large living room window. Through the slits in the purple sheer curtains, she could see that people were starting to make their way back down the street. Desirae huffed as she continued to the dining room.

"I just got my ass beat over some little dick ass nigga!" Desirae yelled and her fists balled with frustration. "I don't fuckin' believe this shit. I just got my ass beat like that, in front of everybody."

Desirae wrapped some ice in a clean washcloth and held it over her swollen eye. She climbed the steps to the second floor after taking a quick glance at her sons, Titan and James. Her legs jiggled as she hurriedly climbed the steps. Much of her spirit was dampened by what she was going to see in the bathroom mirror. With how her face felt, Greg's wife had really given it to her.

Desirae walked into her mother's bathroom at the end of the hall. "Fuck!" she yelled, upon seeing her face.

Scratches slashed across the smooth, brown skin of her cheeks. Both eyes were somewhat blackened, with the left one being far more noticeable than the right eye. Above her eyes, at just about the middle of her forehead, was a leaf of some sort. She pushed it away then went back to assessing the damage. She then noticed how red the sides of her cheeks were under the scratches, not to mention how red and wet her eyes looked.

Desirae's eyes then moved to her lower body. Just like downstairs in the living room, it was very clear that she'd just gotten into a fight while naked. Parts of her body, now in the light and mirror of her mother's bathroom, were blotched with dirt and grass. She quickly wiped them away. Her stinging shins were clear indicators that she'd been drug around a little bit during the fight. A few of her nails had broken off also, while there were patches in her hair where Veronica's unbelievable, and almost manly, grip had taken its toll.

Desirae's chest pumped up and down as she pulled the ice away from her face and looked at herself in the mirror. She couldn't do anything except think about Tron, as he had been

4

Contents

To the Reader

Do you remember as a small child listening to folktales? Perhaps later, when you could read on your own, you enjoyed reading favorite folktales.

In *World Folktales*, you will discover stories from many differ-ent countries around the world. You may be familiar with one or two folktales in this collection, but you will discover new stories as well. And before you read a folktale, you will learn something about life in the country from which the story comes. You will also find a variety of activities before and after each tale to help you improve your reading, writing, listening, and speaking.

Each story in *World Folktales* explores a common theme in the lives of people everywhere: birth and childhood, challenge and adventure, love and marriage, or death and inheritance. You will enjoy discovering how the themes of these folktales relate to your life, too.

Birth and Childhood

PART ONE

Why the Baby Says "Goo"

Native American

Why are things the way they are? Native Americans, who have inhabited what is now the United States since long before the arrival of Columbus, told many stories to try to answer this question. This story, for example, tells how babies act—and why.

_____

Before You Read

Discuss these questions.

1. What facts do you know about Native Americans?
2. How do babies act? What do they like to do?
3. What, do you think, does the word *goo* in the title mean? Clue: It is a sound word.

the last person whose eyes she'd seen before rushing back into the house.

"So, he just gon' watch me, the mother of his children, get her ass beat by some crazy bitch?" Desirae said out loud to herself. There was something about that idea that just didn't sit well with her.

Not giving much thought to what she was going to do next, Desirae turned around. She grabbed her cell phone in the bedroom and called Tron as quickly as she could. She stood in the open space of the bedroom and bit her bottom lip as the phone rang. The light shined in through the blinds, causing bright slits to cross over her bruised, dirty body.

"Wassup?" Tron answered, his voice sounding as if nothing was going on but the rent.

"What the fuck you mean *what's up*?" Desirae asked with her voice already elevated. "What the fuck was your problem, Tron? Huh? What the fuck was your problem, nigga?"

"What you mean?" Tron asked. This time, he sounded as if he were using his library voice. "There you go, gettin' loud again, Desirae. What you mean what is my problem? You called me."

"Nigga, you know what the fuck I'm talkin' bout," Desirae told him. "You know exactly what the fuck I'm talkin' bout. I don't even know why you try'na act brand new and act like you ain't see what was happenin' to me fuckin' ten minutes ago and shit, out on my front yard and shit."

"I didn't know what was goin' on," Tron said. "Who was the chick on top though? Damn, that bitch could fight!"

"Nigga, you lucky you not in front of me right now or else I'd slap the shit out of you," Desirae said, picking up on what he was insinuating. "That fuckin' bitch is crazy, nigga. She crazy. She coulda killed me or some shit."

"Who the fuck is she anyway?" Tron asked. "She came walkin' all up on the porch and shit, lookin' mad as fuck, like she was about to beat some ass. Next thing I know, just when I hopped in the ride, I look back, and there are two chicks out in the front yard with niggas from up and down the street

5

comin' to watch and shit, you know. What the fuck you do to her, Desirae? You had to do something."

Desirae paused for a minute. "Nigga, I ain't do shit to that bitch," she said. "I ain't do shit to her."

"See, there you go again, Desirae," Tron said. "You and that lyin' ass is prolly what got that ass beat. That's why I ain't wanna help. You done did somethin'. Who was ole dude that was sittin' in the house like he fuckin' stayin' there and shit?"

"That ain't none of your fuckin' business, Tron," Desirae said. "I don't belong to you. Remember, you ain't even want me." She sniffled – not because of her feelings toward Tron, but because of how much pain her body was in at that moment. To compound these feelings, her soul was emotionally crushed from the humiliation of it all. In so many ways, Desirae still felt as if the eyes of her mother's neighbors were on her, watching a cat fight turn into a straight beat down. "Plus, I got a life too."

"I know you do," Tron sound, sounding as if he were snickering on the other end. "And that's why I'mma let you live."

Desirae snapped her neck then pressed her lips together tightly. "Listen to me you no good, lyin' ass nigga," she said with so much confidence. "I'm the fuckin' mother to your baby twins and all you do, nigga, is watch me get my ass beat on the front lawn like ain't shit go on and like it don't affect you or nothin'."

"Oh, it do affect me," Tron said. "I felt bad for you, Desirae. I did. Man, that shit looked rough from across the street. I can only imagine how that shit would look from up close. I swear, once people walked up and started blockin' my view by standin' in front of the fence and shit, I really couldn't see much to know all of what was goin' on. All I saw was flinging arms and hair pullin' and somebody on the ground."

"Fuck you, nigga!" Desirae yelled. "Fuck you! I swear to God, I don't ever wanna see you again in life, Tron. You hear me? I don't ever wanna see you again in life. Oh, and by the way, if you think you gon' be seein' your sons, think again." She smiled. "You gon' act like it don't affect you, then okay. It won't. You ain't gon' never see your sons again, Tron. Not after what you just did, or didn't do."

"What?" Tron asked. His voice was now elevated to the point where it let Desirae know that she'd gotten his attention. "Desirae, you can't do that shit. Them my fuckin' kids, too. Not just yours. You not gon' stop me from' seein' my kids, Desirae. I don't give a fuck what you say. You not gon' stop me from seein' my sons."

Desirae giggled. "Nigga, what the fuck you gon' do? Pull up and watch them from the other side of the street. Fuck you, nigga. Dick wasn't even that good no way."

As Tron was starting to speak in response, Desirae hung up the phone. She was so frustrated and angry, not only from the fight with Greg's wife but also with Tron, that she balled her fists together then hurled her phone at the wall. The lit-up screen went dark when the phone collided with the white plaster then fell to the floor. Desirae turned away, shaking her head. Never in her life had she lost a fight that badly. Sure, she'd had some that were not her favorites, per se. However, to outright get her ass beat by some chick, and in her mother's front yard, stung.

Desirae attended to her wounds in the bathroom mirror. As she stood there, she pressed cotton balls swelled with alcohol into the scratches and wounds on her head. Once her cuts were good and tingling, she slid into some pajama clothing and took her hair down. Parts of her head hurt simply just to touch. However, Desirae pushed through it until she got to the point where she could pull her hair back and put it into a ponytail. Now, with her face more exposed that before, she looked at what could only be described as a woman down. Immediately, she bawled out in tears.

"I don't even wanna go outside again," she said to herself. "I swear to God I don't. That shit was just too much for me."

Desirae knew she needed to feel the warmth of a hot shower. Sure, she'd wiped her body off with a wash cloth just to calm herself down. However, doing that certainly wasn't the same as the feeling of hot, steamy water hitting her body. She slid out of her clothes, turned on the water, and stepped inside. While washing her body, Desirae could not fight off the feelings of worthlessness. Rather, the true meaning of being alone in the world was coming to her in a big way. If this had happened to her months ago, she would have been able to call Reese. Reese would have been right over to talk to her and be a good friend. That was all gone now since Desirae had caught Reese trying to get with Tron, only to wind up having to beat her ass in the snow back in February.

When Desirae finished and stepped out of the show, wrapping her white towel around her body, she looked back in the mirror again.

Girl, why do you do this to yourself? She thought. *You too good for this and you know it. You could have any man that you want, from the Wall Street banker guy to the guy who owns the corporations downtown to the NFL or any other sort of sports players. Look at the women in your life now or who have been in your life in recent years, girl. None of them are as fucking beautiful as you are. None of them have the body you have, either.*

Desirae stood there, reflecting on her thoughts. She couldn't help but shake her head. She felt as if she'd been stripped of her womanhood. The result of being Tron's side chick was her two, beautiful twin boys. However, she was not going to deny the fact that they weren't planned, nor was she going to say that having the twins at her station in life didn't hurt her one bit.

The result of messing around with Greg and knowing that he was married, wound up being the most embarrassing and humiliating experience of her life.

"Why bitches gotta be that way?" Desirae said. "I mean, she was just stupid. She jumped on my ass when she shoulda been jumpin' on his ass."

Desirae wondered how she was ever going to go back to work. She already knew that the next couple of days would be a long two days for her. She had the rest of Saturday, and all of Sunday, to let this experience sit with her and her spirit. Her soul would hopefully chime in and tell her what the right move was. Should she go back to Family Dollar or just let it go and find something else?

8

No sooner than Desirae had begun to think about such a question, one of the twins began to softly cry from their basinet. Desirae closed her eyes for a moment, hating how her job as a mother could really interrupt her personal time. She shrugged, deciding that since she knew that Titan and James were in a safe place she could let them cry for a few minutes. Her mother's words came back to her, about how just because a baby cries does not mean that you have to go running to tend to him.

Desirae leaned against the bathroom door as she looked at the mirror.

"Fuck, I need to smoke," she said. "A bitch need to fuckin' smoke after that shit. Shit, I don't even know if I'mma go back to work."

She needed the job, and there was no denying that. However, Desirae also knew that if she went back to Family Dollar on Monday for her shift, as if nothing had happened, then something probably would happen. She'd seen Veronica just a couple of days ago when she'd come to the store to see Greg. That let her know right then and there that all of the things Nalique had said to her, in warning, were indeed true. Something was off about that bitch Veronica, and there was no doubt in Desirae's mind that if she were to go back to work there, Veronica would come up to the store and cause a problem for her. Desirae sighed, hating the price that she had to pay for being so pretty and having the body that so many women lust for, especially after having had twins.

Feeling rather low, Desirae went back downstairs. By the time she'd gotten to the dining room to check on Titan and James, whichever one had been crying just minutes earlier was now silent. Desirae smiled, knowing that now everything she lived for was basically for them. As she walked into the kitchen, still on the edge of a cliff when it came to her rage, she thought about how she'd really given Greg the works. Now, after the fact – and because he wasn't really her type to begin with, in many ways – Desirae began to feel a little dirty. The only good thing about sex with her store manager was the fact that he could eat pussy as if it was his last meal on this earth.

9

Desirae poured herself a glass of lemonade, pulled a chair out, and sat at the kitchen table. The house was so quiet. The clusters of neighbors from up and down the street had long disappeared. The only sound Desirae could here was the clicking of the clock above her mother's China cabinet. She wondered how Veronica even knew that Greg had come over to chill with Desirae. Desirae wanted to find some way – any possible way – to connect Tron to this. However, she knew that this probably wasn't possible. After all, she was the one who had purposely invited Tron and Greg over on the same day. Her entire goal with doing so had been to get Tron to notice her by letting him know that so many other men would gladly take her if he wouldn't. Desirae's shook her head as she took a sip of her lemonade. *This is some fucked up shit*, she thought. *I ain't even do nothing. How the fuck is it my fault when a bitch can't please her man, and that man gotta go looking elsewhere? Jump on his ass, not mine.*

Unable to sit down anymore, Desirae slid out of the chair and stood up. She paced around the kitchen, wishing that she'd been more prepared for Veronica when she'd come walking up to the door. She thought about why she'd lost the fight so badly, and blamed it all on the fact that it was unprovoked and a complete surprise.

Just then Desirae's eyes landed on a family barbeque photo from 2002 that hung on the kitchen wall. Seeing a few neighbors in the background having a good time, she thought about the social impact of all of this. Every time she went outside from now on, she'd be able to feel the eyes on her – the eyes of her mother's neighbors. She'd walk out to her car while they stared at her, and know that they were playing the entire front yard beat-down scene in their heads again as if it had all happened just the day before. Whenever they spoke softly to one another, Desirae would know that they were talking about her. After all, who would watch a chick get her ass beat naked and not talk about it for the next decade?

Video footage then popped into her head. Desirae's eyes bulged, knowing that she lived in a world where so many fights were caught on camera. Once this happened, they would inevitably be shared with everyone as well as be uploaded to World Star or YouTube. Desirae wanted to break down and cry so badly that her fingers and wrists hurt from how hard she balled her fists.

The mental anguish was proving to be just too much for Desirae. With a hell of a headache brewing – the kind that manifests itself dead between the eyes – she went to her bed and lay down. In the silence of the room, the scene in the front yard played over and over again. It all seemed so unreal at this point; it almost seemed as if it didn't happen. However, Desirae knew that it did indeed happen. Furthermore, she knew that she'd be reminded of it happening very soon, as she'd have to leave the house and show her scratched up, bruised face to the rest of the world. With this in mind, Desirae drifted off to sleep.

Chapter 2

When Desirae had called Tron, he'd just been pulling into the parking lot of his residential community. With rows of mid-range townhouses touching all four sides of the parking lot, Tron's eyes fixed on the red brick as he called Desirae back. He called again. And again. Finally, he shrugged it off, knowing that she was probably close to the edge from the beating that she took in the front yard. Even for Tron, the scene played over and over again in his head. The part where the other chick had snatched Desirae's robe off was the best. With Desirae stabbing Tron up at Honeys East back in January, as well as her other antics that were too much to even think about, Tron felt in his gut that Desirae got exactly what she deserved.

Seeing that Desirae wasn't going to answer his calls, Tron stepped out of his car and went into the house. Once inside, he pushed the door closed, against the brisk fall wind.

"That was some fucked up shit," he said to himself. The visualization of Desirae's naked body in the grass was just too much for him. He cracked a smile, knowing that it really wasn't funny.

"What's some fucked up shit?" Tyrese asked.

Tyrese sat in the living room, wearing only his gray gym shorts. At medium height with a D.C. fade, he rubbed oil on a new tattoo he'd gotten on his left shoulder. Tron walked into the room.

"Man, you not gon' believe the shit a nigga just seen," Tron said, shaking his head.

Immediately, Tyrese was alert. Just like women, men talk to one another too about what they've seen or heard. It may come out differently, or not occur in very public places like it does with women, but it does indeed occur. Tyrese put the bottle of ointment down onto the floor next to the couch. Tron crossed the living room and plopped down at the other end of the couch, facing the entertainment system.

"Nigga," Tron said, with a smile on his face.

This one word alone let Tyrese know that whatever his boy Tron was about to say had to be good and worth hearing. "What?"

"I just watched Desirae get that ass beat," Tron said. "Man, that shit was so bad."

Tyrese looked at Tron, shaking his head. "No," he said. "You lyin'. The bitch who came up to the club, stabbin' niggas with forks and shit? Your baby mama? She got her ass beat? Where? When?"

"Damn, nigga," Tron said. "Who the fuck you supposed to be? Goddamn Wendy Williams or somebody."

"Did they get to tearin' clothes and shit off?" Tyrese asked. "You see a titty or somethin'?"

Tron shook his head, smiling. He lifted his balled fist to his mouth and covered it as he spoke. "A titty?" he said, still shaking his head. "Nigga, ya' boy saw more than that."

Tyrese looked surprised. "What?" he asked. "Was one of the bitches wearin' a dress or some shit and her pussy was out and showin' or somethin'? Damn, can a nigga get some details?"

"Man, I was over seein' my sons and shit, right," Tron said. "Nothing more, nothing less. Put that on everything I own. I told myself that when I went up into that house, I wasn't gon' fuck her. She don't even deserve the dick at this point, and I just knew she would want some."

"Duh, nigga," Tyrese said. "You know these thots out here love the D. They act like they don't, but they do."

"They do," Tron said, agreeing. "So, tell me why when I walk through the door and shit, she got some other nigga sittin' on her mama's couch like ain't shit happenin'?"

"She had another nigga?" Tyrese said. "Another nigga, sittin' over there with her and your sons, and she ain't even tell you or nothin'?"

"Nope," Tron said. "Exactly, a nigga walked up in there and saw this halfway outta shape, ugly motherfucka sittin' on the couch lookin' like he was nervous about bein' there or some shit. I was a man about my shit, though. I nodded at the nigga and kept on walkin'."

"So when the fight happen, then?" Tyrese asked.

"I'm gettin' there, I'm gettin' there," Tron said. "As usual, the bitch pissed me off with some of the shit she was sayin'. I

13

was just there try'na see my sons and shit, like a real nigga would do, and I could tell she was try'na push up on me."

"With the otha nigga in the otha room?" Tyrese asked.

"Hell yeah," Tron said. "So, I'm on my way out the door. Desirae mad about some shit. Don't know, don't care. And when I get out on the porch and start makin' my way back to my car, this bitch pulls up in this gray car – mighta been a Kia or some shit like that. And she came marchin' up and walkin' right on past me. This bitch had that deranged look in her eyes. That look that tell you whatever the fuck she doin' there done been on her mind for a minute."

"Damn," Tyrese said.

"Yeah," Tron said. "So, I get into my car and shit and just sit and watch and next thing I know, Desirae open the door for the lady and is gettin' that ass pulled out onto the front porch. Then the other bitch pulled her out into the middle of the front yard and just started goin' in and shit."

"Damn, that's cold," Tyrese said. "You know you 'bout to get that ass beat when somebody come to your door and pull you out your own damn house."

"I know," Tron said. "That's why I ain't pull off cause I knew some shit was about to happen to that trappin' ass bitch. Well, nigga, get this." Tron smiled and leaned forward. "The chick who came up to the door was beatin' Desirae's ass out in the yard. People from up and down the street came rushin' down and shit to watch. Plus, ain't no damn trees or nothin' in the front yard, so the shit was as bright as fuckin' day with no fuckin' shade, you feel me?"

"Damn," Tyrese said. "That's fucked up."

"I sat in my car and watched as Desirae just kept missin' and was gettin' tossed around and shit," Tron said. "Next thing a nigga know, though, the other chick done snatched Desirae's robe off and tossed it somewhere over or by a fence or something."

Desirae's beautifully carved, thick body popped into Tyrese's mind. He had long known that Desirae would just have to be eye candy for him. There was just no way that he'd ever even think about messing around with a chick that Tron liked, let alone a chick that was the mother of his children. Her

14

body – particularly her ass – was something that Tyrese had thought about from time to time, going over mental snapshots from the few times she'd been up to Honeys East.

Tyrese stood up, imagining Desirae's thick body rolling around in grass. "Nigga, is you fuckin' serious?" he asked. "Nigga, you lyin'."

"I swear to God," Tron said. "I fuckin' swear, I wouldn't have believed this shit, my nigga, if I ain't see it for my damn self. The chick snatched Desirae's robe off and beat that ass in the front yard, in front of everybody, while she was naked. When Desirae got up, she was cryin' like a big baby and shit, practically beggin' the other chick to stop givin' it to her."

Tyrese smiled. "Damn," he said, "you shoulda got that shit on tape."

"Man, I wasn't thinkin'," Tron said. "I saw some otha niggas, standin' out on the sidewalk, with theirs out and shit. I know that shit is gon' be on YouTube and World Star."

"Nigga, that shit is gon' go viral," Tyrese said. "I'mma be watchin' that shit. I'mma keep an eye out for it just so I can watch. But who was the chick that was beatin' her ass? You know her?"

Tron shook his head. "No, I don't know her," he responded. "But, based on some of the stuff I could kinda hear her sayin', because the bitch was shitty as fuck and talkin' loud as shit, it sound like the dude inside the house was her husband."

"Damnnnnn," Tyrese said. "Desirae fuckin' around with a married nigga. The wife find out and came over and got in that ass."

Tron nodded, looking ahead at the television. "Hmm, hmm," he said. "And I mean, nigga, she got that ass beat. That shit was brutal. Desirae had scratches and bruises and shit all over her body. The other chick looked like she'd just gotten ready to head into work or something. I mean, it looked like nothin'. Like she was on break from work and came to beat a bitch's ass on her lunch break."

Tron and Tyrese broke into laughter.

"Wait a second, though," Tyrese said. "If she had another nigga over there, and the nigga was married, then

15

why the fuck would she have you come over to see your sons at the same time?"

"You know, I was thinkin' that same shit myself now that you mention it," Tron said. "When I walked in the door, with the way Desirae was lookin' around and shit, it was like she wanted me to see that she had a nigga over. I mean, if they was fuckin' and shit cause her mama wasn't home or somethin', then his ass coulda been upstairs or somethin', and I woulda never even known that he was fuckin' there."

"Yeah, she crazy," Tyrese said. "I think she did that shit on purpose, and now it done backfired on her ass. Man, I can't wait to see that video. For real," Tyrese rushed back over to the couch and grabbed his cell phone, "let me see if that shit is on the internet yet. If that was me who had recorded that shit, I woulda went right home and uploaded it."

"Yeah, I ain't never seen a chick get her ass beat naked," Tron said, shaking his head. "It was some fucked up shit, I will say that. But, yeah, she probably did set that shit up. You know how chicks be. They be doin' shit to try to make a nigga jealous and shit. Like you said, it backfired on her big time."

"Yeah, but if you wanna make a nigga jealous, that's one thing," Tyrese said as he typed different keywords into YouTube, "but why the fuck you gon' use somebody else's husband to do it." He laughed. "That's how you know she stupid. No offense, I know she the mother to your boys and shit, but I'm just callin' it how I see it. How you gon' make a nigga jealous with another nigga that belong to somebody else?"

Tron shrugged. "Man, I don't know," he said. "I really don't. I swear, I don't know what be goin' through her head sometimes. I swear there be times I think that she crazy. Like just before I came in the door."

"Just before you came in the door?" Tyrese asked. "What? Did she follow you home or some shit?"

"Naw," Tron said. "She called me try'na act like the shit was my fault or somethin'. She called me, shitty as fuck, as you can expect, that I ain't get outta the car and stop it."

16

Tyrese snickered. "I ain't gon' lie, man," he said. "I was thinkin' the same thing. Why you ain't get out and stop it from happenin' and shit?"

Tron looked at his boy and wondered where he'd suddenly gotten the holy bone. "What the fuck you mean?" he said. "It wasn't my place. First, she gon' have some otha nigga around my kids and get mad at me when I ask her about him and shit. Then, come to find out, the otha nigga is some otha bitch's husband. She deserved to get that ass beat. Shit, if I was a chick, I'd do it my damn self. I swear I would. She really want me to want her, and that body do look good considerin' that she just had Titan and James a little over a month ago, but she just too much trouble and the bitch is crazy. Before I came in the house, when I was talkin' to her on the phone out in the parkin' lot, she told me that I ain't gon' never see my sons again."

"She try'na play that game, huh?" Tyrese said, shaking his head. "You know how these chicks be out here. So, what she want you to do now? Apologize or some shit that you ain't jump in and stop that ass from gettin' worn out?"

"Fuck if I know," Tron said. "She prolly want some of the damn dick. For all I know, that bitch could be over there cryin' in a corner or somethin'. I don't know how she gon' ever show her face again."

"She betta leave at nighttime or somethin' and wear a hood over her head and not hang out or stop and shop in any Kroger, Walgreens, or whatever in the entire zip code. Damn, I ain't seein' this video yet. I'mma check later on. I gotta see that shit." In Tyrese's mind, seeing a chick built like Desirae rolling around naked in the grass, even if she was the loser in a fight, would make his day – maybe even his week.

Tron felt his phone vibrate in his pocket. Thinking that it would be Desirae returning one of his several calls to her, he pulled his phone out and saw that it was Reese.

"Chill out real quick," he said. "It's Reese."

Tyrese laughed and shook his head. "Nigga, somebody gon' kill you one day with all this jugglin' shit you doin'. I might need to go head and get up outta here before you got some niggas after you. Hell, she might get her daddy again to come find you."

Tron's eyes cut to Tyrese as he answered Reese's call, not liking how he'd just brought up the incident with Desirae's father. While it had happened several months ago at this point, just talking about it was a sore spot for him.

"Hello," Tron answered.

"Hey, what you doin'?" Reese asked, sounding as if she were smiling while she spoke.

"Just got home," Tron answered. He stood up and walked toward the stairs so he could go up to his bedroom. "What you doin'?"

"Shit," Reese responded. "Just chillin'. Just got done takin' one of my aunties to the grocery store up on Michigan Road. I'm just tired from havin' to move with her slow-moving ass. I swear I am."

"I got somethin' I wanna tell you," Tron said as he stepped into his bedroom. "You wanna come over or somethin'?"

"Yeah, I'll come over," Reese answered. "I just gotta get something to eat first, and then I'll be over. I didn't get a chance to get nothin' to eat today."

"Is that so?" Tron said. "Okay, let's do something else then. I'm hungry too."

***

Tron pulled into the parking lot of Bob Evans at just about the same time as Reese. While it was well into the afternoon, he had a taste for some breakfast food. They met in the parking lot and walked into the restaurant, taking a booth over to the side. After a little bit of chit chat, Tron decided to finally tell Reese about the fight out in the front yard of Desirae's mother's house.

"Is you fuckin' serious?" Reese asked. "That bitch got her ass beat naked, in the fuckin' front yard of her mama's house. Was her mama there?"

Tron looked around and shushed Reese. "Don't go talkin' like that too loud," he warned, "before these white folks come and put us out or somethin'."

"My bad," Reese said.

18

"Naw, her mama wasn't there," Tron said. "Just her, the nigga, and the chick who got in that ass."

"Good, that's what she deserve," Reese said, wanting to crack a smile badly. The night Desirae had jumped on her for no reason in the snow still sat front and center in Reese's mind. Part of her wished that she'd been there with Tron, even if she'd been asked to only sit in the car while he visited with Titan and James. If she would've seen what Tron had described going down in the yard, she wouldn't have been able to contain herself from jumping out of the car and going and getting her piece. "All she do is fuck around, and she will fuck around with any woman's man. She used to do that shit when we was friends. And yes, to answer your question that you brought up during the story, I do think that she was probably try'na make you jealous. I mean, what other reason would she have for having some dude that she fuckin' around with over at the very same time that her baby daddy is comin' over to see his kids? That sound like some sneaky shit by its damn self. She knew just what she was doin' and that's why the shit crashed on that ass. I wonder how the wife knew to come find her husband there."

Tron shrugged. "Fuck if I know," he said. "I never even seen the other chick before."

"Well, I hope that God blesses whoever made that possible," Reese said. "I'm just mad that I wasn't there to see it. That bitch is so desperate, I don't know what to think of her sometimes."

Tron nodded, looking at Reese for a couple of seconds too long. Just as he was thinking about how the two of them had met, the waitress – a perky, suburban-looking, teenaged white girl – came over to take their orders. Once the waitress walked away, Tron went back to looking at Reese.

"Why you say she desperate?" Tron asked. "I mean, after everything that done happened and shit over the last year between the two of us, why is she still even try'in?"

"Cause," Reese said, her forehead wrinkled. "She so used to thinkin' that everythin' is about her, and that any nigga out here should want her because everybody always want her,

19

and she just got such a beautiful body. And that ass… Fuck, that's all she talked about."

Tron chuckled softly, looking away as he took a sip of his orange juice. That ass, he thought. That ass was part of the reason he didn't pull off. Now that she was even plumper, and in all the right areas, watching that robe get snatched away from her body in broad daylight surely was a sight to see. Tron even recalled seeing Desirae's ass and legs jiggle on a few occasions during the fight. But Desirae's attitude and demeanor, not to mention her way of forcing herself on people, nearly negated every positive physical trait she had going for herself.

Tron and Reese chatted while they waited on their food to arrive at their table. As Tron was cutting his pancakes and Reese spread grape jelly on her slices of toast, Reese looked up at Tron. Things were going rather nicely between the two of them, especially since it wasn't serious but rather a friend with benefits relationship. While they saw each other on a regular basis, different thoughts had begun to pop into Reese's mind. There was a question Reese really wanted to ask Tron.

"Tron," Reese said. "I got somethin' I wanna ask you, since we doin' all this talk about Desirae."

"Yeah, what?" Tron said.

"How do you see me?" Reese asked. "I mean, since you was sort of talkin' to Desirae when we met and stuff. How do you see me?"

Tron looked up at Reese, pausing. This was a question he didn't have an answer for, and he really wished that she wouldn't have asked.

***

Nalique was resting at her apartment out on 38th Street. She'd just gotten home from having what she'd thought of as a "fun aunty" day with her niece and nephew. She'd taken them to the Children's Museum as well as out to eat then the park before the temperature began to dip a little. After dropping them off with her sister, she came back home and plopped down into her couch.

Nalique's apartment was pretty nicely designed, especially since so much of the furniture was from when she'd

20

lived with her no good ex-boyfriend, Tyrese. She'd added a couple pieces of furniture to the two-bedroom, as well as permission from the landlord to repaint the walls. They had been a plain, bland white. Now the walls were a rich, creamy color that was much more pleasing to the eyes.

A mirror rested on the wall, across the kitchenette. When Nalique had sat down, she could see her reflection.

"Damn," she said. "A bitch look tore up, don't she?"

Nalique got up and approached the mirror. She didn't like what she was seeing. It was definitely time to get some new hair and take the old out. She also wanted to change up the style, and maybe try something a little longer. Fuzzy hair with a lot of new growth was something Nalique rarely showed to the rest of the world.

Shawna, who had been with Nalique's ex's best friend for some years, popped into her mind. Nalique remembered that she had made a mental note to call Shawna and see about getting the hook up with her hair. In fact, the last time Nalique had gone to Shawna's salon, which was the night she and Shawna had gone up to Honeys East – the night that Nalique had to get in that stripper Diamond's ass about her little favors for Tyrese – she had noticed that Shawna did pretty good work.

Nalique grabbed her phone and looked through her contacts, hoping that she still had Shawna's number saved after all of these months. When she found it, she tapped it and waited.

"Hello?" Shawna answered.

"Girl, what is up?" Nalique asked. "It's Nalique, girl. How you been?"

"Nalique?" Shawna said. "Girl, I been good. How you been?"

"Been okay, been okay, girl," Nalique said. "Been a lot betta since I got that no good nigga, Tyrese, outta my life for good."

"I know that's right," Shawna said. "I was kinda hurt at first, but now I know I made the right choice."

"Girl, well, I was callin' you to see when I could get an appointment," Nalique said. She then pushed the tips of her fingers into her thick hair, feeling the roots. "A bitch need these roots done ASAP, and…Shit, fuck it. I just need it all redone. Every fuckin' thing."

Shawna chuckled. "Girl, when you wanna come in?" she asked. "I'm free tonight, actually. I thought about goin' out and stuff, but I just don't feel like it. Tomorrow, I won't be free until the afternoon. How soon were you try'na get in and get it done?"

Nalique thought about it. The weekend would be better considering the weekdays could be a little unpredictable. "Girl, I can come today," she said. "Just tell me what time and I'll be over there. I remember where it is, on Thirtieth Street, off of Central, right? You still over there, ain't you?"

"Girl, yes," Shawna said. "I'm not gon' leave that place. All my clients know it and are used to coming there. You wanna meet me over at the shop around six, or is that too soon, too late? What?"

"Six is coo," Nalique said. "I'll be over there in a little bit. I'mma stop by the ATM and get your money for you, okay girl? I'll be over there."

When Nalique walked into the salon, she was instantly greeted by Shawna. Nalique, who was noticeably bigger than Shawna, hugged her. The two realized how cool they'd been for those years that they dated Tyrese and Tron at the same time. However, in the back of her mind Shawna still didn't like the fact that Nalique was the kind of chick to start some stuff. Yes, Nalique could be sweet and very likeable. She was also hood to the very core. In many ways, Nalique could only be described as the epitome of ghetto to Shawna.

"Long time no see," Shawna said as she led Nalique over to her chair. Nalique nodded and waved at the other stylists who were busy with their own clients.

"Girl, I know," Nalique said as she sat down. "When the last time we saw each other?"

Shawna twirled the chair toward the mirror to where she now looked into Nalique's eyes. "Girl, you know when," she said. "That night you caused that shit and got the club on the news. You know damn well when. I knew I shouldn't have gone up in there with your ass."

"Don't say it like that," Nalique said, smiling. "I ain't mean for all that to happen. I didn't think I was gonna shoot at her."

"You didn't think that you were gonna shoot at her?" Shawna asked. "Why the hell were you carrying the gun if you were just going up there to see what was going on?"

"Girl, I don't know," Nalique said, waving her hand in dismissing the topic. "Something stupid. I caught a charge over that. I shoulda just beat the bitch some more. Hell, I might not be done, especially if I see her ass again I just might be liable to get in that shit again. Maybe not. I'mma lady with class now."

Shawna smiled and rolled her eyes as she asked Nalique what she wanted to do with her hair. Nalique explained that she wanted to take the hair extensions out and, on second thought, do something with her real hair.

"Oh, really?" Shawna asked, surprised. "You gon' let the real show."

Nalique nodded. "Yeah," she answered. "I think a bitch need to let the real show once in a while. Need to let these niggas out here know that I got some hair, and I got that good shit. Just take the weave out and we can go from there. I want my shit laid, though. I know that."

Shawna took the hair extensions out of Nalique's hair. Nalique looked at Shawna in the mirror, noticing that she looked a little more rejuvenated than she remembered. Shawna's thick black hair had grown even longer, now reaching beyond her shoulders. The red highlights were so cute while still being professional. Shawna also looked as if she'd been working out. Her figure was nice, with her waist dipping in above her hips.

"Girl, what you been up to all these months?" Nalique asked. "I see you back there, lookin' all healthy and shit. What you do now? You one of them chicks that be in the parks downtown with them white girls doin' that yoga shit or somethin'?"

"Girl, stop it, Nalique," Shawna said. "You know damn well I ain't in no parks downtown doin' yoga with them white people. I don't know. I just been takin' care of me and stuff.

23

Doin' hair. My sister got married, so I'm not stayin' with her no more. I got my own place. What about you? What you been up to?"

Nalique let out a deep breath. "Shit," she answered. "A bitch just been workin', for real. Up at this dollar store."

"Oh, yeah?" Shawna asked. "How is that goin'?" Deep down, Shawna wondered how well a person like Nalique got by in customer service environments. She simply didn't strike Shawna as the kind of woman who would want to work in that kind of place.

"It's alright," Nalique explained. "I ain't had no shit happen yet. Made a little buddy up there. This chick they hired like a couple weeks ago or somethin'."

"Oh, yeah?" Shawna said. "That's good. I like that I got a couple of friends up here in the salon, too. It's definitely nice to have somebody you work with that you can talk to. I've had some jobs where the people weren't friends and everything was all stale. It definitely makes a difference."

"Yeah, but I can't say that I trust her," Nalique said. "I mean, she my buddy and stuff, but she one of them side-piece bitches, you know. Like the one I had to run up into Honeys East and handle, like you so lovingly remember."

Shawna tapped Nalique's shoulder. "Girl, I remember," she said, rolling her eyes and shaking her head. "Ain't no need in you remindin' me. But, um, why you say that she one of them side chick-kinda bitches? You know that's why me and Tron broke up. He had a side chick and even got her pregnant."

"I heard," Nalique said. "And that's some fucked-up shit, girl. I don't know what I woulda done if some bitch woulda trapped Tyrese back when we was together."

"Maybe you woulda actually shot her," Shawna said, sarcastically. "Girl, I'm just playin'."

Nalique squinted her eyes in the mirror at Shawna. "Hmm, hmm," she said. "So, yeah, I mean we coo and stuff, but I don't trust her cus she one of them side chick bitches. Niggas be hittin' on her ass left and right when they come up in that Family Dollar. One of her first days, or maybe it was later in her first week or somethin', she had this fine ass nigga

24

hittin' on her in her line. Next thing we know, the nigga done walked out the door and in come his wife. And girl, let me tell you, this bitch was ready to jump on my buddy like she had nothing to do tomorrow but sit in jail. I felt sorry for the girl—my friend—because I really don't think she knew he was married or whatever, which I understand that. It's one thing if you know, another if you don't. But she is kinda provocative."

"She's hot?" Shawna asked, wanting clarification. "Girl, you know how them older people be using the term hot when they're talkin' about a girl or woman who gets the attention of a lot of men."

"Exactly," Nalique said. "She is hot, I guess in more ways than one. I wanna tell the girl to tone it down a little bit before she get that ass beat by the manager's wife. Now that is one woman who don't play."

"What? Is the manager fine himself or something?" Shawna asked. "Why she gotta watch out for the manager's wife?"

"Hell naw that nigga Greg ain't fine," Nalique said. "In fact, I heard the nigga was a freak and got into some trouble at another Family Dollar location, or at least that's what they say, anyway. But, naw girl, I just say that she betta watch out cause it look like the store manager might have a little thing for Miss Thang. He be out on the floor, lookin' at her ass and stuff. He be havin' talks," Nalique made the quotation marks hand gesture, "in his office damn near every other day or some shit. She say that he just talkin' to her about the incident, because it did get kinda loud and make the store look bad, but girl, I think that something else is goin' on between the two of them. I think he prolly back in that office fuckin' her or somethin'. I heard his dick little too, so I wonder what she gettin' outta it."

Shawna playfully tapped Nalique's shoulder. "Girl, be nice," she said. "And it sound like you really got this girl profiled as a hoe."

"I swear to you, Shawna, she is coo people," Nalique said. "I will give her that. We be talkin' and shit, and one time we even hung out at the mall. She just had twins, but she lost a lot of weight fast. I be lookin' at her like *damn, Desirae,* thinkin' to myself *you are a pretty girl, but you sho are a thot.*"

Desirae? Shawna thought. *Did Nalique just say Desirae?*

For a few moments, Nalique went on and on – her talking became zoned-out background noise to Shawna. After about a minute, Shawna leaned up from Nalique's head and stopped what she was doing. She looked at Nalique in the mirror, telling her that something was up.

"Girl, what?" Nalique asked. "What's wrong? Why you look all serious all of the sudden?"

"Did you just say Desirae?" Shawna asked. "Is that the name I heard you say?"

Nalique, appearing confused, looked around for a moment. She shrugged. "Yeah," she answered. "That's her name…Desirae. Uh oh, you don't know her, do you? My bad, Shawna. If she yo cousin, girl, I take back everything I said. I ain't mean it like that. I…"

"Girl, stop," Shawna said, shaking her head. "She ain't my cousin or nothin' like that. What she look like?"

Nalique described Desirae to Shawna. First she brought up how smooth her skin was, as well as its unique shade of brown. Nalique then went on to describe her 5'2 height, how much of a shape she has (something that could not be left out), and her demeanor. She told Shawna about how her coworker and friend had just had twins by some dude that didn't even want to be bothered with her in the first place. "Do you know her?" Nalique asked Shawna.

Shawna grinned, thinking of how the last time she'd seen Desirae was when the two of them had been coming out of the store at the same time. Shawna had asked her how she could be okay with just being a side chick, as her favorite client Miss Susan had just begun to secretly see a married man over in Dayton, Ohio. That chapter of Shawna's life seemed to be closed for good now. She smirked, thinking about how easily old memories can be brought back to life.

"Yeah, I know her," Shawna responded. "That's the chick Tron was fuckin' around with and got pregnant."

The mirror was no longer good enough to serve as a means of proper eye contact. Instantly, Nalique turned around in her chair. As she turned, her eyes locked with Shawna's eyes.

"What?" she said. "Are you fuckin' serious, Shawna? Desirae is the side chick that Tron was fuckin' around with and got pregnant?"

"She full of herself, ain't she?" Shawna asked.

Nalique didn't respond. Rather, she nodded her head.

"Yeah, that's her," Shawna said, shaking her head. "And she just might be fuckin' around with the nigga in charge. I ain't got nothin' against her, especially not at this point. But she prolly is gon' catch it from the wife sooner or later. She don't care who man she sleep with, I can tell you that. I wound up finding out that Tron was messing around with her for months. I wound up going up to the mall, where she used to work."

"In Clarke's?" Nalique asked. She thought back to just days ago when she and Desirae had gone to the mall.

Shawna shook her head. "Yep," she said. "You know her, that's for sure. Like I was sayin', I wound up gettin' into it with her at her job, like fightin' and everythin'. She was beggin' for it, but we realized how stupid we were bein'. I let her have Tron. If that's what he wanted, over me, then that is fine with me."

"Over you?" Nalique asked, clearly surprised. She turned back around and faced the mirror. "She coo people and stuff, I guess, but Shawna she ain't got nothin' on you. I mean, you got class and are accomplished and stuff. Pretty. Like the wifey kinda chick, if you know what I mean. This Desirae chick." She shook her head. "Even with how she stands, you can tell that she give it up to just about any nigga if his dick is big enough. She has a deep arch in her back that I think she done developed from years of walkin' with her butt out stuck out."

"Hmm, hmm," Shawna said, nodding her head. "She walk like her shit don't stink and like any man within eyesight is about to come runnin' up and wanting her to fall into their arms."

27

"Girl, I'm just shocked that you know her," Nalique said. "That she is the same chick that messed up your relationship with Tron."

"She ain't mess it up, girl," Shawna said. "Tron is the one who messed it up. All that I was doin' for him, I can't believe that he would go over onto the south side and get some side chick to mess around with. The straw that broke the camel's back for me as far as gettin' back with Tron was the fact that he got her pregnant. I don't know if he meant to do it, or if she one of them girls who is into try'na trap these men to her, but I didn't care. I didn't even like that I'd given it the time of day to even think about it."

"That make me look at her in a totally different way," Nalique said. "I mean, I had my guard up before, like I do with any chick that I don't know, but now I'mma really be havin' my eyes open. Somethin' about her not only remind me of the chick whose ass I had to beat that night up at Honeys East but she just seem like she thirsty. I'm tellin' you girl, I really do think that she messin' around with the manager. Don't nobody have that many meetings with Greg's ole ugly ass and not come runnin' out the door complainin'."

"And you said that his wife is a crazy bitch?" Shawna asked.

Nalique opened her eyes wider and nodded her head. "Hmm, hmm," she responded. "I can already see it now. Greg's wife, Veronica, would fuck that bitch up, any time of day, any place. If she fuckin' around with Greg, she don't know what is liable to happen to her."

"Girl, don't warn her," Shawna suggested. "I'm tellin' you, she need somebody to get in that ass again. She a home wrecker and she know it. I'm over it now, but I feel bad for you. You gotta work with her every day. She didn't seem that coo to me to where I'd wanna be bothered with her on a daily basis. Watch whatever man you bring around her, I guess."

"That I will," Nalique said. "You know how niggas eyes wonder a little too much, so that I sure will."

Chapter 3

That weekend was the longest weekend of Desirae's life. She slept for a couple of hours on Saturday before waking up to a wailing baby. Quickly, she'd rushed out of bed, only to come downstairs and find them both crying. Titan and James continued their back and forth crying well into the night, causing Desirae to not get the kind of sleep she'd wanted. On Sunday, she woke up and paced her mother's quiet house for most of the morning. Every so often, Desirae would stop in the living room and look out of the large picture window. The yard and the street on the other side looked so empty compared to Saturday mid-day. The scene of being stripped of her dignity and losing a fight naked played over and over again in her mind. At times during her aimless pacing she'd just have to turn away from the window and walk to a different part of the house.

Desirae cooked herself something to eat around 4 pm or so. Just as she was finishing up, she heard keys jingling at the back door. Her heartbeat increased. She knew it was her mother coming back from seeing her cousins up in Chicago. In a matter of minutes, Desirae would be pulled out of her mindset – the mindset she'd been in for the last couple of days with not leaving the house. Quickly, she wondered if her mother had ridden down the street and talked to any of her neighbors. That wouldn't be unusual for her mother.

Karen walked onto the back porch then into the kitchen. There, she was greeted by the back of her daughter Desirae. She pulled her suitcases into the kitchen, pushing them over to the side so they could be out of the way. After checking to make sure that she'd locked the back door, she came back into the kitchen and slid out of her jacket.

"Well hello, Desirae," Karen said. There was obviously a clear, positive tone in Karen's voice. Since she'd always been about family, going to see her family in Chicago really did give her a break. The lives of a social worker and a grandmother who has her daughter and the daughter's twins living with her were hard to bring together. "How are you today?"

Desirae slowly turned around and smiled. "I'm okay, Mama," she responded.

Karen's thin, beautifully moisturized face went flat. All excitement she'd felt coming through the door from her weekend trip to the Windy City had flushed out of her body, making room for worry and confusion. The average-height, thin woman approached her daughter and reached out toward her face. "Desirae?" Karen said. "What the hell happened to you? What happened, Desirae?"

Desirae stepped away. "I don't wanna talk about it," she said. "I mean... I just don't wanna talk about it, Mama."

Desirae stepped into the dining room. Karen followed, putting her hands on her hips as she stood in the doorway. "Desirae," she said, "tell me, baby. What happened? Did you go to the hospital to get some of that looked at or what?"

"No, I ain't go to no hospital," Desirae said, shaking her head. "I'mma be okay."

"I know you'll be okay," Karen said, "but I just wanna know what happened to you. Did somebody break in here in the night or something?" Karen looked around. "Did somebody attack you at the store?"

Desirae simply continued to shake her head. The scene in the front yard played over and over again in her mind. The humiliation, the embarrassment; once again she was feeling the pit of her stomach fall out. It was all just too much to deal with, let alone think about. And with each passing hour, she was getting closer to Monday – closer to the day where if she wanted to keep her job, she'd have to step outside. The sunlight would shine on her in the open world as she walked to her car. The scratches and bruises on her face would tell everyone that somebody had gotten the best of her, and they did it in a big way.

Karen leaned her head back as she thought about what was going on before her eyes. Something was clearly off about Desirae. Yes, she wasn't always the most open daughter, particularly because of some of the things she'd been into as a teenage girl and young woman. Now, as Karen stood in the dining room feet away from her daughter, she knew something was up.

"What happened, Desirae?" Karen asked. "I'm not playing with you. Tell me what happened. With how your face is looking, it would seem as if you need to be pressing charges on somebody. What happened?"

Tears rolled down Desirae's face. She hadn't cried since falling asleep yesterday in the bed upstairs. She simply couldn't help it right now. The tears were just going to have to fall as she turned and looked her mother in the eyes.

"I got my ass beat, Mama," Desirae said, in a very emotional way. "I got my ass beat." She began full blown crying, her fists at her sides. "That bitch beat my ass right out there in the front yard!" She pointed toward the front of the house. "Right there in the fuckin' yard, Mama! She came up to the door and beat my ass like it was nothin'! She even tore my robe off and shit and threw it, Mama. Right out there in the front yard."

Desirae buried her face in the palms of her hands and cried loudly. She could feel the anger building inside of her, almost to the point where she wanted to go find the chick and go for a round two. She could feel her mother coming closer, then hugging her.

"Desirae, what are you talkin' about?" Karen asked. "She who? When did all of this happen, Desirae?"

"It happened yesterday, Mama," Desirae said. "Yesterday, right out there in the front yard. She beat my ass, naked, and people from up and down the street came down and just watched. They didn't even do anything. They just came down and watched it all happen like it was nothin'."

"What were you doing going to the door in your robe?" Karen asked. "That's not something you usually do if the person at the door is somebody that you don't know, Desirae. And who is she? You keep avoiding that question, and I'm really starting to wonder why, if you want to know the truth. Tell me, Desirae, who is she and why would she be coming to my house to jump on you to where she'd be pulling you out of the front door and out into the damn front yard? That doesn't even make sense to me, Desirae. What really happened? I don't know if I'm buying the idea of some serial, woman attacker going door to door and snatching people out of their

31

homes to fight in the middle of the front yard in broad daylight."

Desirae shook her head, knowing that she was going to have to tell her mother the truth eventually. There was no better time than the present at this point. "It was his wife," she said, practically having to force the words out of her mouth. "It was his fuckin' wife, Mama."

"Look, I know you all upset and everything, and I understand that," Karen said, "but you're not going to be talking like that in my house, at least not to my face…at least." She smiled. "Calm down, Desirae. Calm down. It's going to be okay. At least you're still alive."

"Still alive?" Desirae asked, her bruised eyelids opening somewhat wider. "Damn, Mama. Do I look that bad?"

Karen's mouth opened, but then she paused. She'd realized what she said and how it could have come across to Desirae, especially considering if this fight happened in the middle of the yard in broad daylight with people watching. Karen quickly wrapped her arms around Desirae's shoulders and guided her to the nicest couch in the living room. Within a matter of seconds, the two of them were descending into a pink, Victorian chaise lounge that Desirae's great grandfather had shipped back from his deployment in France during World War II.

"Just calm down, Desirae," Karen said. "I promise, I won't be mad. Just tell me the truth so I can know and tell you if you need to press charges or anything. At the very least, let me know something so I can look at who is coming to my door."

"Okay," Desirae said, hoping that what her mother had just said to her was true. "It was Greg's wife, Veronica, or whatever her name is. She is the one who came to the door and pulled me out when I opened it."

"Greg?" Karen asked, sounding very confused. "Desirae, who is Greg? I don't even know if you've ever mentioned the name Greg, or at least not that I can think of at the moment."

"Yeah, I have, Mama," Desirae said. "Greg… The store manager up at the Family Dollar."

"The store manager at the Family Dollar?" Karen asked. "Why in the world would his wife be coming up to my door and looking for you?" Karen looked at her daughter, wondering if she still hadn't learned her lesson from the situation with Tron. "Desirae, spill. Are you messing around with some woman's husband? And how would she know that you were here?"

"Cause, Mama," Desirae said, "he was here."

"He who was here?" Karen asked. "This Greg person was here, in my house?"

Karen nodded – a nod that was followed by a groan. "Okay," she said, having to force herself to not be as angry as she wanted to be. "So, this Greg person, who is your supervisor at Family Dollar, was over here. His wife somehow finds out, as they usually do, and comes up to the door and knocks and you open it for her. She pulls you out into the yard and so on." Karen decided to end the sentence for the sake of sensitivity.

Desirae nodded, wondering what her mother was really thinking. "Well, Tron was leavin', so I was already sort of at the door. I just kinda thought it was him coming back or something since he'd just been over here to see Titan and James."

Karen's face immediately changed from understanding to simply shocked. She shook her head as she stood up. Once she turned back to her daughter, she looked as if she were about business. "Desirae, you've got to be kidding me," she said, her lips tight. "How would you just so happen to be having another woman's husband over when Tron just so happens to be coming over to see the twins? That seems so damn coincidental, if you ask me, and I'll tell you whether you asked me or not. That really sounds, shall we say, *interesting* to me, Desirae. I won't even ask about that because I think I already know what is going on here."

"What?" Desirae snapped back, feeling a little upset. She was getting this feeling deep down that her mother was judging her – thinking of her as promiscuous or something like that. "What you mean you think you already know what is going on here?"

"Just what I said, Desirae," Karen said. "I was young once too, you know. And I know these games that these young girls play when it comes to these men out here, especially in your age group and whatnot, if you know what I mean." She shook her head and looked away in disappointment. "It's time you let it go, Desirae," Karen said. "It's really time, I think, that you let it go. Let go of the thugs and the married men and the men who belong to some other girl or woman or whatever. At this point, I really think you need to focus on Desirae. Do something with your life because you're not going to be living here with your children forever. Understand me? That's not happening here. I'm not going to be that grandmother, I'm just not."

"I know, Mama," Desirae said. "I know."

"Girl, I can't believe you," Karen said. "And I was just riding down the street on my way around back to the alley and garage, and I did notice a couple of people walking who looked at me for a couple of seconds too long. Desirae, why don't you focus on taking care of them two babies you got and getting your life back together before you go chasing men and stuff? What were you messing around with this Greg person for, huh? Why? I can only think of one reason a married man, who is the store manager at a Family Dollar, would want to be spending any sort of time with a twenty-something year old girl who has two newborn twins. I really can only think of one reason. But I would like to know your reasoning. Cause you wanna know what I see?"

"Girl, I don't care what you see," Desirae said, standing up. She just couldn't take her mother's righteous attitude. She brushed past her mother and headed toward the stairs.

"What was that?" Karen asked. "Desirae, don't walk away from me when I'm talking to you. Girl, what were you getting out of doing that?"

"Don't worry about it," Desirae said. She knew that if she were to tell her mother what she was getting out of messing around with Greg, she'd have to mention what happened with the man and his wife her first couple of days at Family Dollar.

34

"Look here, Desirae," Karen said. "This is not going to be a hoe house. This—"

Desirae cut her mother off saying, "Mama, I ain't no hoe."

"I didn't say that you were a hoe, Desirae," Karen explained. "You're not listening to me. I'm just saying, you're not going to be bringing men in and out of here when I'm not around. And especially not married men. That's not the kind of reputation I want for my house and where I live."

"Dang, Mama," Desirae said, as she began to climb the steps. "You really did just basically call me a hoe to my face, saying men, like it would be more than one."

"I'm just telling how it looks," Karen responded. "Desirae, I swear. That's all I'm doing. I'm just telling how I see it and how other people will see it. I just don't want you getting attacked the same way again like you did. I can tell the woman was mad and rightfully so."

Desirae was feeling more and more offended at her mother's brash remarks. She felt as if her mother was not really being all that supportive. Something about her tone, as well as how she stood and talked in such an authoritative way just did not sit well with Desirae. "Fuck whatever you got to say, Mama," Desirae said, boldly. "She didn't have to beat my ass in the yard like that! And you one to talk, especially since you a baby killer."

Karen's eyes bulged. Her chest pumped up as she felt her blood pressure rise. Giving very little thought to her actions, Karen lunged forward and headed upstairs. She quickly gained ground on Desirae, rushing up behind her just as the two of them came to the top of the steps. Desirae turned around, snapping her neck as she could practically feel her mother's body heat very close to herself.

"Desirae," Karen said, grabbing her daughter's shirt. "Who the hell are you calling a baby killer?" Karen knew that Desirae's comment was in reference to when she'd revealed that she'd had an abortion back when she was younger, as to not ruin her chances for various opportunities in life. However, the last reason she would ever be telling her daughter such a delicate part of her past was so that she could throw it up in her face.

"I'm just telling it how I see it," Desirae said, looking into her mother's eyes. The two of them stood across from one another, at the top of the steps, just outside of Karen's master bedroom door. "You are one to talk about some of the things I'm doing. Sounds to me like you did a little worse. I at least let mine live. I was woman enough to take on the two babies I created. You wouldn't even take on the one."

There was a long pause. The only sounds in the house were the ticking of the clock downstairs in the dining room and the heavy breathing from both Karen and Desirae. There they stood, looking into one another's eyes. Karen's nostrils flared, as she realized she was about to do something she'd never thought of doing. In the flash of a second, she'd raised her hand and slapped Desirae across the face. Desirae's face turned to the side. It stung, almost just as bad as one of Veronica's slaps. The breathing and ticking of the dining room clock continued. Slowly, Desirae turned her face and looked back into her mother's face. Before she could open her mouth to say anything, Karen beat her too it.

"I wish you would," Karen said. "I wish you would slap your mother. Go right ahead and see what happens to you, Desirae." She lowered her voice, clearly angrier than she'd been in years, if not decades. "I really wish you would. See how hard I *go in*," she said, referencing sayings she'd heard younger people using, "and you're going to see how easy Veronica went on you."

Desirae stood there frozen in place. Her adrenaline rushed so badly that it took every fiber of her being to refrain from reaching out and slapping the holy shit out of her mother. At that moment in time, she saw her mother as another grown woman – a grown woman who had just disrespected her. In Desirae's eyes, there was nothing wrong with what she'd just said. She'd only given her mother a taste of her own medicine. It wasn't her fault if she couldn't take it.

Desirae's body trembled from the energy building up inside of her. "You didn't have to slap me, Mama," she said. "You ain't have to slap me."

"If I didn't have to do it, Desirae," Karen said, "then it wouldn't have happened. Don't you ever talk to me like that again. I don't care how grown you get. You understand me? I wasn't calling you a hoe, Desirae. I was just saying that with your history of men and whatnot, maybe it's time that you lay off of that. Maybe it's time that you refocus, let's say, on something else that will get you a little further than a relationship with a married man will – a married man who is also your supervisor at work, Desirae. Your supervisor at work."

"I know who he is, Mama," Desirae said, calming down. There was just no way she was going to be that girl who attacked her own parents. She thought of herself as being better than that; she thought of herself as having more class than anyone who would do something like that. "And I know, it probably wasn't a good idea."

"Can I be honest with you so that maybe you can learn something?" Karen asked, not really planning to wait on an answer. "I think you had him over so that you could make Tron jealous, is that what it was? Are you trying to make Tron jealous or something? I've seen this kind of thing before, you know."

Desirae hesitated. "I don't know," she said, not wanting to give the real answer.

Karen knew what Desirae's response really meant. "Desirae, listen to me," she said, now sounding more loving. "You don't want Tron back, so don't act like you do."

"He just watched, Mama," Desirae said, her eyes swelling with tears. "I was out in the yard, naked, and he just watched from his car and didn't even do anything."

"Hold up," Karen said. "He was still here, or out there, when it happened?"

Desirae nodded.

"Desirae, it's time to move on," Karen told her, shaking her head. "It's time to move on. Work on yourself and taking care of your kids. The right guy will come into your life. A guy who will want to help you improve yourself, not help, or not try to stop, you from breaking down. Trust me, just let it come to you instead of you looking or trying to get something back that just isn't there at this point."

Desirae knew that her mother was right. She took in her encouraging words. The two hugged and finished up their deep mother-daughter conversation before Karen went to unpack her suitcase. They'd agreed to talk some more over dinner, which would be Karen going and getting carryout from a restaurant nearby. Desirae went and checked on Titan and James. As she changed their diapers, thoughts swirled around about the direction of her life. She knew that there was no way she'd be able to keep her dignity with going back to Family Dollar. She'd go in and get her last check, but actually going back to work there was out of the question. The looks that people would give her would be too much. Knowing that Veronica could come back into the store at any moment, or even before or after work, was only the cherry on top. Desirae couldn't begin to imagine losing a fight that badly in a more-public place.

Video footage then popped into her mind. Off and on, since yesterday, she'd thought about how likely it was that someone would upload the footage of the fight to World Star or YouTube. That was another monster to tackle. Sure, Desirae would try to shrug it off. She'd go with the idea that there was no need for her to worry if there was nothing she could do about it. However, at the end of the day, she couldn't help but think about it. And it worried her a lot more than she wanted to admit.

Chapter 4

Desirae woke up Monday morning and could feel it in her soul: there was just no way she'd go back to Family Dollar. She'd thought about it yesterday, only thinking of it in theory. When her eyes opened on Monday morning, it was as if God had told her that it just wasn't meant to be. Rather, she lay in bed and thought about her options. It didn't take her long to get up out of bed realizing that she needed the money, and get on the computer. At this point, she'd take a fast food job if it was necessary. Some money was better than no money.

She ignored Tron's attempts to contact her. On Monday, he'd called twice. Desirae ignored him. Then, Tuesday rolled around. He sent six text messages. Desirae not only ignored them, but she also didn't bother to open them. By Wednesday, Tron had popped up at her mother's house unannounced. He knocked on the door. Luckily for Desirae, she'd been upstairs in her bedroom when she'd seen Tron pulling up outside. The house was quiet, as it was the middle of the day, and Desirae simply hoped that Titan and James wouldn't make too much noise, or at least not enough for Tron to hear them from the porch.

By Wednesday, however, Desirae's attitude had changed for the better. She now knew what she must do to get herself into a better situation. When she woke up Wednesday, around 10 in the morning, she went ahead and got ready as if she was going to work. She took a shower then got the twins together, ready to leave the house a little before noon. Her goal today was to spend at least a few hours at the library looking for a job. Since she'd already paid her cousin Tiffany for the week to watch Titan and James, as she always paid one week in advance, she knew she might as well use it to her advantage. Aside from that, the little amount of savings she'd had was going to go fast. The child support was surely enough to take care of James and Titan, but Desirae knew that she would need more in the long run.

When Desirae walked out into the front yard, carrying her baby twin boys in her hands, she couldn't help but look at the front yard. Sure, right now it was nothing but a medium-sized front yard with green grass. A couple of leaves blew by, coming from the trees of neighboring yards. Part of her was amazed at how much had happened out there just a few days before.

Desirae's eyes angled to the left as she began to walk down her mother's front walkway. *Well, my robe is gone*, she thought to herself. The scene played over in her mind – the very second where she'd been exposed naked to the rest of the block. Never, in her entire life, had she felt as humiliated as she felt when her robe was yanked from around her body. There were moments she would reflect and try to think of what she could've done to prevent that from happening. At this point, however, there simply was no benefit to thinking this way. Rather, she held her head high, hoping to God that there wouldn't be too many neighbors out, as she walked down the walkway and loaded James and Titan into their car seats. Desirae got behind the wheel and pulled off, feeling a little relieved that she didn't have to make eye contact with anyone. With how she was feeling, even though she was feeling confident, making eye contact with one of the people who saw the naked beat down occur would have totally killed her spirit. Furthermore, her bruised and scratched face, while it had gotten better over the last few days she'd spent in the house, still would have been a picture that told a thousand words.

On the way over to Tiffany's apartment on 16th Street, Desirae went back and forth with herself. To sum it up, she was trying to think up something she could say that would explain her face to her cousin. Up until Desirae pulled into the parking lot of Tiffany's apartment complex, she could only imagine what kind of face would greet her at the door. Desirae had never lost a fight so badly in her life.

When Desirae pulled into a parking spot, she still hadn't come up with anything to say. At this point, she simply shrugged off the situation. She told herself that whatever came out of her mouth at the moment would have to be good enough. Unloading Titan then James, she trudged up the apartment building's steps and knocked on Tiffany's door. Admittedly, she was a little nervous. After all, she hadn't seen her cousin since she'd picked up the twins on Friday, after work.

Tiffany opened the door. "Girl, I was wonderin' when you was gon' come back," she said, moving out of the way as the door opened. "I was just about to…"

Tiffany's worlds trailed off as Desirae walked into the light of Tiffany's living room. Her eyes were glued to Desirae's face.

"Desirae," Tiffany said, sounding very alarmed. "What the fuck happened, girl?"

Now was the time of panic – fight or flight, so to speak. Desirae knew she'd have to come up with something and something quick.

Desirae waved her hand, trying to dismiss the situation. "Girl, you wouldn't believe me if I told you," she responded, setting Titan and James down into the crib on the other side of the room. "Some ole stupid bullshit that I can't even believe would happen to me."

Tiffany nodded, sensing something was off. She loved her cousin with all of her heart – just about as much as she loved any other person in her family. However, this love for family didn't make Tiffany blind. Quickly, she recalled the kind of person she remembered Desirae being when the two of them were kids and saw one another on a more regular basis. Desirae was always somewhat of a hoe, but Tiffany would never say such out loud. However, this gut feeling of hers was the very same one that told her Desirae was looking a little too hard in Reggie's direction just last week.

"Oh, okay," Tiffany said.

Desirae could tell that her cousin Tiffany didn't buy her response to the question about her face. Mentally, she shrugged it off, telling herself that she didn't really care what her cousin thought. On the other hand, there was just no way she was going to tell her cousin she'd gotten her ass beat by another man's wife in her mother's front yard. This was especially so considering she knew that Tiffany had a suspicion about Desirae and her boyfriend.

"Yeah, girl," Desirae said, heading back toward the door. "Well, I gotta get to work now. I'll hit you up later on when I'm on my way to pick them up."

Tiffany followed Desirae's face as she walked across the floor in front of her. She wanted to shake her head so badly, knowing that Desirae wasn't keeping it totally real with her. Even with Tiffany maybe not being as attractive as Desirae, she'd been around the block enough to know when she was looking into the eyes of a chick that had gotten into it with some other woman over a man. However, Tiffany decided to just let it go. If Desirae wanted to keep quiet on it, she would just play along so she could keep making this babysitting money.

"Okay, just hit me up," Tiffany said.

Desirae walked out of the door, avoiding eye contact with Tiffany. She tilted her head up a little bit and waved goodbye before she disappeared down the steps. In the car, Desirae took a deep breath. She felt brave for even coming out of the house with how her face looked, let alone walking between the door and the car at both her mother's house and at Tiffany's apartment complex. She also felt like God may have been on her side today, as she hadn't run into anyone she knew from either her past jobs or years in school. Desirae could only look up at the clear, sunny skies and pray to God it stayed that way.

Desirae already knew that if she was going to get out of the house and apply for some jobs, she would need to go to a library far from any hood. The last thing in the entire world she wanted right now was for some of her friends and old acquaintances in the hood to ever see her like this. She was always so beautiful that she honestly thought she looked different with her face bruised and scratched. Having a body that any woman would pay for often made her the target of jealousy from other chicks, especially if their men couldn't control their eyes when she came walking around or passing by.

Desirae quickly drove out of the more urban areas of the city, remembering that she used to ride by a library over on the south side of the city. With it being the middle of the day, it wasn't very likely that the library would be crowded with a bunch of teenagers. What made going there even better was the fact that the library was located in a very white part of the city – a part of town that had always been white. When Desirae pulled into the parking lot and walked into the building, she felt at ease with knowing she wasn't very likely to run into anyone she knew. She simply requested a computer pass from the library staff at the desk and found a computer upstairs in a corner of the building, where she wouldn't have to look face to face with anyone.

For the next few hours, Desirae felt as if she were in a zone of her own. Here she sat at this library she had only ridden by when she lived on this side of the city just months ago. She applied for positions at insurance companies that only required a high school diploma. Several hospitals were hiring for various positions. However, Desirae was careful with what specific hospital she applied to because she knew a lot of the chicks she'd had problems with back in high school worked in hospitals.

By 4 o'clock, Desirae had worked up an appetite for herself. She'd put in for about ten job openings in and around Indianapolis. She crossed her fingers hoping that one of them would at least call her back for an interview. The last place she wanted to work right now was at a fast food restaurant, especially if her face was going to be scratched up. She'd never hear the end of it.

Desirae grabbed her purse, got up, and walked back downstairs to the parking lot. She looked out at the main road, trying to think of what there was to eat around her that sounded good to her stomach. Just as she was coming up with a small, mental list, she felt her phone vibrating in her pocket. She figured it was Tron at first, but knew that since she was a mother now, she'd better at least see who was calling her, in case it was Tiffany needing to tell her something about Titan and James. Desirae pulled her phone out and saw the person calling was just who she'd first thought it would be: Tron.

"Oh, this is just too much," Desirae said. She shook her head as she smirked. Within a matter of seconds, as she watched her phone with the screen lighting up, Desirae had pressed her fingers up to her lips from how badly she wanted to burst into laughter. "I swear... This is just too much. Now that the nigga gon' sit back in his fuckin' car out on the street and watch the mother of his children get her ass beat, here he come wanna call me and see what the fuck is goin' on with me."

Desirae pressed IGNORE then dropped her phone into her purse. "Fuck him," she said, the scene from the front yard only making her angrier as it played in her mind. "Fuck that nigga," she said, turning her car on. "That nigga ain't 'bout shit, no way. Fuck him."

Desirae pulled out of the library parking lot and headed out to the main road. After turning down Wendy's and missing the turn to get into the strip mall where there was a Burger King and Long John Silver's, Desirae gave into her hunger pains. She turned into a McDonald's parking lot and jumped into the drive thru lane. "I guess this'll be better than nothing," she said to herself.

A few seconds after Desirae had given her order through the speaker; she had pulled closer to the payment window and waited. A nice, flashy SUV caught her eye. It was parked over to the side, in the section of the parking lot that looked as if it were used by the employees. The SUV looked to be a new model, black, and had tinted window. The hubcaps on the wheels looked as if they'd just been cleaned, as Desirae could see the reflection of passing cars in them.

Desirae spent a few seconds too long gazing at this SUV. She hadn't noticed the line had moved up and snapped out of her trance at the sound of beeping behind her. Quickly, Desirae pulled up to the cashier window. She paid for her meal then pulled up to the second window. Just as she was putting her car into park and leaning back into her seat, the drive thru windows opened. She turned and looked, saying hello to a darker-skinned guy holding her Sprite.

Desirae smiled, grabbing the Sprite. "Thank you," she said, looking the guy in the eyes.

The guy, who looked to be about six feet tall, was easily a couple of shades darker than Tron. His shoulder muscles bulged under his red McDonald's uniform shirt. His arms were bulky and chiseled, but not too buff to where he looked like an anxious figure. Upon having a bit of a closer look at his ebony

44

skin, Desirae could see that tattoos virtually crawled up his arms – just the kind of man that turned her on.

"No problem," he said. "Your meal will be up and ready in a minute."

Desirae smiled, practically forgetting or not caring, how her face looked. "Thank you," she said. Her eyes then dropped to the man's name tag. It read *D'Mann*. "I like your name," she said.

The guy nodded and chuckled. "Thank you," he said. D'Mann's eyes then lowered, looking deeper into Desirae's car. He couldn't help but notice, as any man would, just how bad of a body Desirae had. It took him only seconds to see how thick Desirae was, as her thighs were pressing against one another. D'Mann licked his lips, imagining what those thighs looked like not being covered in black jeans. "I'm ready to fuckin' get off."

Desirae could hear the exhaustion in D'Mann's voice. "I bet," she said. "What is it like workin' in there, if you don't mind me askin'?"

"Fuckin' hell," D'Mann responded. "It's fuckin' hell workin' up in the bitch. I guess it's prolly work cause a nigga ain't really gotta do this shit, but I do. You know, so I ain't got the fuckin' police breathin' down my neck and shit."

Desirae nodded, understanding just what kind of situation this D'Mann guy was in. She shook her head, smiling. "I bet," she said.

"Yeah, I just use this shit as gas money," D'Mann said, moving some bags around inside of the restaurant. "For my truck…this shit is just gas money."

Desirae realized he must have been talking about the nice truck parked out in the parking lot.

"Oh, is that your truck over there?" Desirae asked. "I was lookin' at that, over there."

"Yeah," D'Mann said, smiling. "That's my truck. That's my baby." He chuckled as he handed Desirae her bag. "Well, here's your food."

"Thank you," Desirae said.

"Have a good day," D'Mann said, his eyes focused on Desirae's thighs. "Thank you for choosing McDonald's."

Desirae pulled over, catching D'Mann's eye contact in her left rearview mirror. He'd poked his head out of the window and nodded, smiling at her. Desirae waved quickly as she pulled out of the parking lot and onto the main road.

Desirae went back to the library, remembering that the sign on the door had said the closing hour was 8 pm. She sat upstairs, in the same spot that she'd been in just about an hour before, and applied for more jobs. However, as she was scouring the internet for job openings in Indianapolis, the dude she'd met at the McDonalds continued to pop into her mind. He was sexy, to say the least, and had swag. Desirae couldn't help but to think about how he was looking at her as if she were a piece of meat, remembering how he'd licked his lips while the two of them had been talking. The last kind of guy that should ever get Desirae going was the kind of guy who worked at McDonald's. She needed a man with money and wouldn't settle for anything less. However, if he was just working there as a front, then that was a different story. Plus, that truck of his had to be one of the nicest Desirae had ever seen. Everything about it was new and sleek, which she liked.

Security did a sweep of the library around 7:45 that evening, reminding all of the library patrons that the building would be closing in fifteen minutes. When he'd come to remind Desirae of the time, she couldn't help but feel his long stare at her face. She simply nodded, not even making eye contact, as she told him she was about to get up and leave.

The sun was setting, slowly descending over the top of the city as Desirae walked out to her car and got in. For whatever reason, something was telling her to go back to McDonalds and see if that guy was still there. She wasn't really looking for a relationship of any kind, but she sure didn't want to turn down the right thing. If nothing else, he might really have some money and just be working at McDonalds as a front. If that truly was the case, Desirae didn't wanna miss the chance to give the nigga a chance. She pulled out of the parking lot and headed back down the road toward the McDonald's. She'd told herself that if the truck was still in the parking lot, she'd pull into the drive-thru and order something cheap, like a milk shake.

46

Desirae did just that. She'd seen the SUV still parked in the lot and pulled into the drive thru. She'd pulled up to the second window and saw that she was in luck. The double windows opened, and Desirae saw a surprised look on D'Mann's face.

"You back again?" he asked, sarcastically.

Desirae snickered and said, "Well, I ain't think you would be here still. I thought you was about to get off."

D'Mann shook his head and chuckled. "Naw, I get off in fifteen minutes though," he said. "And a nigga is really ready to get the fuck out here and smoke or somethin'."

"Oh, yeah," Desirae said. "Shit, a bitch need to smoke her damn self. I ain't smoked in," she took a moment to think, "maybe ten months now."

"Damn," D'Mann said, hanging the strawberry milkshake to Desirae. "Well, shit. I got that fire if you wanna chill with me for a second, I mean, if you got time and stuff. I can look at you and tell that you pretty busy and stuff."

"You say you get off in fifteen minutes?" Desirae asked. She checked the drive thru line and saw that there weren't any cars behind her.

"Yeah," D'Mann responded.

"Well, shit," Desirae said. "I can just pull over and wait, if that's coo with you."

D'Mann leaned out of the window and pointed toward the parking lot. "Yeah, that's my truck back there," he said. "Just park over by it, and I'll be over there when I clock out in a second."

"Okay," Desirae said. D'Mann leaning out of the window allowed her to hear just how deep his voice was. It was the kind of deep that she found to be so sexy. She'd also gotten a closer look at D'Mann's tattoos, noticing how some of them were those she'd recognized from people who lived over in an area on Indianapolis' west side called "The Land."

Desirae pulled off and drove around the building until she pulled into a parking spot a couple of spots down from D'Mann's truck. Now that she was parked closer to it, she could see some more of the intricacies of its design. More and more, she could see that D'Mann must've had some deep pockets to be able to afford an SUV that was so nice. She sat there thinking as she gulped down her milkshake. Again, she heard her phone vibrating from her purse. She dug it out, shaking her head. And yet again, it was Tron.

"This nigga is somethin' else," Desirae said, snickering. "Now he wanna see a bitch. Now he wanna see a bitch." Against her better judgment, Desirae went ahead and answered. She put on the nicest voice she could and said, "Hello?"

"Why you ain't been answerin' my calls, Desirae?" Tron asked, clearly sounding angry.

"Hold up," Desirae said. "Don't you come callin' my phone just thinkin' that you can talk to me any ole kind of way, and it's just gon' be okay. Let's not forget that you is callin' my phone. And since we ain't together, you ain't really got no right to be try'na ask me why I do this and why I do that."

Tron let out a deep but quiet groan. "You know what I mean, Desirae," he said. "I know you'd seen that I'd been calling you, so why you even gotta front with a nigga. How are my sons? How are Titan and James?"

"They okay," Desirae said, shaking her head. "Thanks for fuckin' askin' about me. I could be sittin' up in the hospital, dyin' from getting' hit by a car or a bus or somethin', and you wouldn't even know or care to know."

"Okay, okay," Tron said. "How are you, Desirae? I was just gettin' around to that?"

"Well, thank you for asking," Desirae said. "I'm doing okay, considering."

Tron knew that she was baiting him to ask considering what. However, he wasn't going to give in. Instead, he moved along with the conversation and asked, "When I'mma come through and see my sons again? You can't stop me from seein' my sons, Desirae."

"Oh calm down, nigga," Desirae said. "Ain't nobody gon' stop you from seein' your sons. You know I was just playin' when I said that. I'm a good mother. I want my sons to grow up knowin' they daddy and to not just wind up bein' another statistic, you know. When you wanna come see

48

them? All you had to do was call and ask. I ain't got no problem with you comin' to see your sons."

"Desirae, you know I been callin' you since you hung up on me on Saturday," Tron said. "Don't act like you ain't seen a nigga callin'."

"I was busy," Desirae said, trying to suppress the giggle in her voice.

Just as Tron was continuing on with the conversation, trying to arrange a time he could come see James and Titan without having to see Desirae's company, Desirae noticed D'Mann. He had just come out of the lobby doors of the McDonalds. With a walked that was definitely swagged out, D'Mann walked over to his truck doors and hopped inside, looking over at Desirae.

"Tron, Tron," Desirae said, cutting him off. "I gotta go. I'll hit you back up later so we can finish whatever you was talkin' about. I'll hit you back, okay?"

"Desirae, I…" Tron began.

Desirae ended the call just as Tron was preparing to speak. She tossed her phone into her purse, grabbed the purse, and hopped out of the car. As she walked around her car then toward the tail of D'Mann's SUV, she saw D'Mann's eyes following her in his rearview mirror. His eyes followed her body as he smiled and nodded. Desirae smiled back, quickly getting around to the passenger front door and hopping inside.

"Damn, thought you was gon' stand a nigga up," D'Mann said, sarcastically. "I was over here waitin' for fuckin' ever."

"Boy, stop," Desirae said, getting comfortable in her seat. "You saw I was on the phone and as soon as I saw you, I got over here."

"Hmm, hmm," D'Mann said, noticing how Desirae's ass pushed down into his seat, practically spilling over the sides. "How was your day today?"

Desirae looked over at D'Mann, this dude she'd just met no more than four hours ago. In a way, she was astonished. Rarely had she ever had a man actually take the time to ask her how her day had been. She smiled and answered, "It's been okay. Just lookin' for a job and shit, but it's been okay."

"Is that right?" D'Mann asked. "What kinda job you lookin' for?"

"Any job I can get," Desirae answered. "Why?"

"Just askin'?" D'Mann said, looking away. "So, you got a nigga?"

Desirae looked over at him, confused. "What kinda question is that?" she asked.

"A real nigga question," D'Mann answered. "Look, it ain't really none of my business, but since a nigga is single and shit, I like to know who I'm hangin' out with is all. You smart, so I know that you can understand that."

Desirae slowly nodded. "Hmm, hmm," she said, thinking about how he'd said that he was single. "I see what you mean. I was actually going to ask you now that I think about it. But, to answer your question, no. I ain't got no man right now."

"That's good, that's good," D'Mann said. He then pulled a cup out of the drink carrier, popped the top off, and pulled out a fat blunt. He smiled as he held it up, looking at Desirae. "You wanna smoke this shit with a nigga?" he asked. "You got anywhere you gotta be?"

"Not for a little while," Desirae answered, not wanting to say that she was the mother of newborn twins just yet. "And hell yeah, let's smoke that shit."

D'Mann's eyes wandered down to Desirae's thighs before he pulled them back up to her face. "Bet," he said. "We can ride around and smoke this blunt and shit while we talk and maybe get to know each other."

"That's coo," Desirae said, shrugging her shoulders. "I just gotta be back at my car by ten, but that's coo."

D'Mann chuckled. "Thought you told a nigga you was single?" he asked. "Why you gotta be back at ten? You look young, but I ain't think you was that young." He looked at Desirae's chest, thinking to himself: *Goddamn she got some big ass titties.*

"I am single, nigga," Desirae said, smiling. "But I gotta be back to so I can get over to my cousin's house."

50

"You got a kid or something?" D'Mann asked. "If you do, a nigga ain't trippin'. I was just askin'."

"Damn, what is this? A background check?" Desirae asked. "But yes, I do. Actually, I got two."

"Damn," D'Mann said.

Desirae shook her head and acted as if she was about to get out of the car. D'Mann chuckled, reaching over and gripping her fat thigh. He squeezed it, keeping Desirae in her place with his strong arm. "Where you goin?" he asked. "A nigga told you that I ain't got no problem with you havin' a kid or whatever. I was just askin', damn. I got one too, in case you wanted to know."

Desirae calmed down and leaned back upright into her seat. She could feel D'Mann's strong hands – hands that came across as being stronger than Tron's hands. She smiled as her arms scrolled up his tattooed arms.

"Okay, I was about to say," Desirae said. "You lucky."

D'Mann broke into laughter as he looked back at the blunt. "You funny," he said. "So, I saw you lookin' at my nametag when you came through the drive thru earlier and shit." He lit the blunt. "You know what a nigga's name is, but I don't know what your name is. That don't seem fair, do it?"

Desirae looked at D'Mann and rolled her eyes. He was just too cute for her to even deal with right now and take seriously. "You are really funny," she said. "And I see you notice shit too. My name is Elizabeth." Desirae tried to keep her face plain.

"Bullshit," D'Mann said. "You ain't no damn Elizabeth. How the fuck you think a nigga supposed to believe that shit? Where they do that at? My name is D'Mann, as I'm sure you know by now. Some people call me D man, but I'll let you call me by my name."

"Well, thank you," Desirae said. "You are so nice. And naw, I was just playin', boy. My name ain't no damn Elizabeth. My name Desirae."

"Desirae, huh?" D'Mann said. He then handed the lit blunt to Desirae and began backing out of the parking space. A few seconds later, they were out on the main road, riding with the evening traffic as the sun had just about dropped out of the sky.

Desirae looked at the interior of D'Mann's SUV and couldn't help but rub her fingers against the door paneling. The dashboard looked so futuristic, like something she'd only seen on television. A few minutes down the road, she'd noticed that the backseats had drop-down television screens. The music, which D'Mann had on at a low volume, played perfectly crisp.

"This is a nice car," Desirae said. "You doin' good up at that McDonald's."

D'Mann chuckled. "Fuck that job," he said. "Like I told you earlier, that shit ain't nothin' but gas money. I burn up more gas with this truck than I make in a month slaving around in there with all them damn Mexicans. I make way more money on my own than I do with that shit."

"That shit just yo' front, huh?" Desirae asked.

D'Mann glanced over in Desirae's direction and shrugged. "Basically," he said. "Once a nigga got out of Marion County downtown, I ain't have no luck findin' no job, so I had to make a way myself. I just keep to myself a lot more now."

"That's what's up," Desirae said, feeling her head get a little light. "That's the shit that I'm on right now. I done had some rough months and shit. I just wanna chill and be coo, you know? I ain't with all the drama no more."

D'Mann glanced at Desirae, wondering what had happened to her face. He knew that he'd eventually find out, but he wanted to have a little strategy with how he went about finding out. "Yeah, I feel you on that shit," he said. "My baby mama." His head shook. "I'm so sick of that bitch, I don't even know what to do, shit."

"I'm in the same fuckin' boat," Desirae said, shaking her head this time. "My baby daddy is a fuckin' piece of work. He don't give two fucks or a shit about me. It's just so damn sad, too."

"Was y'all ever together like that?" D'Mann asked.

Desirae shook her head. "Naw, not really," she answered. "Just got pregnant by the nigga and had his babies."

D'Mann nodded, picking up on the bit of stress in Desirae's voice. "Shit, a nigga woulda thought that the otha nigga, the daddy, woulda snatched your ass up by now," he said. "With how pretty you is, I'm still havin' a hard time believin' that you ain't got no nigga."

Desirae looked at D'Mann. "I know what you try'na do," she said. "You just try'na make me feel better because of how my face look. I can tell by the way you lookin' at me that you wanna know what happened to it."

D'Mann shrugged. "I mean..." he said, hesitantly. "I ain't really think about it like that. I still think you pretty and shit. Just cause you got some bumps and scratches don't mean a nigga can't see that."

Smiling, Desirae said she'd gotten into it with this chick over a dude and the rest was history.

"I see, I see," D'Mann said. "It can happen to the best of us."

"Yeah, well," Desirae said, "if I catch that bitch again, I swear to God I'mma jump on that ass. She caught me off guard last time cause I ain't know she was comin'."

"You know how these hoes out here be," D'Mann said, trying to calm her down. "You know they always wanna get jealous and mad and shit at the pretty chicks or the chicks that got the body. They don't wanna do what they gotta do themselves so they can be on y'all level. That's all that is. Bitches just be intimidated by chicks like you."

Desirae looked at D'Mann, realizing that he was sure more than what met the eye when she'd rolled into McDonalds. "Yeah, well," she said, "I was thinkin' the same about you. I mean, why ain't you got no chick?"

"I don't know," D'Mann said, smiling. "It's just hard to find somebody that really catches my attention and shit. I don't know, maybe I'm just picky or somethin'."

"So, then," Desirae asked, smiling. "How did I catch your attention then? I mean, you is the one who asked me to come and chill with you."

D'Mann let a cloud of smoke billow out of his mouth. It climbed the front of his face before hitting the inside roof of his SUV and slipping out of the slightly lowered window. "Cause, the way you was talkin'," D'Mann explained. "You should see the way some of them black chicks be talkin' to a nigga when they come through the drive thru up there. I mean, damn, I know I work at McDonald's and shit, but that don't mean you gotta be mean and nasty and shit. When you first started talkin' to a nigga, I could hear how sweet you sounded in your voice and shit and how you was just a genuinely nice person. I was like, a nigga gotta say something just in case you wasn't one of them uppity bitches."

Desirae laughed. "Oh, was that what was going through your head?" she asked. "Well, ain't that something."

"So, a nigga gotta know," D'Mann said, "with as pretty as you are and stuff, what really made you wanna chill with a nigga like me... a nigga you met while he was workin' up at McDonald's?"

Desirae shrugged. "I guess the same reason you was lookin' at me, I don't know," she responded. "I mean, I thought you was kinda cute."

"Kinda cute?" D'Mann said, shaking his head. "Is that all you thought about a nigga was that he was kinda cute? Well, I'm honored to hear that."

Desirae playfully slapped D'Mann's shoulder. Even with her tap, however, she could feel how built he was underneath his shirt. He looked to be a good fifty to sixty pounds heavier than Tron, but a few inches shorter in height. Desirae looked down at the fly of D'Mann's pants, allowing her mind to wonder what was underneath, as she always did when meeting a new guy that piqued her interest. She only hoped that, if she and D'Mann got to that point, his manhood would be bigger than Greg's. The odds were in her favor, at least.

"Don't be like that," Desirae said. "You know what I mean, though. I mean, I just thought that you was cute. And since I ain't lookin' for nothin' serious right now, when you asked me if I wanted to chill, I was like fuck it, why not?"

D'Mann nodded. "That's wassup," he said. "So, what kinda shit you like to do?"

D'Mann rolled around the south side of Indianapolis for a good hour or so. He and Desirae chatted back and forth about just about everything. Desirae was really feeling D'Mann, even though she didn't particularly want to date a dude who sold drugs. However, he did seem to be smart about how he did things. Based on what he was saying, he was strategic with how he handled his business. And he really watched what kind of people he hung around.

Further into the conversation, the two of them found out that they'd gone to the same middle school. Since they'd never had any classes together, they didn't directly know one another. However, when either one of them would throw names into the air, many of the names would stick with the both of them. Desirae wondered if D'Mann knew Tron, but she figured it would be best to not even worry about trying to open that door. She was frightened over what could come out of the other side if she chose to do so.

"So, where you stay at?" Desirae asked.

D'Mann was pulling the SUV up to a stoplight on the far south side of downtown. In the distance, rising above the stadium and the interstate, were the high rises that made up downtown Indianapolis. "Actually, not too far from here," D'Mann answered. "I stay over in Haughville. Off of Tenth Street."

"Oh," Desirae said. "I thought you was from The Land." She looked at his arms. "I mean, I looked at some of the tattoos when I came through the drive-thru and thought you lived over off of Thirtieth and MLK or something."

"I knew your ass was smart," D'Mann said, smiling and looking over at Desirae. "But, yeah, a nigga is from over in The Land. But my house had some problems, so I moved over on the west side real quick. It was hard gettin' all my furniture into my place I got now, but I made it work. I'm ready to get somethin' bigger, though, but what I got now is coo. Where you stayin'?"

"I stay with my mama," Desirae asked. She let out a deep sigh. "It's goin' coo and shit, but I'm ready to get my own place again. I moved in with her so she could help me take care of my sons, but it does have its moments. I don't really feel like I can do anything or have company or anything because of it."

"Because she might be there?" D'Mann asked.

"Yeah," Desirae said. "But, it's coo. I'm try'na find me a job right now, as soon as I can, so I can get some money in my pocket and shit. Plus, I need to get back on my routine so I can lose some weight."

"You don't need to lose no weight," D'Mann assured her. "I don't know who you try'na fool and shit, but half these bitches out here wish they was as thick as you."

Desirae smiled, looking over at D'Mann. "I know they do."

"That's what don't make no sense to me is how you say you ain't got no dude," D'Mann said. "I know what you are." He looked at her, smiling and nodding. "I know what kinda chick you is. You prolly one of them real picky chicks that ain't no nigga good enough to please or some shit. I know your type."

"Naw, that ain't me," Desirae said. "Why you say that?"

D'Mann shrugged. "I don't know," he said, laughing. "Just cuz."

Desirae playfully slapped D'Mann's shoulder again. "Don't be like that," she said. "I mean, I been just havin' a real hard time findin' a dude who not gon' dog me out and who gon' give me some attention. My baby daddy, back when I first got pregnant, gon' tell me that I was just somethin' to fuck."

"What?" D'Mann asked, sounding surprised and concerned. "That nigga told you what? How disrespectful is that shit?"

"I know, right!" Desirae said. "I was mad for so long that he told me somethin' like that."

"I am too," D'Mann said. "And I just met you. You too sweet and pretty and smart and shit to be havin' some nigga treat you like you just some side chick or somethin'. I ain't even with that shit. I don't even fuck around out here like that."

Desirae looked over D'Mann, processing what he was saying to her. As he spoke, keeping his eyes on the road as they headed toward the interstate that looped around downtown, Desirae could see the ring of truth in his words; the look of honesty in his eyes. She nodded, even if only to herself, as she picked up on the fact that she was talking to a real man.

"You said you stay over in Haughville?" Desirae asked.

"Yep," D'Mann said.

"Well, shit," Desirae said, "I got a little more time and shit, you know. You ain't gotta ride around burnin' your gas up and shit. I mean, if you want, we can chill a little bit over at your place, or you can take me back to my car, and we can ride around in my car."

"You coo with goin' back to my place?" D'Mann asked. He looked Desirae up and down, knowing that he only needed to say the right things for a little while longer, and he would be deep in that pussy, making her scream at the top of her lungs. "Shit, we can."

Quickly, D'Mann changed lanes then turned a corner. He crossed over the White River and began to make his way north.

"You come over here much?" he asked Desirae.

"Naw, not really," she answered. "I used to talk to this nigga who lived over here, but I don't know if he still live over here or not."

D'Mann was still a little skeptical of Desirae. He simply had a hard time grasping how somebody as thick as she was, and with an ass that could have its own orbiting moon, could not have at least a couple of dudes trying to get with her.

"I know your baby daddy be try'na get back with you," D'Mann said.

"What make you say that?" Desirae said. "Look, let's not even talk about that nigga. Fuck him is all that I got to say. He don't know shit, ain't good for shit, and," she thought about the front yard at her mother's house on Saturday; how Tron had simply watched her get her ass beat from the car, "don't give a shit about me."

D'Mann knew he was hitting a sore spot with Desirae. When she got to talking about the father to her sons, there were definitely hard feelings coming up. In D'Mann's eyes, the dude had clearly done a number on Desirae, probably even making her feel less desirable. *And she got her ass beat, too*, D'Mann thought. *I know she ain't feelin' some type of way.*

When D'Mann drove the SUV into Haughville, Desirae knew where they were right away. The side streets were long and narrow. Houses were small with many yards on slight slopes. Every few houses had cars pulled into the driveway. Some streets had children playing out in the middle of the street as parking on both sides of the street made it seem even tighter.

For most of the journey, Desirae thought about how she felt so connected to this guy with only having met him some hours ago. He seemed like just a really cool, nice, unassuming guy. He pulled the SUV up in front of a two-story, white double.

"This the spot," D'Mann said as he parked his car. "Calm down, calm down. I see that look on your face. I keep the outside plain, but the inside is laid out."

"Boy, I wasn't thinkin' nothin' about that," Desirae said. Rather, she was thinking about who she might know that might come walking down the street. While she felt like the prettiest girl in the world with D'Mann, as he really didn't care about her face at the moment, she was still self-conscious about it. The last thing she needed right now was for people she'd gone to high school with to see her and begin chitchatting about her all over again.

When Desirae stepped inside, her eyes practically jumped out of her face. D'Mann had been telling the truth. While the outside of the house looked nothing more than minimal, the inside was a different story. The living room walls were a rich red color – a red that went well with the cream sectional that commanded much of the room's attention. Spread across the middle of the floor was an area rug made of a fur that Desirae couldn't recognize off the top of her head.

Stepping further inside, she noticed the very large television against the interior wall. Seconds had passed and her eyes were now taking in the medium-sized, but laid out dining room. The dining room table was glass and looked like something she'd seen in a magazine. Of course, she wanted to look upstairs. However, she didn't want to come across as being too nosey.

"Sorry if the place is a little messy," D'Mann said. "I ain't think I was gon' have company when I got off."

"No, you're fine," Desirae said, plopping down into a couch. "It's okay, it's okay. Nice place, D'Mann. I like this."

"Glad you like it," D'Mann said. "If you want, we can smoke again."

Desirae shrugged. "Sure, why not?" she said.

"Okay, let's smoke out back," D'Mann said, motioning toward the kitchen.

Desirae quickly jumped up, and D'Mann led her through the kitchen and to the back door. She noticed how even the kitchen was nice, as all of the appliances were the latest models. Even the dishes in the windowed cabinets looked as if they cost a pretty penny. D'Mann let Desirae out onto his patio, where there was a ten-foot fence dividing his side from his neighbor's side on the other side of the duplex. Much like the front of the house, the backyard was plain and very nondescript. Desirae could tell that he'd put extra energy into his house by making it look as inconspicuous as possible.

The two of them sat down at a cute set of table and chairs as D'Mann pulled another blunt out of his pocket. "A nigga was gon' save this one to go to sleep," he said, "but I'll let you hit it. You seem like you deserve it."

"Oh, do I?" Desirae asked. "Well, isn't that good."

"That nigga, your baby daddy and shit, been doin' you too wrong," D'Mann said. "I can tell by just talkin' to you that he really ain't no fuckin' good."

Desirae shrugged. "I mean, he take care of his sons, I will say that," she said. "But he ain't one for talkin' to or nothin'. Shit, sometime when he call me, he get to talkin' real disrespectful."

D'Mann leaned forward, putting his hand on Desirae's thigh. "Why you let that nigga get you all worked up like that?" he asked. "I mean, it seem like there's more than what you tellin' me for you to be this worked up over some nigga who obviously don't know what kinda woman he coulda had."

Desirae paused for a moment, just as she was going to open her mouth. She learned right then that there were men in this world who could pick up on her feelings and show some

59

concern. Here she sat, right across from one – right across from that kind of guy.

"You don't wanna hear all that," Desirae said. "Trust me, it would only scare you off. I done had me a rough year this year, I swear. The shit has just been unreal, even lost my best friend."

D'Mann insisted that Desirae go ahead and "let a nigga in a little bit." At first, Desirae was hesitant. However, after D'Mann talked to her, she went ahead and opened up. Careful to not give away too many details or say any names as Indianapolis was only so big when you're black, Desirae talked about how she'd met the father or her sons and what kind of relationship the two of them had. However, she did leave out the part about Tron having a chick when they met, Shawna. Desirae surely didn't want to come across as the side chick when meeting a guy who very well could turn out to be a good guy.

They passed the blunt back and forth to one another as Desirae went on to explain what happened with her best friend. She explained it as her best friend was trying to get with the father of her sons behind her back, therefore breaking up the "relationship" she'd had. While this was far from the truth, Desirae knew that D'Mann was eating it all up. He shook his head, just as she'd finished the story on having her sons.

"Damn," D'Mann said. "And the nigga gon' treat you like that when you got his twins. That shit's foul. He lucky I don't know him. I'd beat that nigga's ass for treatin' you like ain't nothin'. I could tell when I met you in the drive-thru, like I said, that you was gon' be betta quality than fifty, sixty percent of these chicks out here right now. I'm tellin' you, you somethin' rare."

Desirae smiled, feeling her confidence rise. She looked across at D'Mann's dark body, a white tank top stretching around his muscled upper body as he slid his red uniform shirt off and hung it on the back of his chair.

"You work out a lot?" Desirae asked.

"I try to," D'Mann said. "A nigga try to. It do get hard sometimes, I can't lie." He looked down at his arms and chest. "But, I go to the gym maybe four times a week. You?"

Desirae shook her head. "I ain't never really been the gym-type of chick, I don't guess," she responded. "I don't know why."

"You don't go to the gym?" D'Mann asked, sounding surprised. "You bullshittin' a nigga. How can you have a body that fuckin' fire and not ever step foot in a gym? Don't tell me your shit fake."

Desirae shook her head. "Oh, hell no," she said, letting him know. "Ain't shit on my face, D'Mann. I ain't one of them chicks. I ain't gotta go addin' in and takin' away."

"So, you just built like that natural?" D'Mann said, licking his lips. "A nigga like that shit. Sometimes, and I hate when this shit happen, but sometimes I'll meet a chick and she'll get me goin' and shit. Next thing I know, when a nigga get home, I find out that she got some fake shit on her or somethin'. I look at it like this, if you wanna nigga to be real with you, then why don't you keep it real with me? I don't play that shit."

"Ain't no shit fake on me," Desirae said. "And I always keep it real. So, you not scared that I got two kids?"

D'Mann shrugged. "I mean, yes and no," he said. "I ain't really think about it like that. You seem like a strong, independent kinda chick who is not gon' go try'na dump that shit on me."

"Naw, you ain't gotta worry about that," Desirae said. "Plus, with all I been through, I ain't really lookin' for nothin' serious, no way. I just can't go through that again. I do get lonely sometime, though."

"Lonely?" D'Mann asked. "Is that so? Shit, I know what you mean, though. I get lonely too sometimes, but you know how it is when a dude get lonely. Don't nobody care. You know how you chicks are. Just do a man so dirty and hit once and never call again, blockin' his number and stuff."

Desirae looked at D'Mann, giving him that look. "Boy, stop," she said. "You funny. I know you got some hoes in your phone."

"No, I don't," D'Mann said. "Swear I don't."

Desirae looked at D'Mann's handsome face and dark, sculpted body. "Nigga, please," she said. "Stop all that lyin'. I

61

know and you know that you got at least a couple hoes in your phone."

"Okay, okay," D'Mann said, holding his hands up. "I may have a couple, but them thots ain't shit. You can't hold a conversation with them or nothin' like that. They a couple airheads, and all they want is the D. Plus, they not even all that good at what they do, for real. Dumb and no fuckin' good."

"What is good to you?" Desirae asked, feeling herself get a little turned on. She noticed how casually D'Mann slouched back in his seat, his legs spread apart like a man who needed extra room.

"What you mean?" D'Mann asked. "Like, with a chick?"
Desirae nodded.

"Well," D'Mann said, having to think. "I definitely like a chick that will let a nigga be a man and take care of her. I don't think of that shit as you not bein' able to do it, but more so as us try'na work together and shit. I also like a woman that knows what she'd doin' with the D. That shit turn me off when they talk a good game, but when we get in the bedroom, they runnin' like they scared and stuff and tellin' me to not go so hard. Fuck that shit."

Desirae looked down at D'Mann's crotch, wondering what was underneath his black pants. "Damn, it's like that?" Desirae asked.

D'Mann chuckled. "Sometimes," he said. "And what about you? What you like in a nigga? What about the last couple niggas you done had?"

"Shit," Desirae said. "I like a dude who treat me like a person and actually wanna talk to me and stuff, see how I'm feelin'. I like a nigga that know what he doin' and is man enough to handle me. The last nigga I got with," Desirae shook her head, thinking about Greg, "well, let's just say that shit damn sure wasn't worth this." She pointed at her face. "All this over some dick that was definitely shorter than a fuckin' dollar bill."

A snicker slipped out of D'Mann's mouth. "Naw, that's fucked up," he said. "You deserve better than that."

"Yeah, that's what I thought," Desirae said.

A few silent moments passed as D'Mann looked Desirae up and down. He eyed her body language, seeing that she was definitely in need of some love and affection.

"Why don't we step in the house and shit?" D'Mann said, standing up. "I don't like the idea of us out here talkin' to each other, and my neighbors might be able to hear. That bitch next door always be try'na be up in people business."

Desirae agreed and D'Mann followed her into the house. Once inside, he quickly pushed the kitchen door closed and grabbed Desirae by her waist. He pulled her closer to him, seeing that she was smiling.

"Nice to meet you," D'Mann said, softly in her ear.

"Hmm, hmm," Desirae said.

D'Mann pushed up against her ass, feeling the massiveness of it. "How much longer you got before you gotta go pick up your sons?"

Desirae pulled her phone out and looked at it. "I gotta be back at my car in an hour," she answered. "Why?"

"You know," D'Mann said. "If you want, we can chill a little bit longer. I gotta get outta these clothes, though."

Desirae turned around and looked into D'Mann's eyes. She soon felt his hands sliding down the middle of her back before spreading out over her ass cheeks.

"Damn, you got a fat ass," D'Mann said. "I know niggas tell you that shit all the time."   "Yeah," Desirae said. "But niggas don't get to see it all the time."

D'Mann gently slapped her ass. "You gon' let me see it?" he asked. "You gon' let a nigga like me see it, do I pass your tests and shit?"

Desirae noticed that D'Mann was getting hard underneath his black pants. She could feel something thick and strong pressing against her.

"I don't know," Desirae said. "I gotta see."

Desirae kept eye contact with D'Mann as she dropped down to her knees, right there in the middle of D'Mann's kitchen floor. D'Mann allowed his hand to rise up her back until the palm of his hand gripped the dome of her head. He looked down at her beaten, swollen face, knowing that he was looking at a chick that just wanted to feel pretty and wanted again. And he was going to do his best to make sure she felt that way.

As Desirae undid D'Mann's belt then zipper, he told her, "You are so pretty. Like, for real. And I mean that shit."

Desirae smiled as she pulled on D'Mann's pants then his gray boxer briefs. Just as she was gripping his dark, muscular thighs, his manhood popped out in front of her. Her face lit up with excitement as she looked at what had to be the fattest dick she'd ever seen. She wrapped her hands around it, holding it as if it were heavy and lifted it up to her lips.

"Fuck," D'Mann said, the word slipping out of his mouth. "Goddamn your mouth feel good as shit."

Desirae giggled as her head bobbed up and down on D'Mann's manhood. His large, heavy balls swayed underneath, slapping against the inside of his thighs. Desirae's slurping noises filled the kitchen as D'Mann turned his back to the kitchen counter, directly next to the sink, and leaned back. He never let up on his grip of Desirae's head.

"Fuck, Desirae," D'Mann said. "Shit. I ain't never had a chick suck this dick like this." A bead of sweat rolled down his face. "Fuck."

Desirae gave it everything she had. D'Mann had made her totally forget about how her face looked right now, as well as the ever-playing scenes in her head of having her robe snatched off of her while Greg's wife beat her ass in her own mother's front yard. Something about D'Mann made him twice the man as Tron. Furthermore, he was caring and was the kind of guy who was willing to take a little bit of time to really get to know a chick by talking to her on a real level. Desirae hadn't really been able to open up about her life since she and Reese had been friends. Now, even Reese was far back in her mind. She focused on D'Mann and the pleasure she was giving to him, as even the way he rubbed the top of her head told her that he really did respect her.

"Stop, stop," D'Mann said. "A nigga gotta taste it." He leaned down and gave Desirae a deep kiss, with a lot of tongue. He liked that he could taste his own dick on her breath.

"Taste what?" Desirae asked, whipping spit away from her mouth.

"That pussy!" D'Mann told her, helping Desirae get up off of her knees. "A nigga gotta taste that pussy."

Giggling, Desirae liked that a dude like D'Mann, who she might've normally thought wouldn't go down on a chick, was thoughtful enough to think of her needs.

"Let me see that pussy," D'Mann said.

D'Mann helped Desirae out of her pants, pulling them all the way down to her ankles. He then yanked her panties down. "Shit," he said. "Look at that ass."

D'Mann lowered himself down to his knees, to where he was now face to face with the glorious anatomy that was Desirae's ass. He slapped and played with it with his hands and watched it jingle. He pressed his face into it before spreading the cheeks and pressing his tongue inside. Desirae moaned, feeling D'Mann's wet tongue push into her asshole.

"Shit, nigga," Desirae said.

D'Mann remained quiet. Rather, he groaned and smiled as he slapped Desirae's ass again. With a quick use of his muscles, D'Mann turned Desirae around and pushed her backward. Desirae now had her back pressed against the kitchen table, her legs in the air. Before she even realized what was going on, D'Mann had pushed his head between her legs and was giving her what could only be described as a hurricane tongue. She squealed and squirmed, pushing his head back from how good it felt. D'Mann, almost as well as Greg, continued eating as if his life depended on it.

When Desirae got to the point where she couldn't take it anymore, she knew that she wanted to please this man as best she could. He was too fine and too thuggish for her to even pretend like she was going to act stuck up with him. Plus, if he still wanted to get with her when her face was bruised and scratched, he had to really be interested in her as a person. Desirae pushed D'Mann back and got back onto her knees in front of him. Quickly, he planted the palm of his hand on the dome of her head and looked down at her.

"Suck on it," D'Mann said. "I don't let just anybody suck on this dick. Suck on it, girl."

Desirae smiled and looked back at D'Mann's manhood. The veins running down the side were so engorged they looked as if they were going to pop. She quickly took him back into her mouth and slurped on his dick as if it were a lollipop.

"Fuck," D'Mann said, tensing up. "You betta stop before you make a nigga bust. Betta quit playin' with a nigga."

Desirae giggled under her breath, her mouth too full to really respond. Instead, she continued giving D'Mann everything she had. She liked how he responded, and how he was so much more respectful. He treated her like the woman she was, rather than the hoe that Tron had tried to make her out to be.

"Fuck," D'Mann groaned, announcing himself. "You 'bout to make a nigga bust! Shit! You bout to make a nigga bust!"

D'Mann gripped the top of Desirae's head, as Desirae gave no resistance to what he was about to do.

***

On the drive back down to the McDonald's where D'Mann worked, he and Desirae talked for the entire ride. It didn't take Desirae long to see just how much she had in common with this dude. They traded phone numbers when D'Mann pulled into the parking lot to drop Desirae off. And, of course, he got one last good look at her ass for the day when she walked back over to her car.

"Damn, nigga!" Desirae said as she was approaching her car. She could see, in the reflection of one of her car windows, that D'Mann was sitting in his truck further back with his eyes glued on her backside. "You ain't gotta just stare at my ass like that."

D'Mann snickered. "You know a nigga gon' look at it," he said. "That shit is too fat."

Desirae climbed into her car and the two of them drove off, waving to one another.

Chapter 5

A range of emotions came over Desirae as she headed back toward downtown to get to 16th Street. Deep down, she felt so freaky. She felt like a little slut and, honestly, she liked to feel that way. D'Mann was sexy in every way possible. He had the body, a cute face, and a dick so thick that Desirae had a hard time getting her mouth around it. The way he walked could only be described as real swag, while at the same time he was very different compared to a lot of the guys that Desirae had messed around with from time to time. There was a look in his eyes that told her that he respected her and not just for her body.

"I wanted to fuck him so bad," Desirae said, smiling. She held on to her steering wheel as she watched for pedestrians and evening traffic downtown. "That dick was so damn good. I shoulda fucked him. Naw, I betta not." Desirae thought about how having unprotected sex with Tron had caused her to wind up being the young mother of twins. "With my luck, I'll fuck around and get pregnant with triplets this time around." She then smiled, imagining how D'Mann would definitely stretch her insides.

When Desirae pulled into the parking lot of Tiffany's apartment complex on 16th Street, she was probably in a better mood than she'd been in for quite some time. Every so often, especially if she was sitting at a stoplight, she would pull her phone out of her pocket and check it. At first, she shrugged it off, telling herself that she was only checking to see if Tiffany had called about her children. Rather, she was really checking to see if D'Mann had messaged her. Knowing how men can be, however, Desirae decided to simply let the chips fall where they may. If he never hit her up again, she'd know then that he was probably just another lying dude who really did have a chick. This was the one thing Desirae struggled with, as she just couldn't believe that a guy as attractive as D'Mann would be single and just so happened to meet her and like her when her face was bruised and scratched up. Desirae shook her head as she got out of her car and walked up the stairs to Tiffany's apartment.

Just as Desirae had gotten about halfway down the hallway from the staircase down to the parking lot, she could hear yelling. The yelling, which was loud and littered with profanity and the word *nigga*, sounded as if it were coming from Tiffany's apartment. Alarmed, mainly because of her motherly instincts when it came to Titan and James, Desirae put a little pep in her step. When she approached the door, she'd just lifted her hand to knock when she heard her cousin say something that stopped her in her tracks.

"So, is that what you want now?" Tiffany said. "You would smash the shit out of my cousin? Huh, nigga?"

Desirae's neck snapped back. Quickly, she looked both ways down the hallway. Nobody was heading her way. She stepped closer to the door, turning the side of her head to it, and listened closely.

"Tiffany, that ain't what I meant!" a man said.

It took Desirae a moment to register the man's voice as Tiffany's nigga, Reggie. She smiled, remembering how he'd greeted her without a shirt on just last week. However, since he belonged to her cousin, Desirae wasn't going to make a move. In fact, much of her felt a little sorry for her cousin. There was no doubt in her mind that her cousin was probably insecure when she came around. With a body like Desirae's, it wasn't unusual for her to intimidate them, especially if said women just didn't have much going on in terms of looks.

"Then what the fuck did you mean?" Tiffany demanded to know. "Huh, Reggie? What the fuck did you mean, nigga? Don't talk to me like I don't speak no damn English or nothin'. I saw the text message you sent your boy Romney. I saw that shit and now you wanna say that it ain't what it seems. Seems to me like your eyes just had a good ole time lookin' at Desirae's ole hoe ass."

Desirae pulled back from the door for a moment. She could feel her temper starting to elevate. Through the years, she'd always thought that she'd been cool with her cousin Tiffany. Growing up, they'd spent just enough time together to where they could get to know one another, but not so much to where they'd have much to go off of if one wanted to say they didn't like the other. For this reason, Desirae had been surprised with Tiffany's reactions lately. First, she insinuated – or accused – Reggie and Desirae of possibly having something going on when she got home from running up to the hospital. Now, based on the pieces of information Desirae had to put together, it sounded as if Reggie had said something about Desirae.

"Look, I was just sayin' that she attractive," Reggie said. "That's all."

"That's all my ass, nigga," Tiffany said, clearly not buying it. "Let me read the text message."

"Tiffany, gimme my phone back," Reggie demanded.

"Not till I'm done readin' this shit, so we can both make sure that we on the same page," Tiffany said. There was a brief pause before she began to read the text message. "Damn nigga, Tiffany's cousin got a big ole fat ass. I'd smash that shit like it was my last."

A smile came over Desirae's face, and she really didn't know why.

"So how am I supposed to read that?" Tiffany asked. "Huh, nigga. You sure you ain't fuck with my cousin. I told you about her. She will fuck any chick's nigga cause won't no respectable dude be with her to begin with. She just a thot. You should see her face. The bitch done clearly got her ass beat by some other nigga's chick and just don't wanna admit it. And now here you are, try'na smash her too. Nigga, I can't believe you."

Hearing her cousin say such harsh things about her definitely did hit a sore spot with Desirae. After letting a few more minutes pass, hearing Tiffany demand some sort of explanation out of Reggie for even looking at Desirae's ass to begin with, Desirae forced herself to go ahead and knock on the door. At the rate Tiffany was going with Reggie, Desirae knew that if she waited until the argument stopped, she could surely be out in the building hallway for at least another hour or so.

Just as Desirae finished knocking on Tiffany's door, the apartment went quiet. Within seconds, the apartment door swung open. Desirae had already made up her mind that she was just going to grin and bear the insults, not wanting to add

69

any more fuel to the fire. She just hoped that Tiffany wouldn't try to start anything with her, as she was feeling pretty good from her unexpected evening with D'Mann.

"Hey girl, come on in," Tiffany said, her lips tight.

"Thanks girl," Desirae said. "I ain't catch you at a bad time, did I? You look mad as hell, girl."

"Naw, girl," Tiffany said. "And no, you didn't. I ain't mad. Just had to talk to Reggie about some things."

As Desirae stepped into the living room, her head caught the back of Reggie. He'd been walking down the hallway, in nothing but a white tank top and gray sweatpants. Desirae couldn't help but look at the muscles on his back and how they moved as he walked down the hallway.

"Okay, okay," Desirae said, smiling. She watched as Tiffany began to gather Titan and James' things from around the living room floor. Badly, Desirae wanted to shake her head. She couldn't help but feel sorry for her cousin, as she was clearly so intimidated and threatened by the fact that Desirae had the body her man Reggie obviously lusted after. "I understand."

"You doin' alright?" Tiffany asked Desirae. "You not in your work uniform? You ain't work today?"

"Girl, I ain't at that Family Dollar no more," Desirae said. "That shit just wasn't for me. I'm lookin' for another job now. Might have some leads."

Tiffany looked Desirae up and down, making sure to take note of her face. Something told her that for her cousin, who is a new mother to infant twin boys, to suddenly not work there anymore that there must have been a major incident at that store. "Oh, okay," Tiffany said. "Well, I wish you luck on that."

"Yeah," Desirae said, shaking her head. "It ain't easy out there, but I'mma find a way. Got they daddy callin' me now, try'na come see the twins."

"Oh, yeah?" Tiffany said. "You never told me much about him. Did you ever bring him to a family function or something and maybe I missed it?"

Desirae's eyes barreled down on Tiffany's back as she lifted Titan then James out of the crib. She shook her head as she knew exactly what Tiffany's motive was for asking such a question. Nonetheless, Desirae wasn't going to let some insecure woman ruffle her feathers.

"No," Desirae said. "I doubt you have seen him. My mama met him, but naw, I ain't never brought him to no family function. We not together like that no way."

"Oh, okay."

As Desirae was headed out and into the hallway, she felt the tension on the back of her like a ray of hot sun. Tiffany was looking at her butt and probably shaking her head. Desirae wanted to snicker, but she knew better than to do such a thing. She decided, instead, to keep it classy.

"Thank you, Tiffany," Desirae said, holding both Titan and James. "I'll be back over here tomorrow."

Tiffany, who stood in the doorway, said goodbye to Titan and James in baby talk. Just as Desirae was smiling at the twins, noticing how well Tiffany interacted with the babies Reggie appeared in the background. He stood in the bedroom hallway, just barely stepping into the light that reached down the hall from the living room. The two of them made eye contact for a second or two too long – a second or two that definitely had some subliminal communication in them. Something about Reggie struck Desirae that he was the kind of guy she probably wouldn't want to mess around with for too long. However, one ride on a pony like that might be all she needed. Desirae looked at Tiffany, thinking, *she lucky that I have respect for my family. She is so lucky.*

Desirae turned away, saying goodbye to Tiffany as she walked down the hall. The door slammed shut and a few seconds later, Desirae heard what sounded like a loud slap. Quickly, feeling the weight of carrying two twin boys in her arms, she rushed back down the hallway to listen.

"Nigga, you just can't get enough of it, can you?" Tiffany asked. "Huh, nigga? Make me slap you again. You just had to come out here and get a good look at it, didn't you?"

Not caring to hear anymore, Desirae walked toward the steps and headed down to the parking lot. She shook her head and giggled, feeling sorry for her cousin.

***

When Desirae walked in the door at home, her mother Karen was in the kitchen. She popped her head into the dining room and smiled. "Hello there," she said.

"Hey, Mama," Desirae said.

"You okay?" Karen asked, speaking loudly from the kitchen.

"Yeah, just tired," Desirae said.

Desirae carried Titan and James upstairs and gently placed them into their basinets. She knew that her mother was probably waiting on her to come back downstairs to talk, as they usually did, but Desirae was just not in the mood. Now, more than anything, she wanted to take a warm shower and get in the bed.

Later that night, as Desirae laid in the dark, she heard her phone vibrate just as she was starting to doze off. She turned over and reached for the bedside table. She couldn't help but smile when she saw that the vibrating was a text message from D'Mann.

D'Mann: *So you not gon' text a nigga. SMH. Just like a chick.*

Desirae chuckled. She loved D'Mann's sense of humor already.

Desirae: *Dang, I just met you today. How soon you want a girl to text you?*

D'Mann: *ASAP. LOL. Was just thinkin' bout you.*

Desirae shook her head. Even if she didn't believe everything D'Mann said, his words were at least nice to hear, or read.

Desirae: *Oh really. What was you thinking about me for?*

D'Mann: *You know. A nigga is just hoping that you ain't one of them crazy chicks you hear about that be given' niggas the business.*

Desirae: *I ain't crazy. Don't play with me, boy. What you doing up anyway? Waiting on your chick to come through or something?*

D'Mann: *You funny. I told you I ain't got no chick. Did you see one when you came over here?*

Desirae: *I ain't see the entire house when I came over. For all I know, she could've been upstairs, sleeping or maybe listening to us talk or something.*

D'Mann: *OMG you funny. Wait till you come over again, if you come see a nigga again. I'll show you the whole house so you ain't gotta think that somebody else be stayin' here. I'll even let you look under the bed for the panties chicks leave.*

"Oh, no he didn't," Desirae said, giggling in the dark as the light from her phone illuminated the room. "This nigga is crazy." She smiled.

As Desirae was typing a response text message to D'Mann, she was interrupted by her phone vibrating. It was a call from Tron.

"Fuck," Desirae said, looking over at the two basinets. She really didn't feel like talking right now because she ran the risk of waking up the twins. She simply decided that she'd speak softly. "Hello?"

"Why you gotta answer like that?" Tron asked.

"Like what?" Desirae asked, shaking her head. "I was just answering the damn phone, and I find you got a fuckin' problem with it. How are you, Tron?"

"I'm fine, Desirae," Tron answered, matching Desirae's sweet voice with his professional voice. "Thank you for asking. Look, here's why I was callin'. I was just callin' to see when I can come over and see my sons, is all. When you don't have company, that is."

Desirae rolled her eyes, knowing that Tron's company comment was in reference to when Greg had been over on Saturday.

"I ain't lookin' for no drama," Tron said. "If you need to, we can meet somewhere if you gotta worry about people showin' up at the house like that."

"Nigga, I'll let you know what I gotta worry about," Desirae said. "And I ain't gotta meet you nowhere. Fuck that bitch. She ain't gon come back up here."

"Yeah, you right," Tron said. "She already made her point."

"What the fuck that supposed to mean?" Desirae asked, feeling offended.

Tron dismissed the comment quickly. "Nothing, Desirae," he said. "Nothing. Look, can I come by tomorrow before you go into work and see my sons or what?"

"Yeah, sure," Desirae said. "Just text me before you come. You know I go into work at three, so just keep that in mind."

"A'ight," Tron said, not knowing that Desirae didn't go back to Family Dollar. "I'll hit you up in the morning."

"Okay," Desirae said. Before Tron could muster up the words to respond, Desirae ended the phone call. She smiled, knowing that she'd hung up on Tron the very same way that he used to hang up on her when she would call. The irony of the situation was just too much for her, to the point where she needed to laugh a little.

No sooner than Desirae began to set her phone down onto the bed, it vibrated again. She assumed that it was Tron calling back. Rather, she found that it was D'Mann sending her a text message. Quickly she opened it and found that he'd sent her a picture of his manhood. She shook her head upon seeing it. "Damn that's a thick dick," Desirae said to herself, feeling herself get wet.

She responded to the picture: *Boy, stop try'na get something started that you can't finish.*

D'Mann: *Haha. Who said I can't finish it? Where you stay? I can come over there and we can park outside.*

Desirae: *Boy, stop. I'm going to sleep. Plus, I can't leave my babies in the house like that.*

D'Mann: *Hmm, hmm. You prolly got some nigga up in there. I know how you chicks be.*

Desirae giggled as she set her phone down, feeling that it was now time for her to go to sleep. Before she allowed herself to get too comfortable, she took one last look at D'Mann's picture. She blew a kiss at the screen, knowing that she'd hit the jackpot.

Chapter 6

On Thursday morning, Tron walked through Circle Centre Mall downtown with Reese. He'd needed to buy some new clothes for a family reunion that was happening over the weekend in a small town just outside of Louisville. Reese, who had spent the night at his townhouse, made it very clear when the two of them had woken up that morning, that she would be more than thrilled to ride along.

Tron wound up caving in and getting Reese a few things out of Forever 21. When the two walked out of the store, they headed toward the mall parking garage.

"I already know she gon' try something when you get over there, Tron," Reese said, thinking about how he'd said something during the morning hours about going over to see James and Titan. "I already know she is. I can just about tell you what I think that bitch is over there doin' right now. She prolly try'na make sure that she puts on something that is sexy and two sizes too tight and too small just so she can show her ass off to you. I know she want you to want her again."

"Well, I don't," Tron told Reese. The visual of Desirae's heavy, swaying backside popped up in Tron's mind. He just couldn't get his mind off of it at times. In fact, while he and Reese had been walking through the mall, every so often the two of them would pass by a chick with an ass like Desirae. And Tron, being the typical black man, just couldn't keep himself from having a look.

"I know you don't," Reese said. "But she gon' try. Do she still not know that the two of us is kickin' it."

"As far as I know, she don't," Tron responded. "I mean, who is gonna tell her?"

"True," Reese said, shrugging. "Ain't like the bitch got friends. In fact, I was probably the only friend she had. And now that's over."

Tron walked Reese out to his SUV. He held the front passenger door and allowed her to climb inside. As she did, however, Tron found himself comparing Reese's ass to Desirae's ass. The two really couldn't be compared, and there were definitely moments that Tron never wanted to see Desirae again. However, as the days went on since he saw her bare ass exposed to the sunlight in the front yard on Saturday, he'd found himself thinking about it more and more. All he needed was one last time to really beat the breaks off of that pussy, and he would be good.

On the way back to Tron's townhouse, he and Reese chitchatted as they usually did when they rolled together. Tron looked over at Reese, feeling a little something stir in his heart. There was something about her that really did make her more of a girlfriend-type of woman, especially when comparing her to Desirae. He also noticed and liked how Reese was religious with making sure she stayed up to date with her birth control. Tron wished that he'd paid closer attention to Desirae when it came to that issue. While he really did love Titan and James with all of his heart, like any father would, Tron still couldn't shake the feeling that Desirae had purposely gotten pregnant by him. That was all water under the bridge at this point, however.

"So, what you got on for the rest of the day?" Tron asked as he pulled his SUV into the parking lot of his community. "Was you try'na come back over later on tonight when I get done at the club."

Reese shrugged. "I don't know," she answered. "I was talkin' to my auntie last night, and she was sayin' something about needin' my help with somethin'. I swear, I'm ready to get my own place again. Them niggas can't do nothin' for themselves."

"I know what you mean," Tron said. He hopped out of his SUV and grabbed his bags out of the backseat. Reese climbed out as well and walked around to the back of the SUV, approaching Tron.

"I'm tellin' you," Reese said. "That hoe is thirsty. She gon' try something."

"Trust me," Tron said, neither one of them seeing the irony in him making such a statement, "she is not gon' try anything with me. We not even cool like that. And I know she probably still feelin' some kind of way about gettin' that ass beat out in the front yard the other day."

Reese snickered. "I bet she is," she said. "And that bitch got her robe ripped off." She shook her head. "Well, she always did like showin' her body off. You never know… You just might see her try'na come up the club and dance."

"Naw," Tron said, thinking about how Desirae, even with having had twins recently, could very well steal the show from the other girls. There was no doubt in Tron's mind that Desirae would be grabbing the attention of plenty of the men who came into the club. She had just the right build. Just then, for whatever reason, Tron imagined giving Desirae's big round and wide ass long shots from the back. He couldn't deny how he missed gripping her hips and holding her in place. "She ain't gon' do nothin' like that. You know she got a attitude when I call her now. I'm just goin' over there to see Titan and James and nothin' else. I swear to God, I hope she don't try to start no shit with me. She prolly gon' have some nigga layin' up over there."

"You know she got some nigga already," Reese said. "You might not see him, but that bitch keeps her mouth on the mic, if you know what I mean."

Sensing the bitterness coming out in Reese's voice. "A'ight then," he said, cutting the conversation short. "I betta get over there so I can have enough time with the twins."

"Text me when you get there or whatever," Reese said.

The two of them kissed before Tron watched her walk across the parking lot and get into her car. As she pulled out of her parking spot, Tron waved goodbye to her and carried his shopping bags into the house so he could get ready to go again.

Just as Tron stepped into the entryway of his townhouse, he could smell weed. He walked into the living room and saw that Tyrese hadn't left yet. Rather, he was sitting on the couch, in nothing but black sweatpants as he smoked a blunt.

"Wassup baby daddy?" Tyrese asked, sounding very sarcastic.

Tron looked at his boy as he dropped his shopping bags onto the floor. He knew that Tyrese's comments were in reference to when he'd stepped out of the club last night to call Desirae. Just as he'd been walking back into the back door, Tyrese was coming out of the dancers' dressing room and Tron quickly filled him in.

"Fuck you, nigga," Tron said. "What the fuck you doin' today? Just layin' around and not doin' shit?"

"Naw, nigga," Tyrese said. "Fuck you. I got plenty of shit to do as a matter of fact. Dude, last night I met this one bitch, her name is Lauren, or some shit like that. Anyway, this bitch got the biggest damn lips I done ever seen."

Tron shook his head. "I already know what that mean," he said.

"Exactly," Tyrese said. "A nigga is try'na see what that mouth feel like." He held up his phone, signaling to Tron that he'd been texting her before he came walking inside. "But you know how bitches be actin'. She keep talkin' that shit about how she ain't no hoe, but I'm like, damn, bitch, with some lips like that, I know you suckin' some damn dick. Stop playin' with a nigga."

Tron shook his head. "Damn, nigga," he said. "All you think about is fuckin', don't you."

"Man, whatever," Tyrese said as Tron got himself something to drink. "A nigga need his dick sucked and that's all. Is that too much to ask for?"

"Maybe it is for her," Tron said.

"Man, whatever," Tyrese said. "Hey, ain't you supposed to be headed over to your baby mama house? You gon' be late. You betta hurry up before she go crazy on that ass again and have you runnin'."

"Naw," Tron said, shaking his head. "After me seeing that ass get beat out in the yard on Saturday, she prolly ain't gon' be try'na do too much no more. As far as I'm concerned, based on what I saw, she need to be goin' to one of them white people churches downtown – them big stone ones – and see about becoming a damn nun or something."

"Oh, oh, I forgot," Tyrese said. He quickly scrolled through his phone. "I was lookin' for the video on World Star and shit, and I think I might'a found it."

Tron poked his head out of the kitchen. "Word?" he said. "You think you found that shit. Man, I'd hate to be her. That shit was embarrassing as fuck, my nigga."

"Yeah, this shit I saw was too," Tyrese said. "It was a chick in a robe and she came outside and got her ass beat bad, but I couldn't make out what nobody was sayin'." He looked through his bookmarks. "Here it go."

Tron stepped back over to the couch and looked into Tyrese's phone. As he leaned up, he called Tyrese stupid. "Nigga, you know that ain't Desirae," he said. "And look at that shit, nigga. Is you stupid? We live in fuckin' Indiana, not Florida or California or some shit. You see them damn palm trees in the background and shit. How you not see that shit?"

"Oh," Tyrese said, realizing that his boy Tron was right. "I will note that. I'mma keep this one saved, but I'll let you know as soon as I find the Desirae one. I know that somebody, after this many fuckin' days, done uploaded that shit to YouTube or somewhere by now. I can't believe I ain't found it."

"Why you wanna see it for, nigga?" Tron asked, acting serious.

Tyrese looked up at Tron. "Nigga, you know," he responded. "Look, I know she your baby moms and shit, but a nigga ain't gon' miss the chance to see some ass and titties out in the air like you say they was. Sorry man, don't take it personal."

Tron shook his head and snickered. A visual image of Desirae's backside popped into his mind. "That ass done got even bigger," he said, not realizing that he'd been talking out loud.

"I know," Tyrese said. "I remember you tellin' me that shit. That's why a nigga need to see so I can get a betta understandin' of what you talkin' bout."

"Nigga, whatever," Tron said. He then turned around, grabbed his keys off of the coffee table, and headed back toward the front door. "I'm out. Gon' head over there and see this chick before I don't even feel like it again."

"Don't do anything I wouldn't do," Tyrese said. "I know you gon' smash that shit again, so I don't even know why you playin' around and shit. You might as well go ahead and admit it. We both know what it is."

79

"Man, whatever," Tron said. "I'm so through with that chick. I know she want the D, but I ain't gon give it to her. Not with the way she act."

Just as Tron climbed into his SUV, he pulled his phone out of his pocket. At first, he was going to text message Desirae and tell her that he was on his way. However, just as he was doing so, a text message from Reese popped up: *Get a picture of that bitch's face so I can see it.*

Tron shook his head and laughed. In many ways, he found it so funny how Reese had been Desirae's best friend just months ago and now felt free enough to talk about how much she couldn't stand being her friend. He responded to Reese: *Okay.*

After Tron messaged Desirae that he was on his way, he zigzagged out of his community parking lot and headed over to Desirae's mother's house.

***

Tron pulled up and parked outside of the two-story house, his SUV in just about the same place it'd been on Saturday. Upon putting his truck into PARK, he looked at the yard. Compared to the last time he'd seen it, which was Saturday, it looked so calm. When he'd pulled off on Saturday and made his way down to the stop sign at the corner, Desirae's arms were wrapped around her chest as she rushed up the walkway, onto the front porch, and into the house.

Over the last couple of days, Tron had been giving a little more thought to his own actions. While there was no doubt in Tron's mind that Desirae was probably doing something that she had no business doing, he started to feel a little guilty about his inaction. Instead of just sitting in the car and watching the mother of his sons have her dignity stripped from her in front of everybody, he could have gotten out and gone up to stop the attack. However, Tron also knew that Desirae's planned and surprised ambush with her father when he'd gone over to her place to help her move was all he needed to sit in the SUV and not make a move. All he could think about was how he'd woken up, on the ground in the snow, after being knocked out by Desirae's father. Desirae sure didn't seem to care about the welfare of the father of her children when all of that was going down.

Tron stepped out of his truck and walked up to the porch. Seconds after he knocked on the glass window of the front door, the curtains moved to the side and his eyes met with Desirae's bruised and scratched face. She opened the door.

"Oh, hey," Desirae said. "I ain't think you would get here so fast. Come in."

Tron was a little cautious about stepping inside of the house. There was a certain tone in Desirae's voice that came across as being very suspicious. She was being very nice and very calm, which was usually how she started any interaction between the two of them.

As Tron stepped further into the living room, he became more and more comfortable. He didn't get the vibe that any other man was in the house, but he wanted to be sure.

"A nigga ain't catch you at a bad time, did he?" Tron asked, looking around.

Desirae rolled her eyes as she pushed the door closed, noticing how cute Tron looked in black jeans, a blue button-up shirt, and a black suede, mid-weight jacket. "No," she said. I ain't got no company today."

Just as the front door closed completely, Tron had gotten a better look at Desirae. A black tank top stretched across her round chest, doing little to nothing to keep it from bouncing as she moved. Tron's eyes then lowered to the red pajama pants that hugged Desirae's wide hips and fat thighs. He thought about Reese's comments, about how she was sure that Desirae would be wearing something too small. Tron shook his head, not being able to decide if what Desirae had on was indeed too small or if she was just too thick for any normal sized clothing. Even with the little bit of stomach she had from the pregnancy, her chest and lower body made it all definitely look proportionate.

Desirae turned around and led Tron into the dining room. For the entire ten feet or so that he followed behind her, Tron's eyes zoomed in on the dimples. Not only did Desirae's ass sway from side to side when she walked but with every step she took, the dimples on the side indented and expanded. When Desirae came to a halt in her path, Tron almost ran into her. His eyes had been too fixated on the way she moved; his dick began to stir a little when he saw the way her ass jiggled even more than he remembered when she would stop moving.

When Tron stepped around Desirae to approach his son's basinets, he'd brushed against the backside of Desirae. Even in the millisecond that the front of his body was pressed against the back of her, Tron could only imagine dicking her down unmercifully. In those red pajama pants, her ass looked as if it had grown an inch or two in size since Tron had seen it last. Quickly, as Tron picked up James out of his basinet first, he made eye contact with Desirae. In her cold, uncaring eyes, he could see that her demeanor had not changed.

Tron talked baby talk to James then did the same with Titan. He asked Desirae if they were sleeping through the night or if they were waking up and hollering the way the two of them had the time Desirae called him to hear it over the phone. Desirae simply shook her head and responded, "What difference does it make to you, Tron? It's not like you here no way to help me when they do wake up in the middle of the night."

Tron grinned, not liking the tone in Desirae's voice. He then asked her, as she pulled out a dining room chair and plopped down, how low on diapers she'd become. Desirae rolled her eyes and answered, "I'm over here taking care of twins, Tron. What you think? Of course I need more diapers. I just ain't wanna call you and bother you, cause you know how busy you be getting."

With his back to Desirae, the word *bitch* slipped out of his lips, but silently. At that moment, Tron realized that Desirae had to probably be the most uncooperative woman in the world. The only good thing about her was her body at this point, seeing as her face was bruised and scratched pretty badly. It wasn't as bad as on Saturday, when Tron watched the shamed and humiliated woman run into the house. However, it was very clear to the outside world that whoever beat Desirae's ass did a good and thorough job. Tron looked at her face and knew that he needed to say something to make the situation a little better. Now holding Titan in his arms, he placed him back down into his basinet.

"I'mma be the bigger person here and actually say sorry," Tron said, looking over at Desirae. He couldn't help but notice how her thighs were pushing together so hard they pushed one another further up into the air.

With folded arms, Desirae snapped her neck. "What you mean you sorry?" she asked. "What the fuck you sorry for, Tron?"

"Saturday," Tron said, trying to sound as supportive as possible. "I been thinkin' bout that shit a lot over the last couple days."

"Oh, really?" Desirae said. She then rolled her eyes and shook her head. "You ain't gotta go rubbin' it in, Tron."

"I ain't try'na rub it in," Tron said. "I was just lettin' you know that you were right."

Right? Desirae thought. *For once, is this nigga respecting me? For once, is this nigga actually trying to come around and see my point of view?* Desirae was astonished. Before she could really process his apology of sorts, she had begun to wonder about Tron's true intentions. "No, it's okay," Desirae said. "It wasn't your fight, obviously."

"Yes, it was," Tron said, looking dead into Desirae's eyes. "It was. Like you said, you the mother of my children. At first, I really didn't realize what was going on, but when I saw that chick coming up into your yard, followed by the people comin' up the block, I shoulda got out and made sure that everything was okay. I can't believe I just sat there like I ain't see shit goin' on."

"You can't believe it?" Desirae asked. "You can't believe it?" She snickered. "I was the one out there gettin' my ass beat in my birthday suit. And now you wanna say that you can't believe that you ain't do nothin'."

"Look, Desirae," Tron said, holding his hands up in the surrender motion. "I know how you feelin' and…"

"Don't tell me you know how the fuck I'm feelin', Tron," Desirae said, now sounding a bit angry. "I'm the one who gotta walk around with my face ass fucked up and shit. You shoulda seen the way my mama looked at me and the people at the library and my cousin, Tiffany. I ain't even leave the house for like three days after that."

Tron looked at Desirae's face. Not wanting to add any salt to the already open wound in her pride, he turned and looked back at Titan and James. "Yeah," he said. "Well, I just thought that I would say that."

"Well, thanks," Desirae said, clearly forcing a smile. "It's good that you thought you would say that."

Tron paused, his nostrils flaring. "What is your problem?" he asked angrily. "Every time I come over here and try to keep the peace, you always got some chip on your shoulder."

Desirae shook her head and said, "I ain't got no damn chip on my shoulder. I just…it just ain't worth my time anymore to try to get you to even see and respect me."

"Who said I don't respect you?" Tron asked.

"Ain't you the one who told me that I was just somethin' to fuck?" Desirae asked.

Tron stepped closer to Desirae, wishing that he'd never made such a comment. He could tell, already, that this particular comment was going to be one that Desirae would probably never forget.

"I know, I know," Tron said, smiling. "I know I shouldn't have said that to you. I'm sorry. You know I was mad and didn't really mean it."

Desirae looked into Tron's eyes, remembering how those very same eyes used to get her panties off when she lived over on the south side.

"Yeah, yeah," Desirae said. "I'm over it now."

Tron nodded, looking down at Desirae's chest then body. She turned away and walked toward the kitchen. "You want something to drink?" she asked. "I'm goin' in there to get somethin', anyway."

"Yeah, I'll take whatever you got," Tron responded. "A nigga don't care like that."

Just as Tron was turning back around to spend a little more time with his sons, he made sure that he watched Desirae walk into the kitchen. *Damn that ass is phat*, he thought. Tron watched the light jiggle in Desirae's backside as she disappeared into the kitchen. Before Desirae could walk back into the room with two glasses of whatever to drink, Tron stepped into the kitchen.

"I really do mean that," Tron said. "I really am sorry. I was talkin' to my boy, Tyrese, about how I was feelin' about Saturday. And he even told me that I shoulda got out the truck and made sure that you was okay since you gotta take care of my sons."

Desirae looked up from the refrigerator, her ass sticking out in the air as she'd been kneeling over to grab a jug of cranberry juice.

"Hmm, hmm," she said. "It's all over with now."

"Who was the chick anyway?" Tron asked, thinking back to when he'd seen her rush up the walkway and toward the front door.

"Nobody," Desirae said.

At this point, Desirae had already grown tired of Tron talking about Saturday. Each time he'd brought it up, she could only think of how much her face hurt when she looked up at Veronica; the way her head hit the grass when Veronica had knocked her to the ground; the chilled fall wind hitting her naked body when the robe had been pulled off and thrown to the side.

"We ain't gotta keep talkin' bout it, Tron," Desirae said, a tear rolling down the side of her face.

Tron noticed that Desirae was getting emotional from him talking about Saturday. He decided to back off the topic. He grabbed a paper towel from the roll setting in the middle of the kitchen table and walked over to Desirae. When he handed the paper towel to Desirae, who was now pouring two glasses of cranberry juice at the kitchen counter, he pushed up on her as soon as she turned around.

"What you doin', nigga?" Desirae asked, snapping her neck back.

Tron, whose eyes had been angled down toward the massiveness that was Desirae's ass, smiled. "You know," he said. "I know just what that ass need."

85

Quickly, Desirae sat the jug of cranberry juice down onto the counter. She turned around, pushing Tron away from her. "Naw," she said, shaking her head. "Don't come over here after everything we've been through and even think that you bout to get up in this pussy."

Tron shook his head. "Stop playin', Desirae," he said. "You know that ass need some of this dick, so I don't even know why you playin'. I ain't try'na start nothin' up with you. I just know that you prolly in need with how you feelin'."

"Need of what?" Desirae asked, wanting to laugh. "More drama and shit, or more disrespect from you? Guess you came over here and saw this ass and just couldn't help yourself."

As much as Tron didn't want to admit it, Desirae's ass was indeed the motivation behind his actions within the last couple of minutes. Even from the front, Tron could see it. It poked out from behind her and called his name, reminding him of how he would drop by her place on the south side and drop several inches of dick into her insides.

"C'mon, Desirae," Tron said. "You know you want some of this dick." Tron stepped closer to Desirae, positioning himself as if he were about to slide his hands around to the back of her then down to her ass cheeks. "Why you gotta play?"

"Stop, Tron," Desirae said. "I don't want you no more. Just like you don't want me no more."

"That don't mean you not try'na fuck," Tron said, sounding a little snappy. "I can see the look in your face that you just need a good dick down."

Desirae paused for a moment, noticing that Tron was getting hard under his pants. She turned around and continued preparing the two glasses of cranberry juice. "Boy, that ship has sailed," she said. "I don't even know why you try'in. Guess you can't get no pussy nowhere else." She shook her head, thinking, *Niggas will do anything to get with a chick when they see she got a ass like this*. She smiled, gloating in the fact that regardless of how messed up her face was at the moment, she still had what it took to make a man lose his mind.

When Desirae turned around to hand Tron his glass of cranberry juice, she was surprised as what she'd seen. Tron was quickly undoing his pants then his zipper. Seconds passed and his semi-hard dick was hanging out of his fly, dangling back and forth against the front of his pants.

"See," Tron said, noticing how Desirae had stopped dead in her tracks, in silence. "You be try'na play with a nigga and shit, but you know you need some of this dick."

Desirae shook her head, trying to look away from Tron's dangling manhood. It was so hard, especially since the last man (Greg) that she'd had inside of her was probably no bigger than six inches in length. As good as Tron's manhood looked to Desirae – and it definitely looked good, she was not going to deny that – she just could not let him think that she was just a vagina he could use when he got to feeling lonely, especially after all these months.

"What the fuck is you doin', Tron?" Desirae asked, still looking down at his penis. "Now, after all these months...after you see that some otha nigga was up in here try'na get with this...you wanna try to get back with me when you ignored me for all these months. Damn, I know my ass got bigger from the weight I gained from carrying the twins, but I ain't think it was like that."

Tron looked down at Desirae's hips. Slowly but surely his dick was rising to the point where it was nearly sticking straight out from his body. "Yeah," he said, smiling. "That shit is huge now."

Desirae, looking down at Tron's rock hard manhood as it pointed out from his body, shook her head. "You really think I'm just a hoe, don't you?"

"Huh?" Tron asked, looking confused. "What you mean? I don't think you no hoe. I just know what you need and when you need it. I don't even know why you gotta go actin' like this." Tron stepped closer to Desirae. The head of his dick pressed against her stomach, an action which he'd done purposely to remind her of what she was missing, and how deep into her pussy he used to dig before they'd fallen out with one another. "Stop," Tron said, softly and suavely. "Why don't you let a nigga get some of that pussy, and we'll all be good?"

Desirae shook her head, not believing what was going on. Instead of coming up with a response to Tron's comments, she tossed the glass of cranberry juice onto his face. Surprised, Tron quickly closed his eyes as his body shuddered lightly under the feeling of cold liquid suddenly hitting his body and rolling down the front of his shirt.

"What the fuck you do that for?" Tron asked.

Desirae pushed past Tron, sipping her cranberry juice and smirking. "You looked a little hot and bothered," she responded. "I thought you just might want something to cool yourself off and stuff. That's all, Tron."

Tron shook his head as he watched Desirae sashay out of the kitchen and back into the dining room. Now going soft, he stuffed his manhood back into his pants and put himself back together. He walked into the dining room and saw how Desirae was bent over the basinet and talking to Titan. Even though she'd just thrown a glass of cranberry juice in his face, he still couldn't deny the fact that he wanted to dick Desirae down as if she'd stolen something from him. He knew that she was just teasing him with how she'd put an extra bit of an arch into her back when she bent over, and it was driving him crazy.

"Plus, I don't know why you try'na get with me anyway," Desirae said. "Ain't like you ain't got a chick already."

"I ain't got no chick," Tron protested. "I don't even know what the fuck you talkin' bout."

"Nigga, you know what the fuck I'm talkin' bout," Desirae said, remembering the one card she had up her sleeve that she could play. "I rolled by your place not too long again, and you won't believe what I saw."

Instantly, Tron became a little nervous. His mind went right to Reese as he tried to think of where Desirae could be going with this conversation. However, Tron also figured that it wasn't likely that Desirae had seen Reese's car in the community parking lot. She always made sure, as far as Tron knew, to park on the other side of the parking lot where there were generally more cars.

"What are you talkin' about, Desirae?" Tron asked. "What the fuck is you talkin' about?"

"Nigga, you know what the fuck I'm talkin' about," Desirae said. She turned around and looked across the dining room table at Tron. He was still standing in the kitchen doorway. "Nigga, I know what I saw. Tell me the truth when I ask you this one question. Is you still fuckin' my old friend Reese?"

Tron could have broken into a sweat at that moment. He'd been so sure that what he and Reese had going was on the low that he wondered how Desirae just so happened to ride through his community and see that Reese's car was somewhere out in the massive parking lot. He'd even made sure that when he and Reese had gone places together, they always went to a mall, restaurant, or store that was in a part of town the two of them were not likely to run into anyone they knew.

Desirae noticed that Tron was having a hard time answering the question. She shook her head, thinking about how some men just were no good. "Exactly," she said. "I saw her car when I rolled through there one day. I know it was her car because she still got that raggedy ass air freshener hanging in the window. Dumb bitch. Make sure you tell her that when I run into her flat chest, no ass havin' self again, I'mma beat that ass again. I don't care what nobody say."

Tron walked over to Desirae. "Look…" he said, trying to think of what to say.

Before Tron could continue his sentence, Desirae reached out and slapped his still-damp face. Tron turned his head, feeling the sting as he had to refrain himself from treating Desirae as if she were a man.

"Why you slap me like that, Desirae?" Tron asked.

"Why you fuckin' around with my best friend still?" Desirae snapped back. "Then, you try'ta come over here and get in this ass like it belong to you or somethin'. Guess some things don't change, huh? That bitch Reese still can't keep no man's attention longer than two seconds. Guess you realized you needed someone with a ass like mine to take all that dick." She shook her head. "You made that bed, so you lay in it."

***

Tron visited with Titan and James for about thirty minutes more before leaving Desirae's mother's house. Most of the time, the two remained silent. Tron was mad that Desirae had gone to extremes by not only throwing a glass of cranberry juice in his face but also by slapping him as hard as she could. When he walked out the door, he walked down the walkway in silence – a silence that was filled with anger and frustration. Desirae watched from the door, as the back of Tron got further and further away from her until he got to his car. She shut the door and burst into laughter.

"Now he want me," Desirae said, shaking her head. "Now that nigga want me. That shit just don't make no damn sense."

Desirae then realized that even with everything she'd gone through on Saturday, the end result was still the same: Tron saw that some other dude was trying to get with her and now he wanted to reclaim his territory.

Desirae closed the front door, knowing that she'd make good on her promise to catch up with Reese sooner or later. Just as she was stepping up to the basinets in the dining room to look at James and Titan, her phone vibrated on the dining room table. She picked it up and answered, not even taking a second to see who was calling her.

"Hello?"

"Damn, girl. Long time no see."

Desirae took a moment to think about the voice that was coming through to her ears. She recognized it as a voice she knew, even if she'd only known it for a little while. "Nalique?" she asked.

"Well, duh, girl," Nalique said. "Who you think it was? Girl, where you been?"

"Girl, I can't work up there no more," Desirae said, thinking quickly. "I just can't do it."

"Why?" Nalique asked. "A bitch over here wonderin' what happened to you and shit. I asked Greg and he always

90

actin' like he too busy to talk about it when I ask him. That's how I knew somethin' was up."

"Girl," Desirae said, pulling a dining room chair out so she could get more comfortable, "you wouldn't believe me if I told you."

"Hmm, hmm," Nalique said. The skepticism was clearly at the base of her voice. "Well, anyway, girl. I was just callin' to tell you that the checks came in if you wanna come up in here and get yours. I can try to slip it out of Greg's office when he goes on break or somethin', if you don't wanna see him."

Desirae gripped her forehead as she looked across the dining room and into the mirror on the wall. She couldn't wait until the scratches and bruises healed so that she could go back to being her beautiful self. With how she was looking right now, the very last thing in the entire world she ever wanted to do was to have that walk of shame into the Family Dollar. She was quite sure that humiliation would be in every step she took. Sitting at her mother's dining room table, she didn't need to expend much energy to imagine how she'd feel with the eyes of her former coworkers looking at her when she walked into the store.

"Girl, I don't know," Desirae said, hesitantly. "I can come up there in a little bit, but would there be any way you could bring my shit out to me real quick? Girl, I really don't wanna see Greg when I come up there. I really don't."

"Girl, I can't make no promises," Nalique said. "I mean, I can try to get it out of his office for you, but you gotta make sure that you tell me when you comin' up here. That way I can try to have it ready instead of just you poppin' up whenever."

"Yeah, I feel you," Desirae said. "I'll be up there around three thirty. I gotta drop the twins off at my cousin's house then I'mma come right on over there. Girl, please try to get my check out of Greg's office so I ain't got to see his ugly ass."

"Three thirty?" Nalique said, in confirmation. "Okay. I'mma try. Hit me up when you on your way so I can know."

"Okay," Desirae said.

The two of them ended the call. Desirae sat at her mother's dining room table, thinking. "God, please," she said, pleading. "Let Nalique have my check so I ain't got to go up in that store and see them people face to face. Good God, please."

Chapter 7

Everything went pretty well when Desirae dropped Titan and James off at Tiffany's place. This time Reggie was not there, and there appeared to be no sign that anyone else was in the apartment except for Tiffany. Desirae really didn't like the idea that she was dropping her twins off with a cousin who secretly didn't think highly of her. However, Desirae also knew that her options were limited when it came to childcare. Any other center in Indianapolis that would take the risk of watching two newborn babies would charge more than Desirae would probably make in a month with the kinds of jobs her qualifications met. Being the strong woman that she was, Desirae simply had to grin and bear it as she dropped Titan and James off.

When Desirae had gotten back into her car, she pulled her phone out of her purse and sent a text message to Nalique saying that she was on her way up to the Family Dollar. Within a matter of seconds, Nalique had responded: *Okay, I'mma try to get that check for you when you get up here.*

Desirae smiled as feelings of guilt came over her. Nalique had been such a good friend to her, even though they'd only worked together for a little over a week. She became nervous just thinking about what Nalique would say when she saw her face. However, Desirae had decided while she was heading up to the Family Dollar, that she would simply explain her face as being the result of getting into it with this chick that lived down the street from her.

Every minute seemed to fly by, but not in a good way, as Desirae rolled up to the entrance of the Family Dollar parking lot. Any other day, there would be droves of traffic coming down the street in the oncoming lane, making it difficult and time consuming for her to turn into the parking lot. However, today – the day that she was going to show her face for the first time to her former coworker and friend – traffic was light. Regrettably, she was able to turn into the parking lot and quickly pull into a spot further back from the store.

Desirae waited in her car for several minutes, sending text message after text message to Nalique. She wanted desperately for Nalique to bring her check out to her as they'd planned. Desirae could see that the parking lot had a quite a few cars, however. She thought that maybe Nalique was too busy with customers to respond to her text message, let alone bring her check out to her in the parking lot.

"Fuck this shit," Desirae said to herself as she climbed out of her car. "Fuck them and whatever they think. I'm goin' in so I can get my fuckin' money. I ain't got time for this shit."

Desirae grabbed her purse, threw it over her shoulder, and walked across the parking lot. Just as she'd stepped inside of the store, she could not only see that it was busy with customers but also that Nalique was the only person with a cash register. Soon enough, of course, Nalique lifted her head up as she was saying, "Welcome to Family…" Her words trailed off as she saw Desirae's face, her own face looking as if she'd seen a ghost.

"Girl, I'm so sorry," Nalique said, trying not look at Desirae's face in such an obvious way. She motioned toward the customers. "It got busy in here and I couldn't answer you."

Desirae nodded, feeling the eyes of customers looking at her bruised and scratched face. "Girl, it's coo," she said. "I understand you busy and stuff. Did you at least have a chance to go back to his office and get it?"

Nalique smiled at a customer then shook her head. "Girl, no," she said. "I'm sorry. Greg been back in his office all day, so when I went back there, there was just no way I was gonna slide out of there with your check without him noticin'."

"Girl, that's coo," Desirae said.

Quickly, Nalique helped the last two customers in her line. She came from behind the counter and walked up to Desirae. This time, however, she made it no secret that she was looking at Desirae's face.

"Girl, what happen?" Nalique asked.

Desirae shook her head. "I don't even wanna talk about it, girl," she answered. "Like I said on the phone. If I told you, you wouldn't believe this shit, I swear. You said Greg is back in his office, right?"

Nalique nodded. "Yeah," she said. "He been back there since I got here earlier in the afternoon. Girl, if you want, I can go back there and tell him that you here and want your check so you ain't got to see him."

Desirae looked toward the back of the store. She shook her head, pushing her chest out. "Naw, girl," she said. "You stay up here. I'll go back there. It ain't no big deal."

Desirae walked past Nalique and made her way through the store aisles until she came to the back of the store. She lightly tapped on Greg's office door, pushing it open and stepping inside when she'd been told to do so. Greg was talking on the phone. As soon as he looked up and realized who had just come into his office, he ended his phone call and stood up.

"Desirae," Greg said, sounding concerned.

"Yeah, it's me," Desirae said, keeping her eyes down. "I ain't come in here for no problems, or to see that crazy bitch you call a wife. I just want my check, nigga, and nothin' else."

Greg sifted through a pile of envelopes on his desk. When he'd come to the envelope with Desirae's name on the front, he held it out to her. Desirae snatched it and began to turn around. No sooner than she'd gotten two feet closer to the office door, Greg had walked from behind his desk. "Desirae?" he said.

Desirae turned around, moving a little of her hair out of the way. "What, Greg?" she asked, clearly not in the mood.

"About Saturday," Greg began.

"What about it, nigga?" Desirae said. "You just gon' sit up in the house and watch your wife do that to me like you ain't have nothin' to do with it. And she probably stayed with your little dick ass too, didn't she."

"You ain't have to go talkin' about my dick," Greg said.

"Fuck you and your dick," Desirae said. "That little ass shit. I can't believe that I even wasted my time on that shit when I coulda been out there with a real nigga with bigger and better. What is it that you want?"

"Look, I know you prolly don't wanna work here no more," Greg said, "but I can help you transfer to another store."

"Oh, can you?" Desirae asked, sarcastically. "You couldn't stop me from gettin' my ass beat *naked* on my mother's front yard like some humiliated bitch, but now you wanna help me transfer. Let me guess, even after what happened on Saturday, you still want us to kick it sometime and hope that your wife don't find out?"

Greg stood there, silently. For the last few days, all he could think about was Desirae. She had the nicest body he'd ever seen, with an ass that he could eat his meals off of and even lay his head down to sleep if he wanted, like it was a couple of plump pillows. "I didn't say that, Desirae," he said.

"Yeah, but you didn't say that wasn't what you wanted," Desirae said. "Nigga, I'm done with that shit. I'm done bein' a side chick. I done found some nigga that might actually be interested in me for me." She thought about D'Mann, remembering that she was going to respond to his text messages from last night when she got on with her day. "You ain't worth shit, nigga. I swear to God you ain't. You saw your wife comin' and just gon' hide in the house while she out there doin' me dirty and shit, pullin' my robe off in the front yard for the whole damn street to see. Hold up...How the fuck she even know where I live? How she know where to come find your little dick havin' ass?"

Greg grunted under his breath, clearly feeling uncomfortable. "Well," he said, "when I came over there that morning, she followed me, or at least that's what she told me. When she got done with the kids at her mother's house, she dropped them off at her brother's house and came over to where she'd followed me to, which was your house."

Desirae squinted at Greg, being able to see right through him. There was no doubt in her mind that he was full of shit – so much so that his eyes were nearly turning brown.

"Fuck you, Greg," Desirae said. At the very moment she'd said that, she'd thought about how ridiculous it was that two men – Greg and Tron – both watched her get humiliated and embarrassed in her mother's front yard. "You prolly slipped up and was tellin' somebody since you know you really can't get none as good as mine nowhere else. That's what I think. Prolly got excited and shit that some woman was gonna pay your little dick any attention and started talkin' too much, and she heard about it. How the fuck you really expect me to believe that she followed you all the way to my mama's house, and you drove all that way, through stoplights and different neighborhoods and shit, and didn't notice your own wife's car following you? Boy, please." Desirae shook her head. "Niggas really be thinkin' I'm stupid, don't they?"

Desirae turned around and headed for the door. Part of her was wondering if it had even been worth coming to get her check. Having to confront Greg and let him know how she felt had proven to take more out of her than she'd originally thought. Just as Desirae was about to step out of the office door, she'd heard Greg say her name. She turned around and said, "What?"

Greg held out two one hundred-dollar bills. Desirae looked down, wondering what was going on. "What is this?"

"Here," Greg said. "You got them twins and you said you need the money. I understand if you got a problem with what happened and all, but if you wanna meet up at hotels or something and whatnot, I can definitely make it worth your while."

Desirae looked at the money then up into Greg's eyes. She'd never had sex for money. However, she didn't necessarily look down on it either. The fact of the matter is that she was well aware of the power between her legs. Many times in her life she'd used it to get men to buy her things, take her out to nice restaurants, or for the occasional shopping trip to the outlet mall an hour south in Indianapolis, in Edinburgh. Desirae simply didn't expect Greg to pull any money out of his pocket and hand it to her right then and there, in his office.

Not knowing what to do, Desirae reached back and pushed the door closed. She stepped closer to Greg.

"So, it's worth that much to you?" Desirae asked Greg. "You like this ass that much you willin' to come up off of that kinda money all the time?"

"I don't know about all the time," Greg said, shrugging his shoulders. "But at least a couple times a week. You the sexiest woman I've ever seen, Desirae." Not being able to help himself, Greg leaned in closer to Desirae's neck. He was leaning in to lick it, but soon found himself practically falling forward as Desirae calmly stepped out of the way.

"Hold up," Desirae said. "I ain't say we could go there, yet." She then looked down at his gray dress pants. In the front was a tent from his hard-on. "I see somebody is really serious, huh?"

Greg chuckled. "I really am sorry about Saturday," he said. "I swear to God I didn't tell anybody and didn't know that she was followin' me. C'mon, Desirae. Tell me what I gotta do. Let a nigga get some more of that pussy." Just then, Greg reached around to Desirae's back and slid his hand down over her behind.

Desirae rolled her eyes, seeing the look of desperation in this man's eyes as he continued holding the hundred dollar bills. She smiled, knowing exactly what she would do. She glanced back at the door then to Greg, smiling. "Take it out," she told him.

Greg, seeming confused, asked her what she meant.

"Take that dick out," Desirae told him again, this time sounding more forceful. It was very clear to her that Greg was being turned on by her taking the lead somewhat. Just as she said to, Greg quickly undid his fly. In a matter of seconds, his hard manhood was poking out of his pants, so hard it almost pointed up at an angle.

Desirae gently tapped the top of Greg's dick, watching it boing up and down like a spring. She giggled then looked up at the money. In a quick snatch, Greg felt the hundred-dollar bills slip from his grip. The moment he looked up and into Desirae's eyes, smiling with anticipation to see what she was going to do now that he'd pulled his dick out in his office, the side of his face stung. In what seemed like the bat of an eye, Desirae had slapped Greg across the face.

"That's what you get from me for two hundred fuckin' dollars after what happened to me on Saturday," Desirae said. She turned around and quickly pulled the office door open, causing Greg to scramble just to get his rock-hard dick back into his pants. The last thing he needed was to be fired, or worse, because an employee or customer just so happened to walk by his office when he was exposed. When Greg had finished getting himself together, having quickly jumped over into a corner of his office, Desirae was gone. Frustrated and a little upset, Greg slammed his office door, telling himself that Desirae wasn't even worth it to begin with.

Feeling confident and bold, Desirae walked with her head high toward the front of the store. For the first time in a couple of days, her bruised and scratched face had literally been the last thing on her mind. She breezed through the cluster of cash registers at the store and out into the parking lot.

Nalique noticed the extra pep in Desirae's step, saw how she marched out of the store. She then looked toward the hygiene aisle and motioned for Shawna to come over to her. Shawna approached Nalique's cash register, having just gotten into the store when Nalique called her, saying that the Desirae chick was in the store if she wanted to swing through.

"Is that the chick that was messin' around with Tron when you and him was together?" Nalique asked.

Shawna nodded, setting some things up onto the counter. "Yeah, Nalique," she said. "That's her. I will give credit where credit is due. She does look good for somebody who just had twins."

"Yeah," Nalique said, nodding, as she and Shawna watched Desirae walk further out into the parking lot. "I admit that she does. I knew something was up with her. She just seem like the biggest hoe I know."

"I wanna know what happened to her face," Shawna said, shaking her head. "Whoever got with her really gave it to her. Poor thing."

"You know who I think it was?" Nalique asked, letting Shawna know that she was about to present one of her theories. "I think that thot been fuckin' around with Greg, the store manager nigga that I was tellin' you about. He back in the office right now."

"That's where she was comin' from when she came walkin' from back there?" Shawna asked.

"Girl, yes," Nalique answered. "And who the fuck you know that need ten fuckin' minutes to go back there and get they check? Girl, in ten minutes, I done got the check, signed the back of it, and am at the nearest bank try'na cash that shit. The ink ain't even dry on my shit. I wouldn't be surprised if she was back there try'na suck his dick to keep her job or somethin'. She seem like she'll do some shit like that."

"Don't be mean, Nalique," Shawna said, feeling sorry that Desirae just couldn't seem to get herself together.

"I ain't bein' mean," Nalique said. "I'm just tellin' it like it is. But, back to what I was sayin', I think Greg's wife Veronica got in that ass. Of course, I ain't never see the chick fight. But I heard she beat some bitch's ass one time so good she sent her runnin' home crying. Poor girl ain't show her face for days after that, or at least that's what I heard. Somethin' tell me, by how she was talkin' on the phone about how she ain't wanna see Greg, that she did somethin' with Greg and got caught up. I even told that bitch to not fuck around with his ole freaky self because that wife of his is crazy. She ain't listen. She like otha bitch's niggas. I can just tell."

"Yeah," Shawna said, shaking her head. "Whoever she did, or whatever she did, they did it back to her good. Her face. It's been a minute since I seen a chick walkin' around with her face beat up like that. She prolly too ashamed to work here, anyway. I know people gotta be lookin' at her when she go places."

"Yeah, well…" Nalique said, beginning to scan Shawna's items. "That's what you get when you a side chick. I don't play that shit. You remember what happened with me and that bitch up at Honeys East when she was fuckin' around with Tyrese and had the nerve to say some ole dumb shit to me."

Shawna's eyes cut to Nalique. She pressed her lips together and put her hand on her hip. "Girl, I know," she said. "You ain't got to remind me what went down at Honeys East that night. Trust me, you ain't got to remind me. You can prolly get on YouTube and see a video of the news coverage and see my ass in the background. I already know how you feel about side chicks. You definitely do not have to remind me."

"Girl, it wasn't that serious," Nalique said.

"It wasn't that serious?" Shawna said. "You almost caught a murder charge."

Nalique snickered. "I was just playin' with the girl. You know I wasn't gon' kill her ass. I was just try'na scare her and make sure that I get my point across is all."

Shawna rolled her eyes and shook her head.

Chapter 8

When Desirae had gotten into her car and pulled out of the Family Dollar parking lot, a little bit of guilt came over her. She felt a guilty for not stopping and taking a moment to talk to Nalique. Nalique had been a good friend to her in the short time they'd known one another; Desirae thought she should at least try to keep in contact with her. However, she also knew that keeping in contact with Nalique would only remind her of what happened with Greg. Desirae wanted nothing more than to put the front yard fiasco behind her.

Twenty minutes later, Desirae was pulling up at the same library she'd sat inside of the day before. She parked her car, went inside, and smiled when she just so happened to find the very same computer open. It was upstairs and in a back corner of the library in an area without a lot of people. Even in a public place, she needed a little bit of privacy. Desirae sat down and, just like yesterday, began her search for open job positions in and around the city.

Around 5 o'clock, Desirae's phone vibrated against the surface of the gray computer table. She looked at the lit screen and saw that a text message had arrived from D'Mann. She quickly picked up her phone and read the message: *WYD*

Desirae: *At the library. You?*

D'Mann: *Work. Ready to get off and go make this money later on tonight. What you got up for later on?*

Desirae: *Just library, looking for a job.*

D'Mann: *Yeah.*

Desirae sat her phone down and went back to scouring the internet for jobs that were a step above McDonald's. Thirty minutes later, her attention was pulled toward the library steps by the sound of swishing pants. As the person came closer to her, she could see that it was D'Mann. Desirae looked him up and down, loving how he walked so confidently. He held the waist of his black uniform pants as he stepped up to the cluster of computers.

"Excuse me," D'Mann said, trying to sound professional. "I was wondering if you could point me to the Harry Potter books and Dr. Seuss."

Desirae giggled. "I didn't know you read books," she said.

D'Mann smiled. "I don't," he said. "They just good places to hide shit when niggas rob your house. You know they don't ever look in books."

The two of them laughed as D'Mann pulled up a chair and sat down next to Desirae.

"How's the job search goin'?" D'Mann asked.

Desirae sighed. "I mean," she said, trying to think of how to explain it. "I'm puttin' in applications and stuff. I got a resume I cleaned up a little bit with the help of my mama, and I been submittin' it. It's only been a couple of days, so we'll see."

D'Mann shook his head.

"What you shakin' your head like that for?" Desirae asked.

"Nothin'," D'Mann answered. "Well, I guess I'm just thinkin' about how you shouldn't even have to be doin' this stuff. That nigga who got you pregnant with them twins should be takin' care of you. If you was the mother of my child, I wouldn't dare have you out there beggin' people for jobs."

"Well," Desirae said, shrugging. "I get child support from him, and he help me out with buyin' stuff when I need it, so I guess I can't complain."

"Shit," D'Mann said, leaning back. "So what? What the fuck that supposed to mean? He still should be takin' care of you so you can be the best mother you can. I don't even know the nigga, and I already ain't even likin' his ass."

Desirae shook her head thinking about how Tron had tried to push up on her in her mother's kitchen. The difference between Tron and D'Mann was becoming very clear to Desirae. Tron just wanted her for sex. She was just an ass that he could hold onto and throw away after he'd came. D'Mann, on the other hand, really got into her character. He talked to her as if she was a person with feelings and real thoughts. Desirae couldn't help but quickly warm up to D'Mann.

"You wanna go downtown?" D'Mann asked.

"Downtown and do what?" Desirae asked.

103

"Shit," D'Mann said, shrugging. "We can go walkin' at the park or somethin'. I been inside all day, since a nigga got to work this mornin'. I fuckin' hate that I gotta work that job so the cops ain't breathin' down my neck and shit. C'mon." He stood up. "I'll bring you back down here to your car in a little bit. I got a few hours to kill before I gotta go meet up with my cousin and get this weight he just got here with. I was gon' go home and just chill, but since you nearby, I figured I'd ask you if you wanna go. I'm so lonely." He made his sad face. "Don't make me go be lonely."

Desirae laughed, putting her hand over her mouth as she realized she was in a library. She playfully slapped D'Mann's thigh. "Boy, calm down," Desirae said. "You be doin' the most. Let me just finish up with this one job application, and I'll go with you."

"Yay," D'Mann said.

Desirae quickly finished up with filling out her information then the two of them walked out into the parking lot. Desirae felt renewed and refreshed as she climbed into D'Mann's SUV. The way he held her when they walked out into the parking lot was nothing short of being a true gentleman. She was even more-so delighted to see him open her car door for her.

D'Mann drove downtown and parked on White River State Parkway, just west of downtown. A long, green park stretched along the White River. D'Mann escorted Desirae over to the trail and the two of them walked. The skyline glittered in the slowly darkening evening sky. D'Mann and Desirae walked side by side.

"So, why you so quiet?" D'Mann asked. "You was talkin' to a nigga a lot more than this yesterday if I remember correctly."

"Oh, I'm sorry," Desirae said. "I just got a lot on my mind. Today been one of them days, I swear it has. I just can't believe the level of disrespect that can come from some of these niggas out here. The shit is just unreal."

"Somebody disrespected you today?" D'Mann asked. "What you talkin' bout?"

104

"Well, I shouldn't say disrespected me," Desirae said. "But you can tell that some niggas…some niggas just see me as somethin' to fuck. I swear, sometimes the price I gotta pay for bein' so pretty and havin' this body is just too much."

D'Mann's eyes angled down to Desirae's ass. He shook his head as he looked at how far it stuck out of her body. He then looked up and into her face, feeling sorry that she had to go through so much.

"Some nigga you used to mess around with try'na get back with you and just fuck you or somethin'?" D'Mann asked.

"Sort of," Desirae said. "Well, two dudes I know. One even tried to offer me some fuckin' money. I ain't no fuckin' prostitute."

"Wait a minute," D'Mann said. "The nigga tried to offer you money for some pussy. I hope you ain't take that shit."

Desirae looked up at D'Mann. "Of course I ain't take that shit," she lied. "I told that nigga I ain't no hoe, and that he could have a good day."

"Yeah, I feel for you," D'Mann said. "I ain't gon' lie, though. I been a little nervous about this shit."

"Nervous about what?" Desirae asked. "What you got to be nervous about?"

"You," D'Mann said. "I mean, not you, but just chillin' with some chick I just met in general. I done ran into a couple of crazy chicks…girls that I wish I'd never met."

"Oh God," Desirae said. She stopped right there on the trail and looked at D'Mann. "Please don't tell me that you got some crazy ex-girlfriend or some shit that I need to be watchin' out for."

"Naw," D'Mann said. "I mean, the bitch is crazy, but you ain't gotta watch out for her. I'm just really guarded right now because of what I had to deal with cause of that chick."

"If you don't mind me askin', what she do to really have you scarred and stuff?" Desirae asked.

D'Mann paused as he gently grabbed Desirae by the arm, and they continued walking down the trail. "Like two years ago, right before I had my daughter," D'Mann explained, "this chick basically wanted me to give her money and buy her stuff. When I told the bitch to fuck off and that I wasn't gonna

105

do no shit like that, she went to the police and told them that I raped her."

"What?" Desirae asked, surprised. "You not serious are you?"

"Yeah," D'Mann said. "Cops came wakin' me up out my sleep and everything. Turned out the shit is false. I ain't never raped no chick in my life and never would. Ever since then, I only date a certain type. They gotta give me the right vibe for me to even take the risk."

"I feel you on that," Desirae said. "Some chicks really are crazy. I got a cousin whose nigga be lookin' at me too hard, and now I can tell that she mad at me."

"Yeah," D'Mann said. "She just mad that you beautiful with a body like that."

"Oh, so all you see is my body, too, huh?" Desirae asked, sounding defensive.

D'Mann grabbed Desirae by her waist. "Don't you start that stuff," he said. "If you really wanna know the truth, you gotta think about how we met. When you came through the drive-thru, I really couldn't see your body like that. All I could see was your face and listen to the way you talked."

"Awe," Desirae said, in her sweet voice. "Ain't you so nice."

D'Mann chuckled. "Well, I try to be."

D'Mann and Desirae walked down the trail a little while longer before D'Mann stopped. "I got this blunt back at the house," he said. "If you got time, we roll over there and smoke it if you want."

Desirae agreed. The two of them walked back to D'Mann's parked truck. Ten minutes later, they were pulling up to D'Mann's place and headed inside. Inside, Desirae felt at home once again. She was so impressed with how clean and neat D'Mann's place was, especially since he was a man. Desirae sat down onto the couch as D'Mann walked into another room and reappeared with a blunt.

"Here," D'Mann said, handing the blunt to Desirae.

They passed the blunt back and forth to one another. Their eyes slowly reddened as they talked on and on about issues with Desirae's sons' father and the problems that D'Mann had been having with the mother of his daughter.

"Yeah, life is fuckin' tough," D'Mann said. He couldn't help but to look down at how Desirae's ass basically spilled out from underneath her. "I hate that them niggas be treatin' you that way. I felt kinda guilty about yesterday, though, I can't lie."

"Guilty?" Desirae said. "For what?"

D'Mann motioned toward the kitchen. "About what happened in there," he said.

Desirae place her hand on D'Mann thigh and rubbed up and down. "You ain't have to feel guilty," she said. "Trust me, I ain't do nothin' that I ain't wanna do yesterday in there. I woulda did more."

"Oh, yeah?" D'Mann said, smiling. Desirae instantly picked up on what he was suggesting, seeing how his eyes continued to glance down at his crotch. "Is that right?"

Desirae handed the blunt to D'Mann as she slid off of the couch and down onto her knees, all the while never breaking eye contact. "Hmm, hmm," she said, nodding.

Knowing what was about to happen, D'Mann leaned back into the couch and enjoyed the feeling of the fire weed he was smoking, and how it was really going to his head. "This shit fire," he said.

Moving quietly, Desirae used her knees to position herself between D'Mann's legs. With an arch in her back and her ass up in the air, toward the middle of the living room, Desirae unfastened D'Mann's pants then undid his zipper. He eventually lifted up, allowing Desirae to pull his pants and underwear down to his ankles. When she looked up at his manhood, having heard it thump against his lower stomach, she reached up and wrapped her hands around it. She looked into D'Mann's eyes.

"Yeah, nigga," Desirae said. "I ain't do nothin' I ain't wanna do."

Desirae gripped the base of D'Mann's fat, veiny dick as she took it into her mouth. A groan slipped out of D'Mann's mouth, followed by a couple of curse words. "Shit, your throat feel like silk," he said. The slurping noises that Desirae made filled the quiet room. D'Mann, as a gesture of encouragement, placed the palm of his hand on Desirae's head and pushed her further down on his dick. She gagged.

"There you go," D'Mann said, looking down at Desirae as she tried to take as much of him into her mouth as was humanly possible. "Suck that dick. There you go. Just suck that dick."

Desirae went nonstop for the next twenty minutes before D'Mann was pulling her head up out of his lap. "Stop," he said. "Hold up." He reached over her back and slapped each of her ass cheeks a couple of times, saying how unbelievably fat she was in the back. "A nigga gotta get in that pussy. A nigga got to."

D'Mann gently moved Desirae out of the way and stood up. Holding the waist of his pants, he waddled into the kitchen. When he returned, Desirae saw a golden-colored XL magnum condom wrapper in his hand. He looked at Desirae and smiled. "Put that head up on the couch for a nigga, okay," he told her.

Smiling, Desirae did just as she was told. She inched forward until her chest was flat against the seat of the couch, and her ass was arched up in the air. D'Mann walked behind her as he ripped the condom wrapper open and stretched the condom to get it over the head of his dick.

"Goddamn you got a big ass," D'Mann said. "A nigga is about to tear this shit up."

A squeal slipped out of Desirae's mouth when she felt D'Mann push his way into her insides. "Fuck, nigga!" she exclaimed, squirming as she felt herself stretch. "This dick is so thick."

"Hmm, hmm," D'Mann said, gripping her waist. "I'm 'bout to stretch this pussy out. Just be quiet and keep that ass up in the air."

D'Mann slowly worked himself into Desirae, feeling motivated by the moans of pleasure that slipped out of her mouth. Once he'd gotten balls deep into her pussy, he slid his right hand up her back and gripped the back side of her neck. The moment Desirae was officially held into place, under the strong arm and grip of D'Mann, he pounded her as if there were no tomorrow. His dick throbbed inside of her from just the sight of her bouncing ass cheeks.

"Throw it back for a nigga," D'Mann told her.

Desirae, who was so gone that she could barely think, could only do as she'd been told. She looked back at D'Mann's bulging muscles as she pushed her ass into his body in a slow, grinding rhythm. D'Mann dropped his arms to the side and looked down, slapping her ass cheeks every few seconds.

"I can't take this shit no more," D'Mann said five minutes later. "I'm bout to beat this pussy up."

Before Desirae could really process what he'd said, she felt herself being pinned down to the couch. Even if she wanted to move, she would have been powerless to even try. With all of his force, D'Mann pressed Desirae's chest into the couch as he stroked into her as fast and hard as he could, showing no mercy.

"Fuckkkk!" D'Mann exclaimed. "A nigga is about to bust! A nigga is about to bust!"

"Fuck this pussy!" Desirae told him.

Into his stroke, D'Mann gripped Desirae's waist again, just above her ass cheeks. He went as hard and fast as he could, loving the way Desirae's body flailed about; loving the way she encouraged him. This was the first chick he'd gotten with in a while who could take all of his dick without complaining that she was hurting.

D'Mann tensed up and let go, wiping the sweat away from his face. He slapped Desirae's ass as hard as he could one last time before pulling out of her and standing up. "Fuck," he said, beads of sweat rolling down his body. "Damn you got some good pussy, girl. Shit!"

Desirae quickly leaned up and turned around. In the flash of a second, she'd grabbed D'Mann's dick by the base and was sucking on it again. She'd never put a man's dick into her mouth just after it had come out of her pussy. However, D'Mann was different. He showed that he was interested in her even when she didn't look her best. She sucked D'Mann's heavy, deflating dick until he just couldn't take anymore.

"Damn, my insides," Desirae said. She rubbed her stomach as she lifted herself up onto D'Mann's couch.

D'Mann snickered. "Shit," he said. "That was nothin'. Just wait till a nigga got a little time. I'mma go balls deep in that pussy for hours, when you can get away from them babies, that is."

"I bet," Desirae said. Based on the quickie D'Mann had just given her, there was no doubt in her mind that he could really go hard if they'd had the time.

"Bet nothing," D'Mann said, pulling his pants up. "Wait till I get that ass in the California King upstairs. You don't know what a nigga gon' do to you then."

"California King!" Desirae said. "That's a big ass bed."

D'Mann looked down at his dick then at Desirae, smiling. He then began to move his hips, causing the head of his dick to slap against his thighs. "Well, a big boy need a big bed," he said. "Don't you think?"

Desirae lounged back into D'Mann's couch, reminiscing more of the days when she'd had an apartment of her own. She missed laying back on her couch, thinking, plotting, and whatnot, as she felt so comfortable in her robe. However, thinking about this only caused her to need to push aside the horrible memories of Saturday – the specific part of the memory when she felt her robe being snatched away from her body in broad daylight.

D'Mann slumped into the couch next to Desirae as the two of them carried a conversation together. There was something about D'Mann that brought a smile to Desirae's face. It was as if he were actually genuine and not one-dimensional. The same, however, in Desirae's eyes, could not be said about Tron. As the months went on, Desirae had quickly seen his true colors. There were moments where she'd think about the difference in his attitude now versus when he couldn't wait to stop by, when his girlfriend Shawna wasn't breathing down his neck, of course. Nonetheless, D'Mann also seemed like just a cool dude. Desirae had only known him for a couple of days. With how they carried on, and how it came so naturally, a stranger passing them on the street would have thought they'd known one another for years.

"Yeah," Desirae said, in response to a comment D'Mann made about Donald Trump. "We'll see what happens, I guess. I mean, what can we really do about it?"

As D'Mann was about to steer the conversation toward finding out what Desirae really wanted out of life, he had to pause the conversation. He felt his phone vibrating in his pocket. "Excuse me," he said. He stood up and walked into the kitchen to take the call.

For the few minutes Desirae sat alone in the living room while D'Mann talked on the phone in the kitchen, she looked around the room. She saw other details of how well laid out this house was that she hadn't noticed the first time walking through the front door. Even more so than before, Desirae could tell that D'Mann must really be on his grind. There was just no way that a guy working at McDonalds would be able to have such a nice place.

D'Mann walked back into the living room. "What time did you say you needed to be back at your car, sexy?" he asked.

Desirae smiled, turning to his bulky body standing in the doorway between the living room and the dining room. "I just gotta pick up my sons from my cousin house around eleven o'clock," she answered. "So, I guess I betta be back at my car by ten thirty or somethin' like that. Why?"

"Bet," D'Mann said, nodding. "If you don't mind, my boy Makim bout to come through. He the nigga that I told you I was gon' meet up with later on when a nigga swooped you up from the library and shit. He bout to bring this money over here, and we gon' go down in the basement. You don't mind, do you? I just ain't think I was gon' wind up chillin' with you for this long. Don't take a nigga the wrong way, I'd rather be chillin' with you then lookin' up in this nigga face. But he already got somethin' on for later on, so a nigga betta go ahead and get this money before somethin' happen."

"Hell yeah," Desirae said. "That's coo with me." She began to slide off of the couch. "Just let me get myself back together before he get over here."

"Yeah," D'Mann said. "If you want, you can actually go chill upstairs." He looked at her bruised, scratched face. "And

111

yeah, gon and put that ass up. I don't want no niggas comin' round my place seein' what I got."

"What you got?" Desirae asked, sarcastically. "So, what are you sayin'? After two days of knowin' each other, I belong to you."

D'Mann shrugged and smiled. "It is what it is," he said. "Just get that pussy up so when the nigga come walkin' through the door, he ain't got his eyes on the wrong prize. Nigga gon' make me slap his ass up over some shit like that, I don't play. I respect women too much."

Desirae slid her pants back on then her shirt. She stepped in front of a window in the dining room to check over her hair. She giggled, seeing that she really did look as if she'd just taken a deep dicking out in the living room. "I'mma have to get myself together," she said.

As these words slipped out of Desirae's mouth, her eyes zoomed in on her face. With time it was getting better, but D'Mann's offer for her to go upstairs was actually not a bad idea. Desirae knew already that she'd be far too self-conscious if this Makim guy were to come into D'Mann's apartment and look at her face. Even if his face didn't say anything, and he never commented on it, Desirae would know what he was thinking. It was very clear that this chick had just recently let someone get the best of her.

"So, you gon' chill upstairs or what?" D'Mann asked, rubbing Desirae's ass.

Desirae nodded. "Yeah," she responded. "I think I will. You sure you don't mind? I don't wanna disturb nothin'."

"Disturb somethin'?" D'Mann asked, shaking his head. "Sexy, you can't disturb anything I got. I ain't got shit to hide from you. And yeah, of course you can chill up there. I know how women can be when it comes to havin' strange dudes comin' around that they don't really know. And a nigga respect that. That's why I offered for you to chill upstairs." His eyes angled toward the ceiling. "Plus, it ain't gon' be that long anyway," he added. "Maybe like fifteen minutes or somethin', or some shit like that."

"Okay," Desirae said. She'd already begun to climb the steps.

"Well damn," D'Mann said, holding his arms open. "A nigga didn't say you had to go runnin' up there already. I mean, shit. It's gon' take my boy Makim at least ten minutes, if not more to get here. Get that sexy ass back down here. That's ten minutes I need."

Desirae hurried back down the steps, giggling. When she got to the bottom, she playfully tapped D'Mann's broad, muscular shoulders. Quickly, he slid his hands around to her lower back then gripped her ass. "Plus," he said. "If you already in the bed when I get done with this nigga and shit, if we got time, I might be able to give this dick to you for real. None of that quickie shit."

"Oh," Desirae said, smiling. "Is that so?"

"You gon' surprise me?" D'Mann asked, giving Desirae the sleep-eyed looked. "You gon' surprise a nigga when he come up there?"

"Surprise you?" Desirae asked, looking confused and snapping her head back. "What you sayin', you want me to be naked and shit when you come up there?"

D'Mann shrugged. "Your words, not mine," he said, playfully.

"Boy, stop," Desirae said. "You are such a freak."

"Ain't that what you liked about me just yesterday?" D'Mann said.

Desirae paused, pushing D'Mann back from her. "Nigga, stop," she said. "Your dude is about to come through here and here you are try'na fuck and shit before he get here."

Moments later, there was a knock at the door. D'Mann slapped Desirae on the ass as she headed upstairs. "I'll be up there in a minute," he told her. "My bedroom is the second door to the right. Get comfortable. It's time for me to get this money."

Desirae climbed the steps, becoming more cautious as she reached the top. There she stood, looking left then right down the upstairs hallway. Behind her, coming from downstairs, she could hear D'Mann greeting Makim, who had a deep, raspy voice. Desirae could hear the two of them shaking hands and hugging before their voices trailed off, the thumping of their feet on the basement stairs in the background.

Desirae turned on the hallway light and saw that the hallway had freshly painted walls, or at least that was how they appeared. She turned to the right, passed one door then came to the second. When she pushed it open, she felt around on the wall to the side until she found the light switch. The room lit up.

"Damn, this shit is wassup," Desirae said, quietly to herself. She stepped into the room, noticing how the cherry hardwood floors were as sleek as the day they were installed. A classy ceiling fan hung in the middle of the room, making its presence known over the top of D'Mann's massive California King-sized bed. Desirae stepped up to the bed and lay down. "This is a fuckin' big bed," she said. "Maybe I will have to surprise the nigga when he come up here. I could get used to layin' in this."

Desirae then stood up, coming back to her senses. She walked down the hallway, looking into the other two smaller bedrooms then the bathroom. After looking around a little bit, not to mention opening a few cabinets and drawers here and there, it became very obvious to Desirae that the chances D'Mann had a chick staying over at his place on a regular basis were very slim. Even though he was clearly a neat and somewhat decorative man, there were no signs of a feminine touch anywhere. "Maybe the nigga really is single," Desirae said, as she tried to push aside the feelings that many women deal with – the feeling that no available man will actually want them.

Desirae went back to D'Mann's bedroom and made herself comfortable. For the next several minutes, she sat there, in silence, as she could faintly hear D'Mann and his friend Makim talking all the way from down in the basement. Just as Desirae was closing her eyes to truly relax, she could hear the two men elevate their voices. Immediately, her eyes opened as she became more alert.

"Nigga, what the fuck I tell you?" one man shouted. Desirae couldn't be sure, but this voice sounded like D'Mann's to her. She stood up, walked back out into the hallway, and approached the top of the staircase. She stood in place, breathing steadily as she looked down toward the dining room and listened.

"What the fuck is this shit?" the voice said again. This time, Desirae was sure it was D'Mann talking. He said, "Nigga, I know you supposed to have more than this. Only one twenty…that's all you fuckin' got for me, nigga? Where the fuck is my money?"

"I told you, D'Mann," the other man, Makim, said. "I told you I ain't take that shit."

D'Mann then said something that Desirae couldn't quite make out. She stepped down one step. Her nerves were tingling as her woman's intuition was telling her that something bad was about to happen. She rarely had this feeling. However, when she did, it was rarely wrong.

"Fuck you, nigga!" D'Mann yelled. "You coulda told me this shit over the phone. Instead, what you do? Come over here and waste my time and shit like I ain't got betta shit I can be doin'. Nigga, why the fuck you try'na fuck with me."

Desirae then heard what sounded like a scuffle.

"Nigga, fuck you!" Makim yelled. "You ain't bout to talk to me like I'm just some bitch or somethin'. Nigga, fuck you!"

Desirae became alarmed as she could hear the two men pushing one another around in the basement. At first, it sounded as if bodies were hitting the wall. Then came the sounds of things breaking and fists hitting faces. Desirae wondered if she should run down there and try to do something about it. Just as she stepped down another step, she realized she was better off upstairs. From her point of view, the two men could only fight for so long before they'd eventually stop on their own.

For the next few minutes, Desirae stood at the top of the steps. Even from two stories up, she could hear Makim and D'Mann in a full-blown fist fight down in the basement. Curse words hurled about as if they were going out of style.

"I don't like when niggas fuck with my money!" D'Mann yelled. "Nigga, fuck you!"

Split seconds after those words slipped out of D'Mann's mouth, Desirae was rattled by a boom. For that moment in time, it seemed as if the entire house shook. She jumped up, a bit of a squeal slipping out of her mouth.

"I fuckin' told you, nigga!" a man's voice said. Desirae was unable to tell who it was this time. The man then said something that Desirae couldn't make out.

Concerned, and quite frankly scared for her own life, Desirae quickly turned around. Walking as lightly and quickly as she could, she hurried back to D'Mann's bedroom. She pushed the door closed, thanking the heavens above that it didn't creak when she pushed it. Within the flash of a second, she'd turned the light off and was now standing in a corner, behind an opened closet door. The anticipation and fear were proving to be too much for her. She had no idea who had actually fired the gun, and no idea which man was still standing.

"Oh my God," Desirae whispered to herself. "Shit, shit, shit." The idea that Makim could have been the one to fire the gun did not sit well with Desirae. She suddenly felt like a prisoner. Her body wanted to make a run for it, rushing down the stairs and out into the streets to fend for herself. She wasn't sure of the time, but she knew that it wasn't too late to still catch a bus if she needed. However, the risk outweighed the reward at this point. If Makim had killed D'Mann and was now leaving the house, he could kill her because she would know something and could tell. Desirae really felt as if she was between a rock and a hard place.

"Oh shit," she whispered to herself. Thumping began, coming up the basement steps. For a few seconds, Desirae tried to think if there was anywhere she could hide that would be better than where she was. She realized thinking about it wouldn't do her much good, as she wasn't in a house that belonged to her or that she knew her way around.

The footsteps sounded as if they made their way across the dining room. The steps of the staircase to the second floor then creaked. Slowly but surely, whoever had survived the fight then shooting was coming up the stairs. As they approached the top, Desirae could hear his heavy breathing.

God, please don't let me die today, Desirae thought. *Titan. James. God, please don't let me die today. What about my sons? What about my twins?* The possible scenarios, or endings to the scenarios, ran rampantly through Desirae's head. She could feel her blood pressure rising as parts of her body broke into a sweat.

As Desirae feared for her life, the bedroom door pushed open and the light popped on. A scream slipped over her lips.

"Desirae?"

It was D'Mann. Hesitantly, she pushed the closet door until her eyes met with D'Mann. He reached for her.

"What the fuck happened down there?" Desirae asked, coming out of the corner. "Huh? What the fuck happened down there? Did you...? Did you kill him, D'Mann?"

D'Mann grunted, not liking that Desirae used the word *kill*. "I ain't kill nobody," he said, sounding defensive. He then calmed down, closing his eyes for a moment so that he could get himself back together. "Look, Desirae," he said. "I had to."

"You had to?" Desirae asked. She now looked at D'Mann's bulky body. He was unable to hide how heavily he was breathing. "What the fuck you mean you had to? Why you have to kill him?"

"That nigga was gon' kill me first," he said. "He pulled a knife out and shit. I had to."

Desirae calmed down. "So?" she said, trying to process everything. "Where is he now? Where is his...his...his body?"

D'Mann looked away. "You know," he said, insinuating the basement. "Look, I'm sorry you had to be here to hear some shit like that happen. I swear to God I am. Now that I look back, I shoulda just waited till I took you back to your car. Oh my God, I feel so bad about this."

"Well...," Desirae said, looking around. "What are you gonna do with him?" she asked, still full of fear. "You can't just leave him layin' down there, D'Mann. In the basement and shit. I mean, what the fuck you gon' do with him?"

"I don' t know," D'Mann said, the words struggling to come out of his mouth. "I don't know what I'mma do with him yet, okay. His body just hit the ground and shit, so I ain't even

117

had time to think about it. I was so worried about you." He stepped closer to her. "You was the first thing I thought about. That's why I had to come up here to make sure that you was okay. I fuckin' hate that I ain't just take you back and do this shit later on like I was gonna do in the first place."

"I can't believe that I'm here for this," Desirae said, shaking her head. "Wait a minute. Ain't you gon' call the police and shit? Maybe if you can get him to the hospital in time and shit, they can do somethin' for him. Save him and shit so he ain't got to die."

"I ain't goin' to no damn police," D'Mann said. "I ain't goin' to no fuckin' police so they can just ask a bunch of questions and twist my answers to use against me. What the fuck? No fuckin' cops."

"So, what are you gon' do?" Desirae said. "What you gon' do with his body? Dump it downtown in the river or somethin'? You gon' do some fuckin' mob shit or somethin'? How you gon' get rid of him without nobody knowin? What about his car?"

"I don't know!" D'Mann snapped, almost scaring Desirae. He then calmed back down. "I don't know. You act like I planned this shit or somethin'. The nigga came at me with a knife. I had to do somethin' or else it would be me down there with my brains and guts and shit spilled out on the floor. Fuck that. Betta him than me, you know. That nigga was askin' for it. Shorted me fifty then gon' have the nerve to threaten my life when I said somethin' to him about it."

"Fifty?" Desirae asked. "Fifty what?"

D'Mann hesitated, looking Desirae in the eyes. Usually, he would be more secretive than James Bond about his business. However, he now realized he'd involved Desirae a little deeper than the usual chicks he kept around. There was no point in not telling her now.

"Fifty thousand," he answered. "The nigga was short fifty thousand dollars, makin' up some bullshit about that's all they gave him. Fuck that nigga. He should not'a been fuckin' with a nigga's money, either. Wastin' my time and shit. Fuck him. I know you scared and shit, but I had to do it. Nigga pull a knife on me, and I'mma definitely kill him. No questions about it."

Desirae stepped across the bedroom floor. Slowly, she sat down on the edge of D'Mann's California King. "Is this really happenin'?" she asked, feeling like a character in a movie. "You just killed him and shit while I was standin' up here?"

"Look," D'Mann said, sitting down. "I ain't mean to put you in some position where you might be in any sort of trouble or somethin'. Trust me... I put it on my life. When that nigga came walkin' through the front door, I swear I never woulda thought that I'd have to kill his ass. Shit, a nigga ain't even think that he'd ever pull a knife on me and shit like we out in the streets or somethin'." He placed his hand on Desirae's thighs.

"So, what?" Desirae asked, looking down at D'Mann's hand. "Now, what does that make me? Your accomplice?"

"Accomplice?" D'Mann asked. "What the fuck you supposed to be an accomplice to? You ain't do shit."

"I'm not callin' the police and shit," Desirae said. "I mean, don't that make me an accomplice?"

"I'm tellin' you, Desirae," D'Mann said. "Callin' the police ain't gon do shit but make our lives worse. Shit, they might even roll up in here and start to shootin' niggas and shit. You know how they are and shit. Look, you can stay up here if you want and chill if you want."

"And chill?" Desirae asked, leaning away from D'Mann. "What you gon' do while I'm up in your bedroom chillin' and shit?"

D'Mann leaned in. "You know," he said, flatly. "You know I can't leave the nigga down there and shit. I'mma have to do something."

"What are you into?" Desirae asked. Normally, she might not get into a man's business like this after only knowing him for a couple of days. However, on the flipside, she probably wouldn't just so happen to be over at a guy's place when he pulled a gun out and had to kill someone down in his basement. All of this was quickly becoming too much for Desirae. One side of her wanted to hide in the closet and act as if she'd never heard a thing. However, she also recognized that D'Mann was making a point. Calling the police would only make things worse and possibly pull the two of them into the legal system trap that was so hard to escape.

"What you mean what I'm into?" D'Mann asked. "You mean, how I make my money?"

Desirae nodded. "You the one who said you just usin' McDonald's for gas money and gotta make money out in these streets, the only way you know how," she said. "I'm just askin'. You ain't gotta go given' me your social security number or nothin'."

D'Mann nodded. There was something about Desirae's confidence that turned him on. She was definitely a strong woman. D'Mann felt that if this had been any other chick, she'd be rolling around on the floor terrified and in tears.

"You really try'na get serious with a nigga, huh?" D'Mann asked. "I don't share my business with just anybody, especially when I only known they ass for a couple days."

"I don't know what I'm try'na be," Desirae said, realizing she was looking at a man who might really want to invest in her, "but I know I need to know what you involved in, if you wanna consider keeping me around after this shit."

D'Mann smirked and leaned back. "You really try'na play hardball with a nigga, ain't you?"

Desirae smiled. "Go hard or go home," she said. "I'm involved in this shit now because I'm not callin' the police, which makes sense. I just wanna know what kinda shit you involved in. I know my face is beat up and shit right now," she shrugged, "but do you like what you see?"

D'Mann looked Desirae up and down. "I liked what I saw when I could only see your face, so don't say shit like that."

"What is it you involved in?" Desirae asked. "I mean, shit, I just heard you have to kill a nigga. At least you could tell me that much."

D'Mann squinted at Desirae as he began to explain.

***

For much of the ride back to the library parking lot, Desirae had a bit of a headache. Hearing such a loud boom,

120

in a relatively small space, had proven to be too much for her ears. Even though D'Mann had made arrangements, for lack of a better word, to do something with Makim's body, Desirae still felt completely shaken up by the entire event. There were moments when the Indiana fall wind would rush into D'Mann's SUV, causing her to think about whether this was some crazy dream or nightmare. Had she fallen asleep at the library while applying for a job and had a dream?

"You okay over there?" D'Mann asked, glancing over at Desirae. "A nigga notice how you over there not talkin' too much. What's on your mind?"

Desirae looked over at D'Mann. While she was still very nervous and shook up at just the thought of being in the same house as a man who'd lost his life, only two floors below her, she couldn't deny the fact that it was a nice change of pace to have a man actually ask her how she was feeling. And D'Mann sounded as if he was genuinely interested.

"Why you into me?" Desirae asked, not realizing she was coming across as insecure. "I need to know."

"Why am I into you?" D'Mann responded, repeating the question back. "What you mean?"

"You got money for days, D'Mann," Desirae said. "You told me about how you was out in these streets, really movin' shit big time and doin' it without havin' to be out in the light and shit. You coulda talked to any chick, but instead you actually hit me back, even after I told you that I got two newborn twins." Desirae looked down at her twiddling fingers. "Any otha nigga woulda ran the otha way. What is it that you want outta me?"

D'Mann snickered, shaking his head. "Awe God," he said. "Females. Y'all always think that a nigga gotta want somethin' out of you for him to be interested. I hope you not over there thinkin' that I really planned on killin' that nigga downstairs like that. Cause that would be wrong. I really didn't."

"I believe you," Desirae insisted. "I swear, I really do. I'm just askin' cause, like I told you, lately I done had a lot of niggas play with my heart and treat me like I'm nothin'."

"And that shit ain't right," D'Mann said. "Like I said when I first startin' talkin' to you in the drive-thru, I could tell that you had somethin' a lotta chicks don't have on their shoulders—a good head. Plus, I liked how you kept your coo with the shit that just went down back at the house. I thought you was gon' freak out and take off runnin'."

"I thought about it," Desirae said. "But I ain't know who was the one that got shot. I was so scared when you was comin' back upstairs cause I ain't know if it was gon' be you or him, comin' up there to kill me or somethin'."

"Naw," D'Mann said. "You the first chick I actually brought back to the spot and shit. I don't care what you say, I wasn't gon' let shit happen to you. You was my first priority when he pulled that knife out if you wanna know the truth. And I ain't perfect either," he said, referring back to her original question. "I don't care that you got them two babies and out here try'na do shit on your own. Shit, you lucky I don't know the nigga who the daddy. Based on some of the stuff you was tellin' a nigga, I'd ride up on that nigga and beat his ass my damn self."

"No, you wouldn't," Desirae said.

"Swear I would," D'Mann said.

"Naw, don't be that way," Desirae said. She began to say that she didn't want Tron to wind up dead, but she decided against it. Since she and D'Mann's emotions were still running high, she didn't want to add fuel to the fire. "I guess I just have a hard time thinkin' that somebody would want me now. I mean, I got my ass beat and am walkin' around with a fuckin' scarlet letter on my face, basically showin' it. You should see the way people look at me now." She looked down. "I can tell what they thinkin'. I swear I can."

"You try'na ride with a nigga?" D'Mann asked, holding the steering wheel and looking over at Desirae.

"What you mean?" Desirae asked. "You not askin' me to be your chick or nothin' after only two days of knowin' each other, is you?"

D'Mann shrugged his shoulder. "You seen, or heard, a nigga kill another nigga in self-defense after only knowin' me for two days and ain't run out and go to the police," he said. "I mean, is you feelin' a nigga or what? If you need more time or whatever, I understand. I ain't trippin'. It ain't like I got no otha chicks or nothin'."

"I don't know," Desirae answered, looking out of her window at the wooded area of the south side of Indianapolis. "I just don't know if I'm up for try'na get involved right now. I gotta get some money comin' in. I got two babies and no job and am stayin' at my mama house. I can't keep livin' like this forever. This shit it too rough. It's already hard enough knowin' that I gotta take care of two babies. If it wasn't for my cousin Tiffany right now, I don't know what I would do. Whoever I do be with next is gon' have to be able to take me for me and all of me. My sons mean too much to me right now. If you wanna know, that's the real reason I ain't go to the police. I ain't got time to be try'na deal with the system right now and take care of two newborn baby boys. Shit, I don't even know what Tron would do if them babies had to go into the system. I just don't."

"Tron?" D'Mann asked, sounding intrigued. "Tron who?"

Desirae wanted to say *damn*; she hadn't meant to say Tron's name.

Chapter 9

Tron walked through the door of his townhouse around 9 o'clock that night. He'd planned on being home much earlier, but since one of his cousins had driven in from Louisville, he spent a good portion of his day chilling with him. In fact, his cousin had wanted to stay in Indianapolis so that he could go to Tron's club, especially since his wife wasn't traveling with him. However, he knew that he'd better go ahead and get back to Louisville before it got too late. The last thing he needed was his wife going off on him because she thought that something could be going on. Tron walked his cousin to his car, hugged him, then headed into the house.

"Nigga, what the fuck you still doin' here?" Tron asked when he walked into his living room and saw his boy Tyrese pulling his pants up.

"Damn, nigga," Tyrese said, smiling. "You missed it."

"Missed what?" Tron asked, shaking his head. "What the fuck did I miss?"

"I just had this bad bitch over here, with a big ole fat ass," Tyrese explained. "All you had to do was tell this bitch to bend that ass over, and she'd let you get up in them guts like it was nothin'."

"Nigga, all you do is fuck big booty bitches," Tron said, snickering. "Nigga, when I text you earlier, you said that you could be up at the club. Do the nigga at the bar up there got a key to get in or what?

"Hell, yeah he got a key," Tyrese responded. "What the fuck you think this is? I done gave that nigga a key. I see you frustrated and shit, walkin' through the door talkin' shit."

"Frustrated?" Tron said. "About what?"

"Nigga, you know," Tyrese said. "You had a nigga prayin' for your safety earlier when you went over to Desirae's mama's house to see them twins and shit. I thought she might come after you after what happened on Saturday."

"Yeah, that shit was pretty bad," Tron said, shaking his head. "But, naw. I smoothed shit over. Actually, now that I think about it, I wanted to ask you somethin'. You think you be seein' Desirae's car ridin' through the parkin' lot at night?"

Tyrese shrugged his shoulders and said, "Fuck if I know. I mean, I see that chick's car and shit, but with all them cars that be out in that parkin' lot, I don't know that I've seen hers and shit. Why? Why you ask some shit like that?"

"Cause," Tron said, about to bring up the thing that had been on his mind since he'd left Desirae earlier in the day. "When I went over there today, she was bein' her usual self and shit, throwing the pussy at a nigga and try'na make me get back with her and shit. And she gon' bring up some shit about how she know that I'm still fuckin' around with her old best friend Reese."

"Uh, oh," Tyrese said, shaking his head. "Nigga, you gon' make me have to move up out this place before you have that bitch comin' over here and shootin' it up and shit. Man, you need to control your hoes. Now you got one ridin' around and seein' who you be havin' at your place. Nigga, I told you that you was foul for even fuckin' around with her best friend and shit. It's only a matter of time before she realize that the two of you is really over, and she start to get in her feelings and shit. You know how bitches be actin' when they feel like some dude done did them wrong. They don't be thinkin' rationally and shit."

"Nigga, fuck you," Tron said, smiling. "I'm just sayin'.'"

Tyrese got up, grabbed his car keys, and headed toward the front door. "Just sayin' nothing," he said. "Nigga, you know that bitch got you scarred. I wouldn't even have them problems, if you asked me. I fuck'em, don't get them pregnant, and don't for one second lead them on to thinkin' that they gon' be more than just somethin' to make my dick feel good."

"Oh, I know," Tron said, hearing his front door open and close. "I know."

Tron got himself something to drink before going upstairs and changing his clothes. Just as he sprayed some cologne onto his neck and wrists, his phone rang. When he looked at the screen, he saw that it was Reese. He was unsure how she would react to Desirae asking if the two of them were still talking to another. Furthermore, Tron wondered how Reese might feel about him lying to Desirae, even after all of these months of him not messing around with her in a sexual way.

"Wassup?" Tron said, answering the call.

"You up at the club yet?" Reese asked. "Ain't heard from you today and was thinkin' that maybe I could come up to the club and see you tonight before things get too hectic and shit."

Tron smiled. He liked that he had a chick who really thought of ways to make his day better. Aside from his ex-girlfriend Shawna, he'd never had a woman who wanted to surprise him wherever he was making money without the real intentions of starting some drama.

"Naw," Tron answered. "I actually just got home. My cousin Brandon came up from Louisville and shit, had some sort of appointment up here or somethin'. He hit me up earlier when I left Desirae's place and was askin' me if I wanted to chill before he headed back. We went and got somethin' to eat and shit. Chilled and smoked in his car and caught up. Hadn't seen the nigga in a while, so it was nice to just see what was goin' on with him and stuff."

"Awe, okay," Reese said. "So, how was it?"

"How was what?" Tron asked, confused. After all, he'd just explained what he'd been doing during the day with his cousin.

"You know what I'm talkin' bout, Tron," Reese said. "Desirae ain't go actin' all crazy and shit on you, did she? I told you how that bitch can be. All she think about is herself and got the nerve to be wonderin' why these niggas ain't try'na be with her in no serious kinda way."

"Naw, everythin' was coo," Tron said, lying. The visual image of Desirae's backside, in those red pajama pants, popped into his mind. Between her nasty attitude and her beat up face, there was nothing he wanted to do more than to bend her over, put her head in a pillow, and dick her down the way he did before she started acting all crazy. "You know, though. I mean, she was throwin' it at me."

"See," Reese said. "Told you. I told you. I told you, I told you, I told you. All that bitch do is fuck, and that's all she wanna do. She prolly don't even care about you bein' a daddy

126

to your sons or nothin'. She gon' do whatever she can to keep you comin' around and in her face. She gon' keep try'na get you back in that bed. Hell, for all you know, she could be try'na trap you again."

Tron looked up at the ceiling. He knew that his weakness was a chick with a big ass, but there were moments he really hated the thought that he may have been trapped by one – trapped by someone that he should've been able to outsmart. "I just ignored her," Tron said. "And you know that."

"How her face look?" Reese asked, clearly sounding a little excited. "Was you able to get a picture of it like I asked you?"

"Stop," Tron said, putting on his fatherly voice. "You ain't gotta be that way."

"Naw," Reese said. "Fuck her. That bitch gon' pull me out the car in the snow then force me to walk home in the cold and shit. I don't give a fuck about her feelins. I wanna see how bad she got that ass beat since she always wanna think that she all tough and shit. That's what she get."

"Yeah, well her face is still pretty fucked up," Tron said. "But I wanted to ask you about somethin' else. Did you know that she been ridin' through the parkin' lot and shit?"

"Ridin' through the parkin' lot?" Reese asked. "What parkin' lot?"

"You know," Tron said, heading downstairs. "The parkin' lot over here, at the house and shit. She said she know that me and you still been seein' each other because she saw your car and some old air freshener you got hangin' in the window."

"Naw, I mean...I ain't never seen her out there," Reese asked. "I just got into the habit of parkin' way over on the other side and shit. What, is she makin' threats now?"

"Naw, she ain't make no threats," Tron said, grabbing his car keys. "She just started to talk about that shit, you know, when I was rejectin' that ass. She kept rubbin' up on me and shit, and goin' in the same room I was in."

"I bet she was bendin' over extra hard too," Reese said. "She was probably archin' her back so damn hard she was walkin' crooked for the rest of the day. I swear, she really think that her ass is the center of the universe and that any and every man she come across just wanna take her clothes off and fuck her from the back."

Fuck her from the back? Tron thought. He shook his head, thinking, *it don't make no damn sense how much ass she got.*

"Yeah," Tron said. "She prolly was, but I wasn't payin' no attention to her."

"So, why you bring up askin' me if I know she been ridin' through and shit?" Reese asked. "You really don't think that she gon' do nothin', do you?"

"Shit, I don't know," Tron said. "That used to be your best friend. I thought that you might be the one to know."

"Shit, I don't put it past her," Reese commented. "I swear, she just so jealous. She prolly will try to do somethin' when she find out about me and you and stuff. She ain't gon' be able to handle the fact that some man wanted ole plain ass me over here. I already know that's what's gon' be goin' through her head."

"Don't say shit like that, Reese," Tron said, knowing that he needed to say something to make Reese feel better about herself. "Desirae ain't nothin' but body. You, on the other hand, actually got a brain and shit. That's somethin' she ain't got."

Reese giggled, almost wanting to laugh. She knew that Tron was telling the absolute truth.

"So, what you doin'?" she asked. "You still up at the house?"

"Headed out the door right now, actually," Tron said. "Tyrese just left and headed up to the club. I'm about to head up there myself. Gotta make this money tonight."

"Oh, okay," Reese said. "Well, I'mma be up. So, just text me."

"I will," he said. "I might even want you to come over and spend the night when I get outta there later on. You down for somethin' like that?"

"Yeah," Reese said. "Just text me and let me know when I need to be over there. If it's too late and I don't answer, then just know that I feel asleep."

When D'Mann dropped Desirae off in the library parking lot, they had roughly ten minutes to kill before Desirae needed to get into her car and head up to Tiffany's apartment. D'Mann pulled into the parking spot next to Desirae's car – the only car in the parking lot. He looked around, feeling somewhat on edge that he was riding around while Makim was lying dead on his basement floor.

"You sure you gon' be okay tonight?" D'Mann asked. "I mean, after what happened and shit?"

Desirae shrugged. "I'mma have to be," she answered. "I mean…What else can I do? You said he pulled a knife on you and shit. I woulda did the same thing. What you gon' do with his body, though? I mean, do you think that he gon' have people that come lookin' for him, seein' that his car is outside of your house?"

"I don't quite know yet," D'Mann said. "I mean, a nigga got his people comin' through to help out in a little bit and shit, but we still ain't one hundred on where and what we gon' do with the nigga's body. The nigga is kinda big, just so you know, since I know that you ain't get a chance to see him."

Desirae felt glad that she hadn't gotten a chance to see him. That could have made things even worse for her, especially since she knew that something had gone down in the basement and was choosing to not go to the police. At this point, the less she knew was probably the better. In light of such, she didn't press the matter much with regard to what D'Mann would be doing with the body.

"Let me ask you somethin'," Desirae said, leaning over the consul. "You ever killed a nigga before?" In so many ways, she felt strange asking such a question.

"I got into a shootout with this one nigga over on the east side one time," D'Mann said, hesitantly. "I don't know if a bullet hit him or not. It was back when I was nineteen and dumb and shit. Once me and the nigga I was with heard them police sirens ring out into the air, we got the fuck up out there and shit. Ain't even look back. But, to answer your question, as far as I know, I ain't kill the dude. At least, I never heard that he died or nothin'."

Desirae nodded, processing what she was being told. "I believe you," she said. "I believe you."

For a long moment, Desirae and D'Mann looked at each other. Without thinking, they leaned toward one another and D'Mann kissed her. "I swear, I like you," he said, putting on a fake country accent. "But, on the real, though, I promise that this shit ain't gon' affect you. I swear to God I would never do nothin' that would put you or the lives of your little boys and shit at risk. I can already tell, from the talks we've had over the last couple days, that you a real chick. I feel bad about how them otha niggas done been doggin' you out and shit."

"Oh, don't," Desirae said. Her eyes glanced down. "It's my fault, really."

"Don't say that," D'Mann said. "And ain't shit your fault, okay? You told me how that nigga treated you. I ain't wanna say nothin', but when you said his name, I think I know him."

"I know," Desirae said. "I could tell. That's why I changed the conversation around so quick. I could tell that you knew him, and I ain't know what that meant. That's why I been so quiet for most of the ride."

"Well, it's a small world," D'Mann said. "I can tell you that. Yeah, I know that nigga, Tron. Don't he own some club over on the east side."

Desirae nodded. "Yeah," she said. "That's him. But how you know him?"

"We used to stay into it when we was younger, actually," D'Mann said. "Back then, we both was out in these streets, and I wasn't doin' as well as I'm doin' now. He already was, and he was Mister Suave and shit. Had all the bitches on his dick, twenty- four seven. He used to say some slick shit when we would cross paths until one time, I had to let him know how the fuck a nigga should be talkin' to another nigga. Since then, I ain't really like that dude. I don't know if he still makin' money out here or what. Ain't heard too much out of him except for that club. Actually, I ain't even know that he owned the club and shit, until me and these niggas I used to know went up in there and saw him walkin' around and shit, bein' Mister Nice Guy. He ain't even hardly say two words to me 'cause he know that I still got a little chip on my shoulder

130

from some of the shit he used to say to me." D'Mann let out a deep sigh. "But, I'm all grown up now. Gotta learn to let that shit go. Ain't got time to be gettin' into with niggas at the club and shit like I used to."

Desirae looked into D'Mann's face and was so sure she was looking into the eyes of a real man. From what she'd seen, D'Mann really didn't want to be out in the light. In fact, he did seem like somewhat of a recluse. He also had some values that Desirae found admirable.

"Don't trip about all that," Desirae said. "You just make sure you do what you gotta do tonight to get rid of that nigga's body. And whatever you do, just make sure that you don't wind up in jail or somethin'. I wouldn't drive this truck 'cause you know how the police are when they see us in somethin' like this."

"Oh, I already know," D'Mann said. "I done thought of that part already. I got this old hoopty I used to drive back before I bought my first new car. I already know that I'mma use that. It got tinted windows. One of them Cavaliers. You know, the cars that look like a little white girl car. Anytime I'm ridin' around in that, the cops don't never pull me over. But, look, you just go ahead and get your sons and shit from your cousin's place. Don't worry about me. I really ain't mean for this shit to go down with you there. I see everything that you been through today, and I hate that I had to do that with you there. I swear to God, I really do."

Desirae showed her appreciation for D'Mann's concern for her well-being as she climbed out of the car. D'Mann watched her walk around the front of his SUV then over to her car. She smiled and waved as she got inside. He then pulled away. Desirae could see the look on his face that he was going to be about business tonight.

Once she'd fastened her seatbelt and started her car, Desirae could do nothing but lean back in her seat and take a few moments to think.

"Did that shit really just happen to me?" she asked herself, out loud. "Was I really just over at his house when he killed some guy in the basement?" The scene played over in her mind – the moments in time when she'd been wedged

131

behind that closet door in D'Mann's bedroom. She recalled how fast her heart was beating when D'Mann was climbing the stairs, not knowing who had been doing the shooting and who had just taken a bullet.

Desirae rested for a few minutes before she got herself together enough to head up north. On her way through downtown, she took in the lit city scenery. Having just been in a house where somebody's life had been taken caused her to look at everything with different eyes, so to speak. She could already feel that she probably wasn't going to get any sleep tonight. As if the humiliating and embarrassing fight on Saturday in her mother's front yard wasn't enough, she now had to deal with her emotions from knowing that she was falling for a guy she'd just met – a guy who, in the two days they'd known one another, had to take another man's life to not only protect himself, but to also protect her as she was hiding upstairs in his bedroom.

When Desirae pulled into the parking lot of Tiffany's apartment complex, she hadn't even thought of the rift she'd had with her cousin just days before. In fact, with everything that was going on at this point, how Tiffany was feeling was far back in her mind. Desirae parked her car and headed inside. Just as she had climbed to the top of the building steps, she felt her phone vibrating in her purse. It was Tiffany calling.

"Hello?" Desirae answered.

"Girl, I'm so sorry," Tiffany said. "Just wait outside. I'm on my way right now, probably about ten minutes away. I had to run up to the hospital real quick, but it ain't nothin' serious. I'll be there in ten minutes, so just wait outside for me."

"Okay, okay," Desirae said. "I'll be outside."

Desirae hung up the phone, knowing that this was another situation where Tiffany's man Reggie must have been in the apartment with James and Titan. As much as she didn't like the idea of her cousin leaving her children with some man she didn't even know herself, Tiffany was the best that she could afford right now in terms of childcare. Just as Desirae was about to turn around and head back downstairs, she decided against it.

"I ain't got time for her shit," Desirae said to herself, snapping her neck. "If that nigga in there with my kids, so what? Tiffany ole insecure ass is just gon' have to be in her feelings. I need to see my babies."

Desirae ignored Tiffany's request for her to wait outside. She went ahead and approached Tiffany's apartment door and knocked. Within seconds, the door opened, and Desirae was looking into Reggie's cold, but sexy eyes.

"Hey," she said. "I ain't come here to cause no problem. I just came here to pick up my sons and stuff. Tiffany just called and said that she was ten minutes away. She wanted me to wait for her and stuff, but I ain't really got time for all that. I done had a long day and just wanna get my ass home."

Desirae brushed past Reggie, who stood to the side. He was dressed in black jeans and a blue, V-neck t-shirt. Standing there in silence, Reggie watched as Desirae moved around the living room and gathered up the things that belonged to Titan and James. No sooner than Desirae had packed her baby bag with everything she'd seen that belonged to her, the front door to the apartment opened. Tiffany came walking in, with a concerned look on her face.

"What is goin' on here?" she asked, looking at Reggie then Desirae.

Desirae looked back at her cousin. "Please, girl," she said, shaking her head. "Not today. With the day I done had, I really don't feel like it. I swear I don't."

"Feel like what?" Tiffany asked, clearly sounding defensive. "Desirae, I told you that I was just around the corner and that I'd be here in like ten minutes, if not sooner. You couldn't even wait to come in here, could you?"

"Girl, what are you talkin' about?" Desirae asked. "How you gon' try to stop me from seein' my kids? Girl, what is wrong with you? Who do you even think that you are? And you one to be talkin' about what I should and shouldn't be doin'. If I recall right, I don't remember you talkin' to me about leavin' my kids with some man that I don't even know."

"I told you, Desirae," Tiffany said, "my grandmother is in the hospital, girl. I have to go up there sometime."

"Okay, that's fine," Desirae said. "But that don't mean that you gotta leave my kids like this. Go up there when you not watchin' them."

"You can cut the little attitude out, Desirae," Tiffany said. "Before I add to that fucked up face you got goin' on right now."

Reggie cracked a smile and shook his head. Even he thought that Tiffany's comments were a bit harsh. "Damn, Tiffany," he said. "Why don't you calm down? You always try'na think that somethin' be goin' on when don't nothin' be goin' on at all."

Tiffany shook her head. "Naw," she said, waving her finger in Reggie's face. "Don't you be the one to fuckin' tell me that I need to fuckin' calm down. I see the way you be lookin' over her way just a little too hard. And I see the way she be lookin' at you. I told you I don't trust her."

"And I heard you too," Desirae said, shaking her head. "Girl, I heard the bullshit you was sayin' about me. When I came over to get Titan and James, I heard what the fuck you was sayin' about me and shit, talkin' bout how I'm just a hoe and stuff. Girl, you couldn't have it further from the truth than some stuff like that. I ain't no hoe."

"Girl, yes you is," Tiffany said, not caring one bit how Desirae felt. "And I know that if I wasn't here right now, you'd prolly drop to your knees and suck his dick. Girl, don't you know that practically the whole damn family can see through that little sweet girl act you got goin' on." Tiffany stepped a few steps closer to Desirae. "So, how did it really happen?" she asked. "How did your face wind up so fucked up? Who man you fuck that they came back and used that face as a punchin' bag?"

"Tiffany, what is wrong with you?" Desirae asked, picking her bag up. "Is you really just that jealous of me to think that I would ever make a move on some nigga that belong to my cousin?" She looked at Reggie and the bulky, chocolate goodness that he was, even though he was only standing in place. "I don't want your man anyway. I wouldn't do that to you. Based on how you actin', I can tell that you would prolly die if he were to ever leave your ass. What is that dick to you? Your damn life support and shit?"

"Bitch, fuck you!" Tiffany said. "Girl, the only reason I agreed to watch them little ugly ass babies of yours is because Auntie said I should do it since you the struggling, broke bitch in the family."

"Ugly?" Desirae said, holding her hand up to her chest and shaking her head. "Whose babies you callin' ugly? If anybody ugly up in here, it's you, Tiffany. Hate to break it to you, girl, but it's the truth. That's why you so mad that I came up in here when your nigga was up in here. Cause you know it wouldn't take much for anybody – and I do mean anybody – to come right along and take your man from right up under you." Desirae looked Tiffany up and down, noticing that she probably hadn't made much effort to even try to stay in shape since popping out her several children back to back. "I mean, let's keep it real. Who you foolin'?"

"Girl, get the fuck out my face," Tiffany said. "I swear, just get the fuck out my face. I know you came runnin' up here so you could have a little more time with my nigga, so you could probably get him to look at you and get his number or somethin'. Girl, I know your type. Just get the fuck out my house before I jump on that ass. There is just somethin' about you that I can't really stand bein' around, I swear."

"Beat my ass then, bitch!" Desirae yelled. "Beat my ass then if you really about it." She held her arms open.

Tiffany began to make her way across the room to Desirae, but Reggie stepped in the way. He now stood between the two of them, moving side to side when he needed to, as long as one could not get to the other. Curse words spilled out of Tiffany's mouth and rolled over Reggie's muscular shoulders.

"Damn, Tiffany," Reggie said. "You trippin'. Girl, you know I love you."

Tiffany pushed Reggie back. "Nigga, please," she said. "You sure wasn't talkin' about how much you love me when you was textin' that one nigga about Desirae's ass and shit. You know you be lookin' a little too hard at her." She looked at

Desirae. "And you know she'll open her legs for any nigga that got a big enough dick."

Desirae snickered and shook her head as she picked up Titan then James out of the crib. "Girl, you crazy," she said. "I mean, for real. You got self-esteem issues." She laughed out loud. "All I do is walk in the door and got some ole insecure bitch comin' for me like I done really did somethin' to you or somethin'."

Desirae walked up to the apartment door and pulled it open.

"Fuck you!" Tiffany said. "For real, fuck you. You lucky you carryin' them babies or else I'd be out in the hallway and draggin' that ass down them steps and around the parkin' lot."

Holding Titan and James, Desirae marched out into the apartment building hallway.

"And I suggest you find somebody else to watch them little niggas," Tiffany said. "I already know what you about. And I can't trust you with what I got goin' on up in here."

"Girl, whatever," Desirae said. "You petty as shit. I ain't got time for this mess."

Desirae walked down to her car, not looking back. At this point, she never wanted to see Tiffany again in her life. She was so angry with her cousin that once she'd gotten Titan and James into their car seats, she got into the driver's seat and took a moment to breathe.

"Fuck!" Desirae yelled, not caring who might be in the parking lot or standing nearby. "I just can't catch a break, can I?"

As Desirae pulled out of Tiffany's parking lot and onto 16th Street, the weight of what had just happened began to fall on her head. In fact, she felt like the world was falling on her head. It didn't take her long to realize that not only had she lost, or given up, her job at Family Dollar, but she had also just lost the most affordable childcare option she had. And the last place she really wanted to send Titan and James to was one of the state-run daycares. It wasn't that they weren't up to standards to take care of newborn twins; she and Tron had agreed they wanted the babies to stay with someone they knew since Desirae wasn't going to be able to stay at home and not work for a year. Her mind zipped through what options she had – a route that led her to nowhere, as she didn't have any family members in town who would have the time, and wherewithal, to watch Titan and James for what she could afford to pay them.

"Why she have to go and fuck up my situation?" Desirae asked as she thought about Tiffany. "Fuck, this shit is fuckin' ridiculous."

Desirae had been talking too loudly and forcefully. Titan woke up and began to cry, then James did the same. Desirae leaned her hand on her folded arm while driving with one hand. She could feel her headache get stronger. Hearing the gunshot in the basement just hours earlier was still too fresh on her mind to even begin to put it aside and try to act as if it didn't happen. Now, when she passed dark, empty parking lots, paranoia would set in. She felt as if at any moment one of the lurking police cars would swing out of a parking lot and jump on her tail.

Desirae wondered if she should have just made a run for it and never responded to another text message from D'Mann. In fact, the more Desirae thought about it, the more it made sense to her. D'Mann didn't know where she lived or who she hung out with. She then bit her lip, thinking about how she'd slipped up and said Tron's name.

"Why the fuck I do that?" Desirae asked herself. She then shook it off, realizing that she wouldn't tell a man anything she really didn't want him to know. Whatever her feelings were regarding the situation in the basement, Desirae still had to keep it real with herself. There was something about D'Mann that was pulling her to him. He had swag, but was unsophisticated, in a good way. He could speak well, but didn't sound like a nerd or lame. He was smart enough to have a front rather than be just another one of these guys out in the streets selling drugs, purchasing cars, and having no source of income to show for it.

For the next twenty minutes or so, as Desirae zigzagged through Indianapolis to her mother's neighborhood, she simply turned on the radio. A Kelly Rowland song had been on at first, then commercials and Meek Mill. A little further down the road, the radio station played a Brandy song followed by one of Drake's many hits. Desirae eventually turned the radio down, happy that the music managed to calm Titan and James down. She rode the west of the way home in silence.

***

When Desirae finally got home and put Titan and James into their basinets, she felt more tired than she'd been in a long time. This fatigue was not physical. It was mental. She'd checked her phone repeatedly since getting back to the house, waiting to see if she'd hear from D'Mann again. At this point, with how she felt about men, she wouldn't be surprised if he never called her again. She shook her head, wondering if another guy had simply talked his way into her panties. She couldn't help but remember Tron doing it. Then, she glanced over at the couple of basinets, knowing that Tron's words were how she got to this pivotal point in her life in the first place. The taste of bitterness came to her, as she thought about how Tron had dissed her like she was nothing, only to try to push up on her when he'd come over to the house earlier in the day to see Titan and James.

Reese then popped into Desirae's mind. Rather, thinking of Tron caused her to only take the next step, mentally, and think of the chick who had been her best friend and confidant for years. Desirae finding Reese's car parked on the other side of the parking lot from Tron's townhouse played over in her mind. She shook her head, thinking of just how trifling of a friend Reese turned out to be. Not realizing her actions, Desirae bit her bottom lip. She wanted to jump on Reese so bad she could almost feel herself lifting up off of the ground.

"And here I am," Desirae said, looking at her circumstance. "Ain't got no place of my own, no job, no babysitter, no nigga to help me. And that bitch over there layin' up with him. He prolly takin' her shopping and out to eat and shit. He ain't even wanna be seen with me in public, even though I'm the baddest chick he ever had. I swear to God, fuck that nigga, Tron."

Desirae felt her phone vibrating on top of the bed from a couple of feet away. She grabbed it, saw that it was D'Mann calling, and answered.

"Hello?" she said, sounding a little disgruntled.

"Hey, wassup?" D'Mann said. "Wassup with you? Why you answer the phone like that? What's on your mind?"

Desirae calmed down. Once again, it was so nice to have a man ask her about her feelings. "Nothing," Desirae answered. "Well, just sittin' here thinkin'. What did you wind up doin', anyway?"

"Hold up," D'Mann said. "I'll get to that. First, I need to know what's goin' on in your mind. What's up with you, sexy? I don't like when you not happy. Tell a nigga what's goin' on."

Desirae took a deep breath then explained what all happened at Tiffany's house.

"Is you serious?" D'Mann asked. "The bitch got to trippin' like that?"

"Hmm, hmm," Desirae said. "And me and her nigga ain't never even messed around. That's what's crazy about this. I can prolly count on my two hands the number of words I've even said to the nigga. She called my babies ugly and said that she ain't gon' watch them no more." Desirae was too deep into her feelings at this point. She sniffled then a couple of rogue tears escaped and rolled down her cheeks. "I swear, D'Mann. It's like no matter how hard I try, I just can't get ahead. I mean, damn. What the fuck did I do to deserve this? I just can't win for losing."

"Calm down, calm down," D'Mann said. "Let me come see you."

"Come see me?" Desirae asked. "When you talkin' bout try'na come see me?"

"Tonight," D'Mann said. "A nigga mean right now. I know we just met and shit, but I can't sit up and listen to you cry without me at least try'na do somethin' about it. Let a nigga come see you. I know you got the babies and stuff so you can't leave, but that don't mean that you can't come outside and sit and talk with a nigga in the truck or somethin'."

"I don't know," Desirae said. She thought about how much of a risk it was to have D'Mann come over to her mother's house and park outside in the middle of the night. But she then thought about the risk she took with Greg coming over – a risk that led to her being humiliated and embarrassed in front of the entire block with the sun acting as a spotlight for the stage.

"How soon can you be here?" Desirae asked. She gave D'Mann the address and he said he'd be on his way right away. Desirae, already dressed in her pajamas, grabbed her cute black jacket with a hood and slid into it. She slid into some Gucci house slippers that she used to wear at her apartment out on the south side of Indianapolis.

Within fifteen minutes, Desirae saw D'Mann pulling up as she watched from her bedroom window. She grabbed her phone, headed downstairs, and out to his car. She climbed into the front passenger seat and looked over at D'Mann.

"I see you been cryin'," D'Mann said. He pulled a small packet of Kleenex out of his glove compartment and handed it to Desirae. "Don't cry. It's gon' be okay."

"Yeah, if you say so," Desirae said, not feeling too hopeful about tomorrow. She decided it was time to change the subject. "Did everything go okay? Do you think your neighbors saw us leavin' earlier?"

D'Mann shook his head. "Naw," he said. "I don't think they saw us. Plus, you know there be gun shots all the time over in Haughville. Knowin' my neighbors, they prolly ain't think nothin' about that shit. Plus, you saw how dark it is around my place."

"Yeah, but that still don't mean that somebody ain't see us when we was leavin' or something, like the people who live on both sides of you or somethin'," Desirae said.

"Chill out, chill out," D'Mann said. "A nigga think he about to move from over there anyway. I don't know. I'm just thinkin' about it." He looked up and down the street, clearly on the edge just as much as Desirae had been. Desirae could relate all too well.

A couple of awkward moments of silence passed. "And just so you know," D'Mann said, "he is gone, and I don't think nobody saw. Had one of my best niggas come over and help me and shit. Trust me, ain't nobody gon' find that nigga even when they do start lookin' for him. I can't let nothin' happen to you. That's all I was thinkin' 'bout when we was movin' and stuff. I felt so bad that I let that happen while you was there when I coulda just had him come through when I took you back to your car."

Desirae told D'Mann to stop worrying about that part. After D'Mann explained what happened with Makim's car, as it was now also well on its way to disappearing, he looked at Desirae. "Look, I know you only known a nigga for a couple days," he said. "Trust me, don't think that I don't think about that shit too. I really don't normally do this kinda shit, but I just keep thinkin' bout how I feel some sort of connection to you. It's like we can relate with some of the things we been through in our own lives."

"Yeah," Desirae said, looking up at her mother's house. "This is some crazy shit." She looked over at D'Mann. "You swear you ain't got no other chick, D'Mann?" she asked. "I mean, if you do, it's coo. I just wanna know cause right now I don't need no more surprises, if you know what I mean. My life is like hell right now."

"I swear to you," D'Mann said, chuckling. "I ain't got no other chick. Ever since that chick tried to accuse me of rape and put me in prison, I been real careful with who I mess around with. Like I used to just fuck to fuck. Now, I'm lookin' more at substance and real shit. I ain't lookin' for no hoe. That's why I knew you was somethin' I might could get with when I met you up at the drive-thru."

Desirae smiled, knowing that she was probably blushing. "Yeah," she said. "A lot of men don't see that about me. That's why sometimes I feel like this body is a curse."

D'Mann began to shake his head immediately as he reached over and pushed his hand down between Desirae's thick thighs. Even in these red pajama pants, it looked as if her hips were spilling over the sides of the car seat. However, D'Mann knew to not get too sexual with Desirae, as she was clearly in need of emotional support rather than physical attention.

"Don't say that," he said. "Just feel sorry for them niggas that can't see what you really bringin' to the table.

Think about what happened with your baby daddy and that chick who you said you was best friends with."

Desirae rolled her eyes. "Don't remind me," she said. "I was just upstairs thinkin' about that shit. Just thinkin' about it gets me mad. I rolled over there and saw her car in the lot, but the nigga gon' come over here and try to lie to my face and say he ain't doin' shit with her. Nigga, I'm not stupid. I know when somebody is lyin' to me."

"Yeah, that's some foul shit," D'Mann said. "I ain't known no niggas to do no shit like that. I mean, that is just some fucked up shit. I'm surprised you don't go beat that bitch's ass for all it's worth."

"I think about it," Desirae said. "But I ain't got time for all that right now. Maybe when I'm back on my feet and stuff, but right now I feel like I'm drowning." She sniffled. "I mean, I feel like every one step I take forward, I get knocked two steps back."

Desirae looked over at D'Mann as he pulled his wallet out of his jacket pocket. She watched as he pulled what looked like at least five or six one hundred-dollar bills out and held them out toward her. "Here," he said.

"What's this for?" Desirae asked, being a little apprehensive.

"I'm helping you," D'Mann said. "And no, don't think of this as charity or whatever shit chicks be try'na say when a man is just try'na help a woman out a little bit."

"But we ain't even known each other long enough like that for me to even think about takin' money from you," Desirae said. "No, that's okay. I done took money from dudes long enough, and it sure ain't doin' shit for me."

D'Mann shrugged. "So what?" he said. "We can get to know each other, just like we are. Hell, I'd say we know each other better than a lot of people know each other. It ain't nothin' to laugh at, but you had to hear me kill a nigga before he kill me. How many people can say that about the person they with?"

Desirae nodded, seeing D'Mann's point. "Look, you not takin' the money," he said. "I'm given' it to you. That is two different things. After what you had to go through tonight

142

because of me, the least I can do is help you out a little bit. At least until we get to know each other a little more."

Desirae looked at the money, knowing that she needed it badly regardless of the source. "Okay," she said as she took it. "Thank you. I appreciate it. I really do. As soon as I'm back workin' again, I promise I will pay you back."

"Naw, don't worry about it," D'Mann said. "It ain't nothin' but five hundred dollars. What the fuck I'mma do with some little shit like five hundred dollars. You can keep it. I promise I won't bring it up again."

Desirae hoped that what D'Mann was saying would turn out to be true.

"Shit, I'm tired," D'Mann said. "That shit from earlier got me paranoid as fuck."

"Is that why you thinkin' that you gotta move from over there, where you stay?" Desirae asked. "Because you feel paranoid? Me, personally, I don't know if I could keep livin' in a house where somebody was shot dead. I mean, I know people who done did stuff like that, but I just can't see myself doin' it."

"Yeah, then there's that too," D'Mann said. He leaned back into this seat. "Can I ask you somethin'?" His voice sounded very philosophical. "Do you ever just wanna start over again?"

Desirae looked at D'Mann and answered, "Every damn day of the week. This has to have been the hardest fuckin' year of my life. I promise you on everything, this shit has been hard. Sometimes I think about just packin' my shit up and goin' to start over somewhere else."

"Exactly," D'Mann said. "I think about the same thing. I be like I don't even wanna be here no more. I mean, sometimes I think about the real reasons I don't really be out there like that, like I used to be. I guess I was just hangin' around until I met a chick or somethin', but I don't know."

"Yeah, well my issue is findin' a dude that's gon' ever wanna be with me, so I know how you feel," Desirae said. "Uncertainty can really be a bitch. For real."

D'Mann looked over at Desirae. Once again, he felt as if he was connecting with her on some level. Sure, he had questions about her past. After all, he really wondered what kind of life she'd been leading that would cause her to have falling outs with so many people in her life. However, he couldn't look beyond the last couple of days. Usually when he'd meet a chick who had a body that looked even a fraction as good as Desirae's, D'Mann would dick her down once, twice, or maybe three times then she'd be history. Now, and especially since the rape accusation, his mindset had changed. He still didn't know how he felt about Desirae having two babies, especially since those two babies were from a dude he used to cross paths with back when they were younger.

"Don't you worry about all that," D'Mann said to Desirae. "If we keep gettin' to know each other, if you want, then I can be there to help you."

"Yeah, right," Desirae said, almost dismissing the idea. "I still gotta see how serious you are."

"Okay," D'Mann said. "See how serious I am then. I got time. You know where to find me."

Desirae glanced at her mother's house then back to D'Mann. "Well, I guess I betta be headin' back in now," she said. "I swear I can't wait until I'm workin' again and don't gotta be here no more. I mean, stuff been coo with my mama so far, but it still ain't the same as livin' on your own. Then I hate that that nigga Tron gotta come over here and look down on me."

"I don't even wanna talk about that nigga no more," D'Mann said. "With how he and that chick that you used to be coo with are soundin', it make me wanna ride up on them and get a little justice for you. But I ain't gon do that."

Before Desirae could respond, D'Mann was pointing toward a window on the second floor of her mother's house. "Is that the room you sleepin' in?" he asked. "That light just popped on."

Desirae turned toward the house and up toward the window. "Fuck," she said. "That mean my mama up. I don't know what she would be goin' in the room for, not unless one of the twins is cryin'. Shit, I betta get in there. Thank you for the money."

"No worries, no worries," D'Mann said, smoothly. "Really, don't even think about it. I know we just gettin' to know each other and shit, but can a nigga get a kiss goodnight? You know I ain't gon' sleep right if I don't get that at least, right?"

Desirae smiled and quickly leaned over to kiss D'Mann on the lips. When she got out of the car, she giggled when D'Mann had reached across the front passenger seat and slapped her ass as hard as he could. "Boy, stop."

D'Mann chuckled. "Hit me up later on or somethin', okay?"

"Okay."

Desirae walked up the walkway and back into the house. With every step she took, D'Mann's eyes zoomed in on her shape, how round her ass was, and how deep her lower back arched in. It was a sight for sore eyes, to say the least. D'Mann could only wait and wonder what it would really be like to work Desirae out in his bed. He wondered how flexible she was, as well as how far she'd go to please a man with a big sexual appetite like him.

When Desirae stepped over the threshold into her mother's living room and closed the door, she heard crying from coming upstairs. Whichever baby was crying he was literally wailing at the top of his lungs. Desirae pushed the front door closed, made sure that it was locked, and rushed upstairs. When she rushed into her bedroom, she was greeted by her mother. Bags under her eyes and her hair up in a doo rag, Karen rocked Titan, trying to get him to calm down.

"This is your responsibility, Desirae," Karen said, in a very scolding way. "These aren't my children."

"Dang, Mama, sorry," Desirae said. "As soon as I heard them, I came rushin' up here to you."

"Girl, don't start with the lies," Karen said. "It's after midnight and I gotta get up and go to work in the mornin'. I know you were outside. I peeked out the window and saw the drug-dealing lookin' truck. You can't be doin' that kinda stuff when you're a mother, Desirae. When you got responsibilities to live up to, like two newborn babies in basinets, you can't just go runnin' out of the house to meet up with some thug you done met."

"Mama, you don't even know what you talkin' bout," Desirae said, taking Titan from her mother. "He wasn't no thug or nothin'. Just a friend of mine."

"A friend of yours?" Karen said, her hands on her hips. "What kinda friend, if that's what you wanna call it, would be comin' to see you after midnight like this when this friend knows that you got two newborn babies?"

"Just a friend of mine, Mama," Desirae said, avoiding eye contact. "I swear, that's all he is."

"Desirae, you listen to me," Karen said. "Don't you be havin' strange men comin' over to my house in the middle of the night in cars and SUVs that cost more than this house does. You hear me? That's dangerous, especially when you have two little children. I know you've heard me talk to you about some of those girls, especially in the black community, who get themselves involved in these less than ideal situations with men they don't really know, only to find out these men are preying not only on them but on their children."

"Okay, okay," Desirae said. "I'm no child, Mama. You ain't got to go talkin' to me like this. All this ain't even necessary."

Karen smacked her lips together, imitating Desirae's rather urban demeanor and mannerisms. "Well I'll tell you what was not even necessary, Desirae," she said. "The fact that I had to get up out of my sleep because one of your children were crying when you were outside in the car with some suspicious-looking man is what is not even necessary, if you want to know the truth. It's time to grow up, Desirae. It's time to grow up."

"I am grown up!" Desirae snapped. "I'm tired of you talkin' to me like I don't know what I'm doin'. I'm tryin', Mama. I'm tryin'. I keep havin' stuff happen to me and it just ain't fair."

Karen noticed the way her daughter's eyes were swelling up, trying to sympathize with her struggle in a situation most women would not be in, young, alone, and with twins.

"Well, I'm sorry you feel that way, Desirae," Karen said. "But that's life. You laid down with some man that really didn't want to be with you. I don't know what you were after, but I

146

know what you've got. Don't make me have to get up out of my sleep again to tend to your responsibilities. I actually have to get up and be at work in the morning. Goodnight."

Karen ended her sentence sharply, turned around, and headed back out into the dark hallway. Seconds passed then Desirae heard her mother's bedroom door close. She rocked Titan in her arms, calming him down before she checked both him and James to see if they needed to be changed. As luck would have it, neither of them did. Desirae set Titan back down in his basinet before shutting her bedroom door, turning the light out, and lying face down in the bed.

"Why me?" Desirae asked herself, her voice muffled by the comforter. She rolled over. "What am I gonna do?"

Just as she had moved her body, she heard the crinkling of the money in her pocket that D'Mann had given to her. She thought about how that money was really just about all the money she had on her. Once she got around to cashing her check, she'd have a couple of hundred dollars more. However, even she knew that she would still be the same level of broke regardless.

As Desirae lay in the dark, the entire situation with D'Mann played over in her mind. She thought about every point, from when she'd gone upstairs, to when she'd heard the gunshot, to when D'Mann had come upstairs to get her. Out of all of the guys she'd messed around with since she was in high school, she could honestly say she'd never been with one who had to take somebody's life while she was in the same vicinity. Even at this point, hours after the fact, it still didn't seem real. Desirae was paranoid that somebody would come knocking on her door in the middle of the night and take her away in handcuffs, charging her as an accessory to murder or something similar.

Thinking about these things only led Desirae to think more about D'Mann. He'd already shown that he was so giving. And it was even better that he didn't want anything in return from her. However, Desirae couldn't look past the fact that D'Mann was obviously doing well for himself financially.

Everything about his house screamed not only that he had money but also that he had some class about him.

When Desirae had grown tired of lying in the dark with only her feelings, she grabbed her phone. Her mother's words echoed in her head, reminding her that desperate times really do call for desperate measures. The entire situation with Greg was a total flop, but Desirae saw that she might have some potential to get something going with D'Mann. At this point, Tron was old news – water under the bridge, so to speak. Desirae texted D'Mann: *I gotta get out of my mama's house, ASAP. I gotta get up out here.*

Chapter 10

Desirae woke up a couple of hours earlier than usual the next morning. She'd gone to sleep with a headache and had woken up feeling a bit angry. Slowly, she worked her way out of bed and headed downstairs. Just as she was making herself some tea, shaking her head at how similar to her mother she could be at times, she heard what sounded like paper hitting the front door. Desirae made her way to the front of the house and opened the door. Just as she'd guessed, it was some sort of neighborhood association publication. It sat smack dab in the middle of the porch.

Desirae stepped out onto the porch, grabbed the magazine, and looked up. To her horror, her eyes met with eyes she'd seen recently. They were the eyes of this teenage boy who lived down the street – the eyes of one of the people who stood by and watched Greg's wife violently have her way with Desirae. Even though this kid was easily only fourteen years old, Desirae could read his eyes and tell what he was thinking. He looked her body up and down, playing the front yard fiasco over in his mind. The kid smiled and nodded, in a very sexually suggestive way.

Desirae rolled her eyes and walked back into the house. Not paying any attention to the sexual innuendo the teenage boy had made from the sidewalk, she closed the door. With her back pressed against her mother's front door, she closed her eyes. It all seemed too real again. She realized why she kind of stayed away from people she knew for the last several days. She could only imagine how other people up and down the street would look at her.

As Desirae went about her morning, forgetting about the teenager out on the sidewalk, she went to the kitchen. There, she cooked herself some bacon, eggs, and a couple of slices of French toast. No sooner than she'd sat down at the table, she realized she'd forgotten her cell phone upstairs. She dashed upstairs to get it and returned to the kitchen. Now, at the table and in front of her plate, she scrolled through her text messages to see what she missed last night while she'd been asleep. Part of her, even if only subconsciously, wondered if

Tiffany would have sent an apology message. Desirae had thought about that entire situation briefly as she fell asleep last night. She'd chalked up Tiffany's sudden and swift attitude change to the fact that she was feeling some kind of way about her grandmother on the other side of the family being in the hospital, as well as her insecurity with having Desirae coming around her man, Reggie.

As Desirae opened her *missed messages* icon, her phone began to vibrate with a call. It was Tron. She rolled her eyes and looked up at the ceiling. "Ain't this somethin'?" she asked herself, rhetorically. "A nigga ignored me at first, and now he can't get enough of me." She quickly thought back to when she and Tron had been standing in this very same kitchen, and she'd thrown her glass of cranberry juice onto his face. The look on Tron's shocked face showed his surprise, as well as the feeling of powerlessness that comes over a man when he is unable to retaliate against a woman for her actions.

"Hello?" Desirae asked, trying to sound pleasant.

"Good morning, Desirae," Tron said. "How are you?"

Desirae shook her head, holding back a giggle. She found it hilarious how she'd practically whipped Tron into being more respectful toward her. Never, in all the months the two of them had known one another, had he actually started a phone conversation by asking her how she was doing.

"Calm down, Tron," Desirae said. "No need to be all formal with me and stuff." She could hear Tron groan. "I'm doin' good. How you doin'?"

"I'm okay," Tron said, flatly. "Look, I was callin' for a reason. My mama is comin' to town."

"Oh," Desirae said, hearing the serious tone in Tron's voice. "So, what are you saying? Are you trying to have us meet or somethin' and we all have a family kind of day out?"

"No, not exactly like that, Desirae," Tron answered. "Actually, I'm callin' you cause I'd like to get James and Tron, and they can spend the night with me and my mama. You know, she is waitin' to get to spend some time with her grandchildren, Desirae. C'mon, don't make this any harder than it has to be."

"I ain't, I ain't," Desirae said. "But where they gon' stay at? I don't want them over there and bein' up in the middle of the night and bein' with that fuckin' hoe I thought was my friend."

"Desirae," Tron said, "it ain't even like that. And no, it won't be over here. My mama is stayin' with one of my great-aunties up here, up north in Nora. She had like three or four kids, so her house is basically set up for kids. She also watch her grandkids and a couple great grandkids or somethin' like that every once in a while."

"Hmm, hmm," Desirae said, still feeling a little skeptical about such a request. "Okay, I guess. When was you try'na come pick them up and stuff? Do you got car seats for them or do you gotta get mine outta my car?"

"Friday," Tron said, answering Desirae's first question. "And I'mma get car seats. It's no problem. You don't need nothin' do you?"

I need to get some fuckin' income goin', Desirae thought. She then filtered her response to Tron. "I'm okay for now," she answered. "Of course, we can always use more diapers. How many nights was you try'na have James and Titan over there with your mama?"

"See, that's the thing," Tron said. "I don't know. She said she might leave Saturday if the weather is bad in the afternoon because it might supposed to be raining, or at least that's what I think I saw on the news when I was gettin' home and shit this mornin'. But I don't know. If the weather is good, of course, you know she'd wanna keep them until Sunday."

"Well, I don't have a problem with that," Desirae said. "But I do gotta say one thing. I do think that I should at least meet your mama since I'm the mother of her two grandsons."

There was a long pause before Tron had even begun to say anything. "Tron?" Desirae said, on the edge as she anticipated his response.

"Yeah, yeah," Tron said. "And okay, we can do that. She'd be delighted." Desirae could hear the latent sarcasm in Tron's voice. "I can bring her with me when I come pick them up on Friday, if that's cool with you."

151

"Friday?" Desirae said. "Okay. I can have them ready and have a bag packed for them and everything. It'll be nice to finally meet your mama, Tron. I'm sure she's a lovely lady and is gonna love me."

"Love you," Tron said, his tone suggested he was lost in a daze of confusion. "Yeah, she'll love you."

"And don't worry," Desirae said, smiling at the phone. "I'mma make sure I wear somethin' real nice so I leave a good impression with the grandmother to my little twins."

"Desirae," Tron said, "don't come out that house wearin' no hoe shit. I swear to God, if you try to pull some shit like that in front of my mama..."

"Nigga, please," Desirae said. "Don't go back to that callin' me a hoe shit, okay? Cause I ain't no hoe and ain't never been one. And don't worry about what I'mma wear when I meet your mama. I'm always classy and never trashy. So, don't even go there with me, okay?"

"Man, whatever," Tron said. "Well, that's all I wanted. I'll text you with the time that me and my mama will be over there on Friday in a little bit. Talk to you later. Bye."

Before Desirae could even respond with a goodbye of her own, the call ended. She set her phone down onto the table, shaking her head and rolling her eyes. The level of disrespect was just unreal.

D'Mann then popped into Desirae's mind. With today being the morning after she'd been at his house, Desirae was able to look at things in a different perspective. While she still struggled to come to grips with knowing that she'd been in the house when another man died, she still couldn't deny that she had feelings for D'Mann. The first thing she did with this new information about Tron and his mother coming to pick up James and Titan was think about calling D'Mann. She knew she'd already be free for one day. If the weather held up, it could wind up being two days. At first, she was going to call D'Mann. However, after realizing that it was probably still early in the morning for him, she decided to send him a text. Within a few minutes, after she'd eaten a good portion of her breakfast, D'Mann was calling.

"Why you text a nigga?" D'Mann asked, clearly sounding as if he'd just woken up. "You know you can just call a nigga. You ain't gotta text."

"I ain't wanna call and wake you up if you was sleepin'," Desirae said. "That's why I text you, you know."

"Yeah, but don't worry about that shit," D'Mann said. "I ain't got no problem gettin' up for you. What you got on for today? Wassup? Is everything okay? I saw the text you sent me a second ago about havin' to get out of your mama's house and shit."

"Yeah," Desirae said. "I sent that last night. My mama gave her usual righteous ass speech to me when I came in the house last night, talkin' to me like I'm some child or somethin'. I can talk to you about that later, but I just wanted to tell you that this Friday night, I'm not gon' have the twins...just in case you wanted to know."

"Is that so, huh?" D'Mann asked. He then chuckled. "A nigga might have to take you out for a little treat or somethin'."

Desirae smiled. "Oh, really?" she asked, in her sweet voice.

"Yeah, really," D'Mann said. "So, what's goin' on with the twins. Is they grandmamma watchin' they asses or somethin'?"

"Yeah, but not my mama," Desirae explained. "Tron's mama is comin' with him to pick up the twins on Friday, prolly in the afternoon, I guess."

"Yeah, I'mma have to come swoop that ass up," D'Mann said.

Desirae leaned back in her chair as the two of them talked about what they could possibly do on Friday night with the free time. At first, Desirae had wanted to tell D'Mann that she'd prefer to not stay the night at his house. Just the thought that a man had been killed in his basement might keep her up at night when she could be sleeping. However, when D'Mann talked about them going to the mall for a little while, Desirae decided to play her cards right and hold off saying some things.

153

Chapter 11

When Friday came, Desirae hadn't even mentioned to her mother that Tron and his mother would be coming to pick up the twins for the weekend. She'd seen her mother, of course, and the conversation between the two of them had become a little cold. Desirae remained cordial, all the while knowing that she needed to get out of her mother's house as soon as possible. With each passing day, there were just too many things to remind her of how stressful her life had become by moving in with her mother. At this point, however, she could only hope and wait that one of the jobs she'd applied for online would call her back. In the meantime, the money that D'Mann had given her was surely needed and very much appreciated. Desirae pitied Tron for this very reason, as he was so reluctant to help her out monetarily. Tron had texted Desirae earlier in the day, saying that he and his mother would be stopping by between 3:30 and 4 o'clock. Desirae looked through her temporary closet, trying to figure out what kind of outfit would be the perfect outfit to wear to meet Tron's mother, while also being what D'Mann would like to see. Desirae had coordinated with D'Mann so that he would come pulling up only a few minutes after Tron and his mother left with the twins.

At first, Desirae tried on a nice red dress she'd bought at a mall a couple of years ago. However, when she squeezed into it, she'd quickly found that it was too tight for her body. The weight that she gained had become more obvious, especially around her hips, butt and thighs. Finally, Desirae found some faded jeans with cute rips around the knees and on the thigh. She slid into a savvy-looking black shirt. Just the right amount of her cleavage showed, only being accentuated more by the fact that she had slid a gold chain around her neck. The charm on the chain, which was Desirae's birth stone, sat perfectly in her cleavage. When she looked in the mirror, she had to take a few moments to turn around and see how she looked. She knew that the way these pants fit her would drive Tron up the wall. It would probably make him want to beg for the pussy, all while feeling helpless because his mother would be standing right there with him.

"Tron, what does this girl look like?" Tron's mother, Brenda asked. She sat in the front passenger seat, looking at the road ahead of her as Tron drove the car down the interstate in Indianapolis.

"What you mean what does she look like?" Tron asked, smiling. "You know, mama. She's cute."

Brenda looked over at Tron and shook her head. "I know what that means," she said. "All these months she been pregnant and done had the twins, and this is the first time I'm seein' them. I ain't even seen the girl herself yet. Somethin' tell me this is not going to be the kinda young lady I'd want to see."

Tron thought it was nice of his mother to even describe Desirae as being a lady. However, he kept his sarcastic thoughts to himself. Part of him hoped and prayed to God that Desirae would at least be appropriately dressed when he pulled up with his mother. If she wasn't, he didn't know what he was going to do.

"So, I noticed that you've been rather quiet on the Shawna front for much of the year," Brenda said, looking out the window. "I take it the two of y'all broke up or somethin'. Would that be the case, son?"

"Yeah," Tron said, shaking his head. "Yeah, mama. That would be the case."

"Well, I'm not gon' ask why," Brenda said. "That's the way it goes, I suppose. They never marry the ones you want to marry, or the ones that they ought to be marrying."

"Yeah, well," Tron said. "It's over at this point, Mama. So ain't no point in even talking about that."

Tron turned off of the main road and onto the street Desirae's mother lived on. He gripped the wheel a little more firmly as he realized in just minutes, his mother would be face to face with Desirae – face to face with the very chick he felt deep down had purposely gotten pregnant by him as a way of trying to keep him around.

"Well, let me ask you this last question and I'll let this subject die, Tron," Brenda said.

155

Tron let out a deep breath. "And what would that be, mother?" he asked.

Brenda glanced sharply over at Tron, knowing that he was being sarcastic when he used the term *mother* in his sentences. "Anyway," she said. "Just tell me this. Are these twins the product of one of them situations you younger people call a break baby?"

Tron snickered. "Not really," he answered, feeling honest and bold. "I wouldn't say that."

"Then what would you say?" Brenda asked. "How did you meet this girl, Tron? What kind of person is she?"

Tron raised his shoulders and extended his arms. "Well, mama," he said. "She was just this chick, you know, that I was kickin' it with. That's all. And then this happened."

"Tron, be honest with me," Brenda said. "Don't talk to me like I'm some old person that don't know what's goin' on out here. Is this young lady the reason that you and Shawna broke up? Was she a, what do you all call it these days since so many of you choose to not get married, a side chick?"

As much as Tron didn't want to admit it, he struggled to think of ways around his mother's questions. In fact, he wished that she wouldn't have even asked them to begin with. He looked over at his mother, realizing that he was a grown man and not a boy. He had to keep it real with his mother and just be honest.

"Yeah," Tron said. "I guess you could say that she was somethin' like that. I ain't too proud of it either, but I'm takin' care of my responsibilities."

"You know how I feel about this kinda mess," Brenda said. "Now you got little Ebony down in Louisville with Andria, who at least has some damn sense and y'all were in some sort of relationship together. Then you got twins up here in Indianapolis with this Desirae person. God, son, please don't have me meetin' some, whatever y'all call it these days, a thot or whatever I hear the kids sayin' now. Please, tell me she ain't some big booty-fied girl with a bunch of fake hair and stuff."

Tron snickered and shook his head. He wanted to laugh out loud, but he knew that such a response would really cause his mother to worry. Instead, he opted to remain silent. Within two or three minutes, he'd pulled his SUV into a parking spot in front of Desirae's mother's house.

"Well," Brenda said, looking at the block. "This doesn't look all that bad I don't guess. Maybe she is a nice girl or somethin' with a nice upbringing."

Tron went ahead and climbed out of his truck, not bothering to say anything to his mother's comments. He just wanted this meeting to be quick and painless. If he had it his way, they'd meet in the parking lot at a busy intersection. That way, the meeting would truly be quick.

As Tron walked his mother up the walkway and toward the front porch, the front door opened. Tron looked at his mother. Barely opening his mouth, he said to her, "Be nice, Mama. Be nice."

"What you mean be nice?" Brenda asked, feeling appalled at such a remark. "I'm always nice."

Tron helped his mother into the house where he and she stepped up to Desirae. She'd been standing in the living room, with her best smile on. Tron quickly looked her up and down, seeing how she looked ghetto in some ways, but was at least presentable. Without realizing it, Tron had licked his lips, seeing that no matter what Desirae wore, her ass and hips would look as if they could have their own zip code.

Desirae looked at Tron's mother and introduced herself. "Hey, I'm Desirae," she said to the older woman, who was in her mid-fifties and still in rather good shape. "I like that haircut on you."

Brenda smiled and hugged Desirae. "I'm Brenda," she said. "I'm Tron's mother. It is so nice to finally meet you, Desirae." Brenda looked Desirae up and down. "Well, I see you must've had a good pregnancy. You're still in shape."

"I did gain some weight," Desirae said, "but a lot of it was proportionate. I still watch what I eat 'cause I don't need to gain no more weight."

"Oh, okay," Brenda said. "Well, if you don't mind, can I please see my grandbabies. I gotta see these grandbabies."

"Of course," Desirae said, smiling. She pointed toward the dining room. "James and Titan are right in there."

As Brenda headed into the dining room, Desirae turned and looked at Tron. She gave him a sharp look, knowing that he was probably having to suffer from looking at something that he couldn't have. Furthermore, minutes before Tron and his mother had come walking through the door, Desirae spent a considerable amount of time and energy in the mirror, making sure that her makeup did a good job of hiding the remaining scratches on her face. "Hello, Tron."

"Hello, De..."

Just as Tron was speaking to Desirae, she had turned around and was now heading into the dining room. For the next ten minutes or so, Tron sat at one end of the dining room table while his mother and Desirae quickly got to know one another. His mother asked Desirae what was her field of work. Of course, Desirae's response could only be that she was looking for a job at the moment. Desirae had decided to simply leave the Family Dollar fiasco out of the equation.

Another question Brenda asked Desirae was what kinds of arrangements she'd had for childcare. Once again, Desirae's true response would not have been favorable. Lying, as she knew she'd need to do considering that she wasn't working, she told Tron's mother that she had a cousin who would watch the twins when she needed and was available full-time once she found a job.

"Alright, well," Brenda said. "I guess we'd better get to going now, huh, Tron?" Brenda stood up and pushed her chair in as she held Titan. Together, Desirae held James as Tron's mother held Titan. Tron grabbed the baby bag that Desirae had made and followed the two women out to his SUV. A little ways back from Desirae and his mother, who chatted to one another, Tron noticed a nice SUV parked up the street, probably four or five spaces down the block from Tron's truck. While he was admiring the detail of the truck, as well as how clean it was, his eyes met with the man behind the wheel. Instantly, Tron recognized those eyes. He squinted, looking closer. Quickly, he figured out what was going on and looked at the back of Desirae, her big ass swaying from left to right.

"Desirae?" he said, quietly. As Desirae did not turn around, Tron looked back to the SUV. The person behind the wheel was a face he remembered from when he was a teenager and out in the streets, dealing drugs: D'Mann. Instantly, Tron locked eyes with him. Never in his life had he needed to use so much energy to keep from saying something to Desirae about it. As there was no doubt in his mind that D'Mann was there to see Desirae, Tron wondered how the two knew one another. Beyond that, he also wondered if Desirae really knew what she was getting into by messing around with a guy like that. All of the memories and the stories Tron used to hear about D'Mann came flooding back into his mind. Actually, he was feeling somewhat surprised that a guy like D'Mann had even managed to avoid prison.

Tron, Desirae, and his mother, all carrying the twins and their baby bag, crossed the sidewalk and approached Tron's SUV. Keeping his eyes on D'Mann up the block, Tron walked around the back of his car and opened the doors. In a very gentlemanly way, Tron helped Desirae and his mother load Titan and James into their car seats and then shut the door.

"Okay, Desirae," Brenda said. "We're gonna get goin' now. It was so nice meetin' you, again. Well, for the first time."

"Yes, it was nice meetin' you too," Desirae said, smiling. "Maybe I'll see you again, like when you two drop them off tomorrow or on Sunday."

"Yeah," Brenda said. "Maybe."

The two hugged before Brenda climbed into the SUV, leaving Tron and Desirae standing out in the street. Tron leaned in closer to her. "Desirae," he said, "Who the fuck is that?" He shifted his eyes toward D'Mann's SUV. Desirae glanced that way then back to Tron.

"What is it to you?" she asked. "What difference does it make to you?"

Tron stood there, biting his lip. He knew that if he said anything, it would only be vindicating what was going

159

through Desirae's mind. Any response he gave would only prove Desirae to be right. "You don't know that nigga," he said, quietly.

"You don't know who I know," Desirae said. She then walked off and back toward the house. Tron's eyes followed the back of her, not forgetting to look at her ass. Desirae looked back and waved at Tron's mother before Tron looked her dead in the eye and nodded. He knew that he was going to talk to her the first chance he got. There was just no way he was going to be able to sleep at night knowing that the mother of his sons was messing around with D'Mann. Even if only half of the things he'd heard about D'Mann were true, Desirae being with him in any way would still be twice as scary.

Tron swallowed his pride and watched Desirae walk back into her mother's house as he climbed back behind the wheel. As he pulled off, he looked in the rearview mirror and back at the other end of the block. He could see D'Mann getting out of the SUV and walking up to the house. Reluctantly, Tron pulled his eyes away and focused on the road ahead of him.

"Everything okay, Tron?" Brenda asked her son, noticing that he seemed preoccupied with something.

Tron nodded. "Yeah," he answered, sounding very unsure. "Everything is okay, Mama."

***

When Desirae went into the house, she waited in the living room for D'Mann to walk up onto the front porch. She smiled when she saw him, watching him walk so confidently into the living room.

"Everything go okay?" D'Mann asked. "That nigga ain't give you no problems, did he?"

"Hell naw, he ain't give me no problems," Desirae said. "You saw his mama when they came out of the house. She was standin' right here, well, in there, next to him the entire time. He ain't say nothin' that he shouldn't say. He ain't even look at me the wrong way."

"The nigga was mean muggin' me when he walked out to his truck," D'Mann said. "With how he was lookin' at me,

160

nigga was lookin' like he wanted me to jump out the truck and across that street so we could box and shit. But yeah, like you said, I saw the older lady he was with and knew that she was probably his mama or auntie or whatever you told me. Enough about that nigga, though." D'Mann leaned in and kissed Desirae softly as he reached around and grabbed a handful of her ass. "You ready to go or what? You think they gon' keep the babies until Saturday or Sunday?"

Desirae moved about the living room then dining room. She gathered her purse then her cell phone and slid into her jacket. "Hell yeah, I'm ready," she answered. "And I still don't know. I gotta watch the news to see. Knowin' him and how he be so busy with stuff, he'll probably be dropping them back off by the early afternoon or somethin'. I'mma just watch for his text and stuff, you know."

Desirae led D'Mann out of the house, locking the door behind her. The two of them climbed into his truck and headed to an upscale mall in Caramel, a small rather-wealthy suburb north of Indianapolis. When D'Mann pulled into a parking spot close to the door, he could already see the look of excitement on Desirae's face.

"Damn," he said, chuckling. "You over there lookin' like you ain't never been to a mall or nothin'. Mister Baby Daddy, Mister Suave never took you and bought you nothin'?"

Desirae looked at D'Mann with the eyes of a brokenhearted woman. "No," she answered, shaking her head. "Shit, when me and him was kickin' it, he never even took me anywhere. Really, he would just come over to my apartment and fuck and then leave. Sometime he would chill and smoke with me, back when I used to keep that good shit on me at my apartment out on the south side. But no, he never took me nowhere or did anythin' with me other than fuck."

D'Mann shook his head. "Yeah, that's some foul shit," he said. "Well, here's what I wanna do. We gon' go in this mall cause I know you done had you a stressful week with everything that happened. We gon' go in this mall, and I want you to only spend a stack, okay?"

"A stack?" Desirae asked. "You want me to go in here and shop with a thousand dollars."

"If that's a problem, then we can go to the dollar store," D'Mann said, sarcastically.

Desirae looked at D'Mann with squinting eyes, smiling. "See, now you try'na be funny."

The two of them headed into the mall. Inside, Desirae nearly lost her mind. There were so many stores, some of which were not located in shopping centers and malls in the city. Desirae felt as if she were in a fantasy or some sort of whimsical dream. With D'Mann at her side, as well as his pockets, the two of them walked into basically any store that piqued Desirae's interest. For once in her life, she felt so sophisticated. She looked around at the white mannequins, who all looked so stylish in the name-brand pants suits. Desirae told herself that when she became successful one day, and maybe a little slimmer, she wanted to be one of those older black women she'd see around the city who looked sharp in a pants suit.

D'Mann liked that he was making Desirae feel better. From where he stood, it seemed as if she'd forgotten about what had happened with her face. When Desirae walked in and out of a store, D'Mann made sure to keep his focus on her ass. No matter where she went, he always knew just how to find her—he simply needed to scan the area and find that ass.

When the two of them walked down the mall and were passing by Victoria's Secret, D'Mann noticed how Desirae didn't even bother to look inside of the store. He grabbed her arm and pointed. "What about here?" he asked, smiling. "You can't let a nigga buy you a little somethin' to wear and shit, since we here already?"

Desirae's neck snapped back as she smiled. "Nigga, what you mean?" she asked.

"You know what a nigga talkin' about," D'Mann said, raising his eyebrows. "I wanna see what that ass look like in somethin' white and see-through."

"Oh, really?" Desirae asked. "Okay." She pushed him back and pointed at some white benches sitting out in the middle of the mall walkway. "Wait right there while I go in there and pick out somethin' you might like then."

D'Mann smiled and backed away, sitting down on one of the benches. While he sat there, checking messages, Desirae browsed Victoria Secret, looking for something white that she could put on that would really have D'Mann eating out of the palm of her hand. Once she'd found something, she used the money he'd given her already and bought it. When she came back out into the mall, she grabbed him and the two of them continued walking.

Later, when D'Mann pulled up at his house, he put the car into PARK and began to get out of the car. Desirae looked at the house then back to D'Mann. "Hold up," she said, thinking about the basement. "You sure that everything is okay? You don't think that we gon' be woken up in the middle of the night and have to be walkin' out the door in handcuffs or stuff like that, do you?"

"Naw," D'Mann said. "Trust me, you coo. A nigga got all night to spend with you and shit. You ain't got nothin' to worry about. I told you, we got rid of him and we got rid of the nigga's car. Ain't even heard shit about it since, if you want the truth."

"You sure we can't just go stay at a hotel or somethin'?" Desirae asked, feeling uneasy. "I mean, you know, so I don't have to sit up and deal with havin' some bad feelin' or nothin'."

"Yeah, we could," D'Mann said. "But then I won't be able to dick you down like a nigga really want to."

Desirae looked at D'Mann then down toward his crotch. She smiled. "Oh, is that so?" she said.

"Look, I know how you feelin'," D'Mann said. "Look, let's do this. We can go grab a Redbox movie since we forgot to before we pulled up outside the house. If you get in there and just feelin' like you not gon' be able to sleep easy, just let a nigga know. I put it on everything I own that I'll get up, put my clothes on, and we can go to a hotel or somethin'. No problem, I swear."

Desirae agreed, trying to be optimistic about the entire situation. They headed to a Kroger on West Washington

Street and got a couple of movies to watch for the night out of the Redbox machine. Between what had been going on with Tron, being pregnant with twins for nine months, then having to cope with being a young, single mother to two baby boys, Desirae was just happy to be out of the house and doing something normal. She was unsure if she would even answer her phone, as she was more than confident that Tron's mother could take care of James and Titan.

Back at D'Mann's house, he and Desirae smoked a blunt and shared a bottle of wine together after they popped in one of the DVDs they'd gotten. They were so interested in one another that they completely forgot to really watch the movies they picked out.

Once the clock struck 11 o'clock, D'Mann knew it was about to go down. He'd shared a blunt with Desirae and had drunk a few glasses of wine. Feeling totally relaxed and very turned on by just being able to look over at Desirae's bodacious thighs, he had had enough of the talking at this point.

"So," D'Mann said, smiling, "when do a nigga get to see that ass in whatever you bought when you went into Victoria's Secret and didn't even wanna let a nigga come in and help you pick somethin' out?"

"Don't say it like that," Desirae said. "Plus, that would've felt awkward. A man walkin' around Victoria's Secret with me. I don't know if I could do that. Plus, you know how them white people up in Caramel be actin' when they see some niggas walkin'. You know they think we all shoplift and can't buy nothin'. They prolly woulda rushed right on over to *assist* you, even though you was with me."

D'Mann nodded. "Yeah," he said. "I bet they would have. But fuck all that at this point. A nigga wanna see what you got."

Desirae stood up and smiled. She'd brought her bags into the house and pushed them all into a corner behind the door. In many ways, it was a lot like Christmas to her. While there was no tree, nor lights, and certainly no snow outside at this time of year, she couldn't help but smile when she looked across the room and saw so many shopping bags.

It seemed unreal, but she was so grateful. Lord knows that she needed to ease her mind and getting some new clothes, jewelry, and purses was surely a way to do it.

"Calm down, nigga," Desirae said. "Calm down. I'mma let you see."

Desirae stepped across the room and bent over, searching through the mountain of shopping bags. Once she'd found the Victoria's Secret bag, she leaned up. Just when she was turning around, D'Mann had gotten up and was across the room. With bloodshot eyes and a bit of sweat on his forehead, he slapped her ass and smiled, leaning in as if he were smelling her like a dog in heat.

Desirae giggled and pushed D'Mann back from her. "Stop," she said, smiling. "You can't see what I got until I put them on."

D'Mann stepped back to the couch and sat down, nodding his head.

Desirae stepped into the downstairs bathroom, which was right on the other side of the basement door. Inside, she slid out of her ripped jeans and cute collared black shirt. She pulled her matching silk white bra and panties out of the bag and slid into them. When she'd gotten them up and over her ass, she twirled around in the mirror, thinking that maybe she should have gotten a bigger size. She didn't think that her ass cheeks would swallow the panties so much so that they nearly looked more like a thong than panties.

When Desirae stepped out of the bathroom, she walked through the dining room and stepped into the light of the living room. Immediately, both of D'Mann's eyes were glued to her body. He stood up, rushed over, and began to kiss on her chest.

"Fuck," D'Mann said. "This shit look so sexy. Goddamn, this body." He looked over her shoulder and slapped both of her ass cheeks before grabbing one with both hands and jiggling them. "This ass is almost eatin' these damn panties, girl."

"I knew it," Desirae said. "I knew that I shoulda got a bigger size and…"

D'Mann cut Desirae's sentence off, shaking his head. "No, no, no," he said. "These panties is perfect. Turn around so a nigga can get a good look at them and that ass."

Desirae slowly turned around and leaned forward. She laughed when D'Mann slapped her ass on the side. "Make that ass clap," he ordered. Desirae did as she was told once again, leaning forward and moving her hips in such a way that caused her ass cheeks to slam together.

D'Mann set his glass of wine down onto an end table at one side of the couch. "This shit is too much," he said. "A nigga need to get you upstairs."

Desirae looked back and could see that D'Mann was as hard as a brick under his pants. She reached back and grabbed his bulge.

"Stop playin' with a nigga," D'Mann said. "I'm bout to tear that pussy up."

Quickly, D'Mann slipped out of his pants and underwear, leaving them in a pile on the floor. He then pulled his long sleeve, gray shirt over his head and tossed it to the side. Desirae looked at his dark, muscular body wearing nothing but a white tank top and white socks. His dick, which looked even thicker than it looked the first time Desirae saw it, stood straight up, veins bulging and calling Desirae's name. D'Mann slapped her ass.

"Get that ass up them steps," D'Mann ordered. "Get in that bed for a nigga."

Desirae rushed upstairs with D'Mann following behind her as she climbed the steps. D'Mann pushed the bedroom door open, and then the two of them jumped into his California King bed. D'Mann laid Desirae on her back and began to kiss her all over her body, causing her to moan with pleasure. Desirae, enjoying the wet but gentle kisses of D'Mann's thick lips, rubbed the top of his head, enjoying the way his hair, which was cut into a fade style, felt under the tips of her fingers.

D'Mann leaned back to the edge of the bed and slid Desirae's panties down to her ankles and over her feet. He held them up to his face, smelling them, before tossing them to the side. "Damn," he said, "that pussy even smell good to a nigga. Let me get a taste."

Very smoothly, D'Mann lay down on the bed and slid between Desirae's legs. With both arms, he held either leg back to where her knees were practically pushing against her torso. Any discomfort Desirae was feeling had gone out the window at this point. D'Mann worked his tongue, slopping in her pussy as if he hadn't eaten anything all day. She even had an orgasm from the sensation being so great.

After ten minutes or so of D'Mann tasting Desirae, she flipped over and arched her back, putting her ass high in the air as she faced the front of the bed. D'Mann slid back, off of the end, and pushed his manhood toward Desirae's mouth. "Suck that dick," he told her, smiling. "You know you wanna suck on it. Go on, suck on that dick."

Desirae smiled and looked up into D'Mann's eyes as she opened her mouth and took him inside. Taking as much as she could into her mouth, and somewhat in her throat, D'Mann placed his hand on the dome of her head. He pushed her head down until she gagged, causing spit to spill out of her lips and run down off of his balls.

"There you go," D'Mann said. "Get that shit nice and wet for that pussy." He leaned over and slapped Desirae's ass. Out of all the chicks he had messed with since he was sixteen years old, Desirae by far had to be the one with the best body. She was thick – rather plump, actually – but it was all very much in proportion. Her chest was big and bouncy while her ass was fat and wide. These were two things that sent D'Mann running up the wall when he met a woman. He encouraged Desirae more, telling her that her throat felt good and that she needed to keep sucking on him. Every so often, just to hear the sound of a woman gagging on his manhood, D'Mann would push her head down. He thought to himself that one day he'd work her in so good that she'd be able to deep throat him all the day down to his balls. Rarely, had a chick been able to do that for D'Mann. This motivated him even more to see it happen one day, as Desirae was looking like a good candidate. When he'd look down at his shaft, she'd managed to get more of it wet than any chick he could think of at that moment who had tried and failed.

D'Mann couldn't take anymore. Desirae's oral skills just felt too good. Once he'd looked down and saw that his manhood was as shiny and slippery as it was going to get, he knew that it was time. "Turn around," he told her.

Desirae did as she was told, thinking that at any moment she'd hear D'Mann pulling a condom out from a dresser drawer and stretching it over his dick. Instead, she felt him climb up onto his knees on the bed and grab her hips.

"Fuck it," D'Mann said. "A nigga gotta see what this shit feel like first before he go puttin' on the plastic." He reached underneath and fingered Desirae, afterward bringing his fingers up to his lips, smelling them before licking them. "Fuck," he said, Desirae's scent driving him wild. "You got that flower pussy, I swear you do."

Desirae giggled, loving that a man could appreciate her and what she had to offer. She kept her back arched and moaned loudly, grabbing the pillows at the top of the bed, as D'Mann pushed inside of her. "Fuck!" Desirae exclaimed, trying to catch her breath. "Damn, you got a fat dick, nigga."

"Hmm, hmm," D'Mann said, nodding his head and smiling as he slowly pushed himself into Desirae until he couldn't go any further. "This pussy is tight as fuck, girl. Fuck, this shit feel good as fuck to a nigga dick. Don't move. Just stay right there so I can feel this pussy."

D'Mann moved his hips in a circular motion, slowly helping to loosen Desirae up a little bit. After a few minutes of this, once he'd seen that she was adjusted to his size, he slapped her ass then grabbed her hips. "I'm bout to beat this pussy up. Fuck!"

Desirae's head yanked back from D'Mann pulling her hair then putting a tight grip around her neck. He held her in place in the doggy style position. He stroked into her with long strokes that had Desirae nearly crying from the pleasure. She squealed and screamed, every so often having to lower her head just to catch her breath. Her breasts swung around wildly until D'Mann had gone into beast mode. He pushed her head into the pillows, held her in place, and stroked as deep and hard as he could. For the next several minutes, D'Mann made music with his stroke. The room filled with nothing but the clapping sound of his pelvis colliding with Desirae's big, round ass.

Sweat dripping down his face, D'Mann grabbed Desirae by the waist and flipped her over onto her back. Feeling as light as air, it all seemed to happen in the blink of an eye. Now, Desirae looked up into D'Mann's eyes as he held her legs open and went as hard as he could.

"Fuck this shit feel good!" Desirae yelled. "Fuck! I think…I think. Oh shit, I'm bout to come. I'm bout to come, nigga. Damn this dick. I'm bout to come."

Desirae had an explosive orgasm – one that left her sweating and almost shaking. However, this did not slow D'Mann down the least bit. Minutes later, he had slid off of the bed and had pulled Desirae toward the edge. He pushed himself inside of her and stroked until she could feel that his body was tensing up.

"Fuck," D'Mann said, squinting his eyes. "A nigga is about to bust. Fuck, this pussy! A nigga is about to bust in this shit. Damn."

Desirae could feel D'Mann drop his load off deep inside of her. As his dick slowly deflated and slid out of her, she could feel throbbing coming from down there. She knew that she'd be sore for at least the next couple of days at least. D'Mann lay down next to her, breathing heavily as he looked over at her. "Fuck, that was good," D'Mann said. "That shit was good as fuck."

Desirae turned over and laid with her hand resting on D'Mann's bulging chest. "You did it," she said, playfully.

"Did what?" D'Mann asked. "I ain't do nothin' but tear that shit up."

"That you did," Desirae said. "That you did. But I'm talkin' bout how I'mma be walkin around sore tomorrow and shit from that dick. Why you do that to me?"

"Naw," D'Mann said, shaking his head. "I'mma get in that pussy again at least another time tonight, maybe twice. Just wait until my shit wake back up after we chill for a minute.

I go even longer when a nigga done already busted his nut. I ain't done with that ass." D'Mann reached over and slapped Desirae's ass cheeks. Even though he had just smashed her, seeing that ass nearly made him get hard again as if it were completely new pussy to him. From his point of view, looking down at how far up in the air Desirae's ass protruded, he could only thank God that he'd had the chance to meet her and get her into his bedroom. She really did have a body that no other could rival.

D'Mann and Desirae lay there and talked as they allowed their bodies to calm down. Desirae felt at home and so comfortable in D'Mann's arms. In fact, the sex had been so good that she hadn't even thought much about the fact that just the other night he had to take a man's life down in his basement. Rather, her mind was still stuck on the massive amount of shopping she'd been able to do today, all thanks to him. She'd never had a man take her to the mall and drop $1,000 on her so that she could get any and everything that she wanted.

"So, what you gon' do about that nigga and his bitch?" D'Mann asked. "You still try'na get after her, the chick you used to be best friends with? I told you, I fuck'em up if you need me to. Plus, I ain't like the way that nigga was lookin' at me when I was sittin' out in the car. I think he think he own you or somethin'."

"That's exactly what it is," Desirae said, smacking her lips together. "That is exactly what it is. Let me tell you about Tron. He the kinda dude that just think he can have me on reserve, so that way, once something goes sour with whoever he try'na call himself being in a relationship with, he can have something to fuck to fall back on. I swear, I'm through with that shit. You shoulda seen the way he was pushin' up on me the other day when he came over to see the twins. He really was comin' at me like he just know for certain that I was gon' bend over and let him get some. Naw, nigga. Them days is gone."

"I feel you on that," D'Mann said. "I could tell by just lookin' at the nigga that he probably one of them selfish little mothafuckas that just ain't used to not gettin' they way."

"Yup," Desirae said, nodding her head. "That's exactly what he is. That's why he be talkin' to me any ole kinda way and shit. I swear, I'm just so done with it. And yeah, about that bitch, Reese, I'mma just let her live. I know she over there fuckin' that nigga cause we all know she can't get no other dude, or at least can't keep no other nigga round long enough to really be entertained with her ass, evidently."

"Why you say that?" D'Mann asked. "What is she? Ugly or somethin'?"

"I mean..." Desirae said, taking a moment to think. "She ain't ugly in the face or nothin', but she just so fuckin' plain lookin'. Plus, she ain't got much of an ass or a chest. I mean, you can just tell that God ain't spend too much time when he was makin' her. She really ain't got a lot goin' for herself. Really, if you want the truth, I feel sorry for her. I know that Tron is just gon' throw her ole simple ass to the side when he get bored. Shit, if he pushin' up on me and shit, it look like he might already be bored for all I know. Fuck him and her as far as I'm concerned. If I wasn't try'na do the right thing and make sure that my sons get to have they daddy in they life, I swear I woulda never answered that nigga's phone calls or texts, and he wouldn't even know where I live. I'mma just let that bitch, Reese, the one I used to be best friends with, live. It ain't even worth my time no more. I'm done stoopin' down to her level."

D'Mann held Desirae closer to him, making her feel warm and secure. "See, that's the shit I like about you," he told her, in a very complimentary way. "You not just another one of these stupid bitches out here that be doin' crazy shit. You actually got a good head on your shoulders and shit...rational, you know what a nigga mean?"

"Thank you," Desirae said.

D'Mann looked back down at Desirae's body, wanting to keep her locked away in his attic for a century of nights so that he could spend as much time with her as he wanted. With the kind of body that she had, she could get it in the morning when he woke up with a morning erection, for lunch in the early afternoon, then as soon as they finished eating dinner.

Rap music blared from downstairs, telling D'Mann that his phone was ringing. "Fuck," he said.

"What?" Desirae asked.

"My phone," D'Mann responded. "I left it downstairs in my pants and shit. I'm sorry, but I gotta answer it. My bad."

D'Mann slid out of the bed and headed downstairs. Moments later, he'd returned to the top of the staircase and was calling the number he'd missed. "Yeah, wassup?" he said.

Desirae listened from the bedroom. Considering what had happened the other night when D'Mann had gotten a call, she knew she needed to be alert. While his old friend Makim's body and car may have been done away with, Desirae did not allow herself to be fooled. She wanted to make sure that she was on top of her game this time should anything pop off while she was over at D'Mann's place.

"Right now, nigga?" D'Mann said. "A nigga got company. Why we gotta do it right now? What is goin' on?"

Desirae could hear the muffled voice of the other person from D'Mann's bed. A few more minutes passed of D'Mann handling his business before he came back into the bedroom. "I got bad news," D'Mann said. "I'mma have to step out for a minute. Please, don't be mad. I just ain't want them comin' over here while I'm with you, you know?"

Desirae nodded. "Okay," she said, not really in a position to argue with him. After all, he'd taken her to the mall and had allowed her to buy anything that she wanted. She smiled. "So, how long do you think you gon' be gone? Am I gon' have to wait up for you to get back."

"Naw, naw," D'Mann said. "This nigga I'm goin' to meet with actually live right over on Tibbs, like a mile away. I prolly won't even be gone for thirty minutes, I promise."

"Okay," Desirae said. She pulled a sheet up over her body and turned over on her side, causing her ass to practically hang over the edge of the bed. "I'mma just wait here since you said you gon' be back in thirty minutes. If I don't hear from you in like an hour, I'mma just call a cab or somebody and see about getting home."

"It ain't that deep," D'Mann said, approaching the bed. He leaned over and kissed Desirae, her eyes looking at the heavy, dangling meat that was between his legs. "Wait up for a nigga, okay?" he said. "I ain't done with that pussy yet. Wait up for a nigga. Make me have to wake that ass up with this dick, and you really gon' be sore tomorrow."

"Nigga, go on so you can hurry up and get back," Desirae said.

D'Mann smiled, slapped Desirae's ass one more time, then turned around and headed downstairs. From his bedroom, Desirae could hear D'Mann fumbling with his pants then his car keys. The front door opened and closed, letting her know that she was officially alone in his house.

Desirae slipped out of bed, deciding that she could go downstairs and get her phone. Even if D'Mann would only be gone for thirty minutes, she could still use the time to see what text messages she missed or browse Facebook to see if there were any posts that she needed to keep up on. In nothing but the bra she'd gotten at Victoria's Secret, Desirae headed downstairs and back to the living room. She slid into her jeans, feeling a little cold now walking around. She then pulled her shirt over her head, telling herself that she'd just take her clothes back off when D'Mann texted her saying that he was on his way back to her.

For a few minutes, Desirae sat on the couch and scrolled through her phone. Soon, she felt parched, especially after the pounding that D'Mann had just given her. She walked to the kitchen, poured herself a glass of lemonade out of the refrigerator, and headed back toward the living room. Just as she was passing the door to the basement steps, she stopped. She looked at the door, thinking how D'Mann's friend had gone down there alive to never come back up on his own.

Desirae pulled the basement door open and looked down. The staircase, which was wooden and rather narrow, seemed to lead down into a dark abyss of sorts. Desirae wasn't usually the kind of chick who would purposely go exploring basements. But there was something that piqued her curiosity about D'Mann's basement. Seeing as she'd now seen every other part of the house, including the few bedrooms and bathroom upstairs, she wondered what D'Mann had done with the basement. She wondered if it would be as nice as the other two levels of the house.

After feeling around on the wall for the light switch, Desirae watched as the basement lit up. Slowly and cautiously, looking back every few seconds, she made her way down the steps. Once she'd gotten to the bottom, she stood in place for a moment and took in the room. Much of the basement was a large, open room. In the middle sat a few couches, which were centered around a glass coffee table. In one corner of the room was a bar set up, albeit on a miniature scale. On the other side of the room was two doors. One door was open, allowing Desirae to see that inside of it was a bathroom. The other door, however, was closed. Desirae stepped off of the last step and made her way across the room. Just as she'd gotten halfway to the other side, she stopped. She'd seen a counter located underneath the basement steps On top of the counter was a money counting machine, telling her that D'Mann and Makim had been standing there at some point in time. She walked over to the area and saw that there was a new square of carpet a couple of feet out from the bottom of the counter. She put her hand over her mouth, realizing that this must have been the place where Makim had been standing when he pulled the knife on D'Mann.

Desirae shook her head, getting an eerie feeling. To her knowledge, she'd never stood in the same place as a person who had been killed. She stepped around the area lightly, making her way back over to the unopened door. When she pulled the door open, she found another room. This room, while small in size at only about nine feet by eight, was not as well done as the other rooms. In fact, it looked like a leftover room from when D'Mann had moved into the house that he'd simply never done anything with.

Desirae stepped inside of the room and found the light switch to the left on the wall. Once the room lit up, she could have screamed. Her heartbeat jumped as she tried to make sense of what she was seeing. Quickly, she slapped her hand over her mouth. There, in the middle of the floor, was what looked like blood splatter on the concrete. While the other clearly-cleaned-up area of the basement made sense, as it was right next to the money counting machine, this wasn't so clear. In fact, Desirae found herself confused as she stepped forward. She tried to figure out what could have happened down in this basement to where there would be two separate areas that needed to be cleaned up from blood. Furthermore, she began to wonder what D'Mann would be doing having anyone come into this cold, concrete room. In fact, it looked as if there had never been anything in the room.

As Desirae stepped toward the middle of the room, her forehead ran into some sort of rope hanging from the ceiling. Upon taking a closer look, she realized what kind of rope this was before her eyes. To her, it looked like the perfect kind of setup that someone could use to hang or strangle somebody. She had never been so nervous in her life. What had begun as a lovely afternoon and evening with D'Mann suddenly turned into a scary night. Part of her was starting to regret ever coming over to D'Mann's place. He seemed just a little bit too casual when it came to defending himself against Makim. Getting rid of his body and car seemed rather easy for someone who supposedly had never killed anyone before. In fact, the more Desirae thought about it, D'Mann's smoothness of getting rid of a body and vehicle at the last minute was starting to alarm her.

As Desirae stepped further into the room, looking at the cold concrete to see if it told stories of what could have possibly happened in this room, she heard the front door upstairs open and shut. Her eyes opened wide. She couldn't believe that D'Mann would be back so soon. He'd said that he would be gone for at least thirty minutes, and Desirae thought that would wind up being more.

Quickly, Desirae stepped out of the room, turned the light off and closed the door. Above her head, she could hear D'Mann climbing the stairs to the second floor. There was no doubt in Desirae's mind that he was going up there to look for her. In a matter of seconds, upon discovering that she wasn't in bed, Desirae could hear D'Mann calling her name. She rushed for the steps and hurried up them, hearing

D'Mann's footsteps coming back downstairs from the second floor of the house.

Just as Desirae was stepping out of the basement and pushing the door closed, D'Mann walked into the small walkway between the kitchen and the bathroom. Desirae was startled when she turned to find him there, standing over her and looking dead into her eyes. She smiled. "Here I am," she said.

D'Mann looked at the door, very seriously. His eyes looked at Desirae as she tried to casually close the basement door. "What are you doin?" he asked, forcing himself to smile.

"Nothin'," Desirae answered. "I was just lookin' around since I ain't get to see the basement like I seen the rest of the house."

D'Mann nodded. "Hmm, hmm," he said. "Did you like the basement?"

Desirae felt as if that was a strange question to ask. "I mean, it was nice," she answered. "I like that you got a little bar setup going on down there. That was cute as shit."

D'Mann nodded, still wondering what Desirae was doing going down into the basement. "What were you really lookin' for?" he asked Desirae. "Keep it real with me, Desirae. Why was you goin' down in a nigga's basement?"

Instantly, Desirae became nervous. The palms of her hands itched and perspired. "I swear," she said, trying to sound as innocent as possible as the last thing she needed was for D'Mann to think that she'd seen what was in the spare room off to the side. "I got up and came downstairs to get my phone and shit," she said. "I was walkin' into the kitchen, noticin' how much I like what you've done with this place. I simply was wonderin' what the basement looked like since you never really took me down there." She playfully pushed his shoulder. "That's all," she added. "I just wanted to see it."

"Did you see it?" D'Mann asked, his eyes coming across as very cold to Desirae.

Desirae stepped back. "I mean, yeah," she said, shrugging her shoulders. "I just saw the main room, I guess you would call it. And I saw the bathroom. I really just stopped

176

at the bottom of the steps and looked around is all. It ain't all that big of a basement. I mean, you can see it from the bottom of the steps, D'Mann. You know?"

D'Mann smiled and nodded, glancing away. "Yeah," he said. "You can. Did you wanna go back down there?"

Desirae looked at the door and shook her head. "Not really," she answered. "I mean, did you wanna go down there?"

"Not unless you did," D'Mann said. "I was just askin'. You wanna watch another movie? I got halfway over to my nigga's house, and he gon' come callin' me and tellin' me that his chick did this or said that and now the two of them are goin' at it. I told that nigga to not even worry about it, and that I would just come through tomorrow and get with him then. I had to hurry up and get back over here to my baby."

Desirae tried to contain herself as D'Mann leaned forward and kissed her softly. It amazed her how much her perception of him had changed. At first, he seemed like the kind of guy one would see living next door and who had nothing going on but the rent. Now, however, after seeing that strange rope contraption hanging from the ceiling down in the spare room in the basement, she was starting to have second thoughts. She was no detective – not in the least bit. However, she tended to stick with her gut when it was telling her something. Now, at this very moment, she hated that she was ignoring her gut feelings. Something was really setting off her woman's tuition, telling her that she needed to leave because something was just not right with how D'Mann was looking at her.

Gently, D'Mann placed his hand around Desirae's lower back and pulled her toward the dining room. He guided her toward the living room, smiling as he felt his groin press against her ass as she moved. "If you want, we can smoke again," D'Mann said, suggestively. "I can roll one up and we can smoke again and shit. Watch another movie." He shrugged. "You know."

Desirae nodded, not wanting to disagree. She now saw this house as a totally different kind of place. As D'Mann

177

rolled up the second blunt of the night, Desirae looked around. Now that she thought more thoroughly about things, she noticed that D'Mann's house was just a little too perfect. Her eyes then shifted over to the front door, as she noticed something about it that she hadn't seen when she came over the first time, or when she walked through the door earlier that evening: it had the kind of lock where one would need a key to get out as well as to get inside. There was no lock on the actual doorknob itself. This alone made Desirae feel kind of nervous.

"You okay over there?" D'Mann asked. "You over there lookin' like you nervous and shit. What you got on your mind?

Desirae shrugged, pulling her legs up onto the couch. "Nothin'," she said, shaking her head. "I was just surprised that you came back so soon. When I heard that front door open, with what happened over here, I was so nervous. Almost hid again until I realized it was you."

D'Mann chuckled. "Oh, chill out," he said, smiling. "I told you that you'll be safe with me. A nigga ain't gon' let nothin' happen to you, okay? Just relax."

D'Mann finished rolling the blunt then handed it to Desirae. As Desirae took the first hit of the blunt, several questions rolled through D'Mann's mind. He not only wondered about Desirae's true intentions for going down into the basement but also what she'd seen when she'd gone down there. If he thought for one second that she'd slip down into the basement when he stepped out for a trip that was only supposed to be thirty minutes, he would have never left her in his house alone. His mind would now have to wonder, for the rest of the night, if she'd gone down there and had seen the very thing he didn't want her to see. There were some areas of his house that he just did not consider for company, and one of those areas was the basement.

D'Mann turned on another movie then turned down the lights. He couldn't help but notice Desirae's silence. Before he'd left, she couldn't stop talking to him about this and that. Now, she seemed as if she were on edge about something.

And D'Mann wanted to find out what it was that was on Desirae's mind.

"Wassup with you?" D'Mann asked. "Since I got back, you been actin' funny."

"Naw," Desirae said, pulling her eyes away from the television and shaking her head. "I'm just sore as shit from the dick before you left. My pussy almost hurts from that shit you did to me up there, nigga."

D'Mann laughed, feeling confident in his ability to please just about any woman. He put his arm around Desirae then let it slide down to where his hand could grip her ass. "I know you like that dick," he said. "And like a nigga told you before he left, I prolly ain't done with that pussy. Wait till I start to feel this weed again. You gon' see my dick rise up again and get up in that pussy again."

Desirae forced herself to giggle. At first, D'Mann had enough swag to make her panties wet from just talking to her. Now there was just something that was too suspicious about him. She really didn't want to have sex again, but she knew that if she refused, he would definitely know she'd seen what she'd seen down in the basement. Once Desirae was high from the weed, as was D'Mann, he reached over and dimmed the living room lights. He smiled at Desirae, the look on his face telling her what was on his mind.

"A nigga wanna see that ass clap again," D'Mann said. "Why don't you get outta them clothes so a nigga can see that ass."

Desirae smiled, her eyes empty compared to what they had been earlier. She stood up, took her clothes off until she stood naked in front of D'Mann. At this point, she would do anything he asked as long as she knew that she could get out of the house safely. Her plan was to let him fall asleep first so she could figure out what she was going to do – if she was going to do anything.

Desirae looked at D'Mann as he motioned for her to turn around. As soon as she did, her ass cheeks stung from how hard he slapped them. "Make that shit clap for a nigga, damn!" he said, clearly feeling good from the weed. "Why you playin' with a nigga?"

Desirae smiled, knowing that she needed to use her charm and her body so that she could be smart about this situation. If D'Mann was like any other man that she'd known in her life, she knew that she'd simply need to keep him happy and satisfied. Desirae dropped to her knees, bent over and arched her back. She looked back into D'Mann's sexy but cold eyes. "Like this?" she asked as she moved her hips as fast as she could, causing her ass to practically give the room a clapping ovation.

"Fuck," D'Mann said, clearly hypnotized by her ass. "Your ass is almost too good to be real. I done met chicks who went and got ass shots, and they don't even look this good. I'm tellin' you."

Desirae smiled and continued moving so that her ass would clap at a steady rhythm. Several seconds later, D'Mann had placed the blunt down into an ashtray. He dropped to his knees on the floor and pressed his face into Desirae's ass. She moaned. Even though she was uncomfortable and unsure about what D'Mann really had going on in his house, she couldn't deny that his tongue felt good in that way. The more she moaned, the harder he slurped. Eventually, he lowered his head, holding her ass cheeks apart with his hands, and licked her pussy from the back. Desirae placed her head down on the floor, on the soft cream-colored carpet.

D'Mann groaned. "Damn, this pussy taste good," he said. "Put that shit in my face. Go ahead, put it in a nigga's face."

Desirae pushed back onto D'Mann's face, being a little more forceful than she might normally be. Fascinated with Desirae's anatomy, D'Mann turned over onto his back and slid under Desirae. He slapped her ass, telling her to lean up and ride his face.

Desirae did as she was told and grinded her pussy into D'Mann's face. He moaned as if he were starving for more. His tongue swirled around so quickly that Desirae could feel his spit flickering off of his tongue and onto the insides of her legs. She giggled a little bit, but wasn't able to really enjoy it. Her senses were too alert after what she'd seen in the basement.

"Ride my face!" D'Mann ordered, slapping Desirae's ass as hard as he could. "Ride a nigga face so he can get up in this wet pussy. Shit this shit taste good."

Desirae moaned, faking her expressions, as she grinded as hard as she could into D'Mann's face. Even for her, considering some of the men in her past that would do anything to get into her pants, sitting on a man's face was unusual. She felt in power in this position, while feeling helpless to leave D'Mann's house even if her life depended on it. Every so often, her eyes would glance over at the door, and she'd think about how even if she wanted to get up and run in the middle of the night, she'd need to find his keys first. Therefore, she would have to take the risk of making too much noise.

"Damn, nigga," Desirae said, upping her game. "You can eat some pussy." She laughed, in a frolicking way. "That tongue feel good. You gettin' this pussy wet as fuck! Shit!"

D'Mann snickered, knowing that Desirae was only a little tense because she missed him so much. He pulled out from underneath her and rose up onto his knees. "I gotta get in this pussy again," he said. "This shit is too good. A nigga gotta get up in it, I swear."

Desirae listened as D'Mann undid his belt and pants then slid them down his thighs. Before she knew it, D'Mann had gripped her hips with all of his energy and was pushing his way inside of her. For the next thirty minutes, Desirae had to see the pleasure she was receiving for what it was and try to not let her fears get in the way. This time, D'Mann had flipped her over several times, doing some positions twice and pounding her unmercifully. He did short strokes, long strokes, and plenty of grinding before finally unloading inside of her. When he finished, he backed away and leaned back on the couch.

"Shit!" D'Mann exclaimed. "That pussy got a nigga seein' stars and shit." He wiped beads of sweat away from his face. Desirae, feeling somewhat vulnerable and even more sore than she'd felt the first time they'd done it, sat back up on the couch. D'Mann looked at her. "You heard from that nigga yet to see if he gon' be droppin' them kids back over at your mama house tomorrow and shit?" he asked.

Desirae shook her head. "Naw," she said. "I checked my phone when you left, try'na see if he was gon' text me or not. I told you how that nigga can be though."

"Prolly ain't even thinkin' shit about you, is he?" he asked.

"Exactly," Desirae said. "I'mma just go home tomorrow and be there in case he drop James and Titan off. I do think that the weather is prolly gon' be bad tomorrow, so I guess I betta just play it safe and be there."

D'Mann nodded, saying that he understood completely.

Chapter 12

Around 1 o'clock that night, Desirae lay in bed next to D'Mann with her eyes closed. He snored heavily – the snore of a man who had just had a couple of orgasms. When Desirae lifted her head up and looked at his chest going up and down, she knew that he was knocked out cold.

"D'Mann?" she said, softly, trying to see if he would wake up. "D'Mann?" she said again.

There was absolutely no reaction from D'Mann, letting Desirae know that if she was even thinking of making a run for it, she'd better get up now. She had no plan for how she would get home, but getting out of D'Mann's house would work just fine at this point. What she'd seen down in the basement had really creeped her out.

"I'm goin' to the bathroom," Desirae said out loud, covering herself in case D'Mann just happened to wake up enough to hear her say something or make a move. She slipped out of bed, pressing the balls of her feet into the hardwood floor as softly as she could as she made her way to the door. She looked back into the bedroom. Even though the second floor of the house was rather dark, she could still see D'Mann's bulky body. His chest rose and fell as he was in a deep sleep.

Desirae hurried down the steps, using the banister as her guide in the dark. Once she'd gotten down to the bottom, now standing in the dining room, she looked back up the stairs. She could still hear D'Mann snoring, heavily and steadily. Quickly, she made her way around the dining room table and into the living room. She gently picked up D'Mann's keys off of an end table and walked over toward the door. She tried various keys, trying to see which one would open the door before she went as far as sliding into her clothes. Never had she felt so nervous and scared as she did right then. In fact, she almost felt twice as fearful as she had felt when she'd heard D'Mann shoot Makim down in the basement.

"Shit, shit, shit," Desirae said. She'd fumbled with three of the four keys within a matter of seconds, still not finding the right key to open the door. "Which one is it?" she whispered. "Which fuckin' key is it?"

Desirae tried a couple more keys before she heard D'Mann's feet hit the floor upstairs, as his bedroom was directly above the living room. Her heart jumped. There was just no telling what he might do if he came downstairs and found Desirae trying to get out of the house. Catching her like this would let him know that she really did see something down in the basement.

Moving quickly, Desirae quietly set the keys back down on the table, careful to not let them jingle. She could hear D'Mann's footsteps coming down the steps, causing her to think quickly. Determined that she could use being a female to her advantage, she grabbed her purse and headed toward the staircase. Just as she was approaching the bottom, D'Mann was coming down. He looked at her. "What you doin' down here?" he asked.

Desirae held up her purse as she forced herself to make a sleepy face. "Woman problems," she said, looking at her purse. "Excuse me, but I gotta handle this."

D'Mann relaxed. He nodded and headed back upstairs as Desirae followed behind him. She went into the bathroom where she pretended to be using her purse. She ran water and even flushed before going back out into the hallway and getting back into the bed with D'Mann. As she lay there, next to him in his strong arms, she struggled to get any sleep for the rest of the night. There was something about D'Mann that didn't sit well with her; she couldn't wait until he dropped her off back at her mother's house in the morning.

**

When D'Mann pulled up outside of Desirae's mother's house, a huge feeling of relief came over her. In a strange way, she'd felt like she survived the night. Now, while she didn't plan on going back over to D'Mann's place, based on what she'd seen in the basement, she would just have to come up with a way to get him to go away.

"A nigga had a nice night with you," D'Mann said.

Desirae looked across the consul and smiled. "Me too," she responded. "Fuck, I'm still sore."

D'Mann chuckled, knowing that he was the man. "Yeah," he said. "You not the first chick to tell me that. That's

184

why I go easy the first couple times. Down the road, I go even harder.

Desirae giggled as she began to open her door.

"Wait a second," D'Mann said, gripping Desirae's thigh. "Why you in a rush to get out the car on a nigga like that? Damn!"

Desirae leaned back into the SUV. "Oh," she said, trying to come across as if she didn't realize what she'd been doing. "I wasn't thinkin' like that. I ain't know if you had somewhere to be yet or what."

"Did you hear from that nigga yet?" D'Mann asked.

Desirae nodded. "Yeah," she answered. "He actually text me while we was sleepin'. He said that he was gon' be bringin' the twins back over around 1 o'clock or so." She glanced at the clock above the radio. "It's about noon now, so I was gon' go in there and get a little somethin' to eat before he show up."

"Somethin' to eat?" D'Mann asked. "Shit, if you wanted somethin' to eat, I coulda stopped and got you somethin' to eat. All you had to do was say so and a nigga coulda took you to get somethin'."

Desirae shook her head. "Naw," she said, "I don't really feel like eatin' out, actually. I just want somethin' simple that don't got a buncha extra shit in it. When Titan and James get back, I'mma prolly lay down and take a nap."

"Okay," D'Mann said, feeling like something was up with Desirae. "If you say so. I do got somethin' I wanna ask you, though. You feelin' a nigga anymore?"

"What you mean?" Desirae asked.

"I mean just what I said," D'Mann said, smiling. "I mean is you feelin' a nigga? Is you into me and stuff?"

Desirae shrugged, not knowing how she wanted to answer at this point because there was nothing she wanted to do more than to get out of the car and get into her mother's house where the world was safe. "I mean, we just kickin' it, ain't we?" she said. "What was you try'na be? We done moved kinda fast with this and ain't really got to know each other."

"There you go with this knowin' each other shit," D'Mann said, chuckling and shaking his head. "Look, I'm the

185

kinda nigga that prides himself in being what you see is what you get. But, okay then, I see how you bein'." He smiled, showing Desirae that he was being sarcastic. "I'mma let you go on and get back into the house and shit so you can get settled in before baby daddy come back around try'na start shit with you."

"Yeah," Desirae said, shaking her head. "I hope he ain't around long for today. Just come and drop my babies off and we good."

"Remember what I told you," D'Mann said. "Let me know if that nigga disrespect you even the littlest bit. I'll jump on that ass. Shit, with the way that nigga was lookin' at me yesterday, you woulda thought he was lookin' into the eyes of some crazy nigga or somethin'."

Desirae looked at D'Mann then thought about the rope she'd seen dangling in the room in the basement. Furthermore, the look on D'Mann's face when she'd run into him as she'd come upstairs let her know that he could very well be crazy. She kept her cool and told him that she was going to hit him up when she woke up from her nap later on. D'Mann went ahead and watched her get out of the car and grab her shopping bags out of the back. He'd offered to help Desirae, but she declined. Instead, his eyes following her plump ass as her belt looked as if it were about to pop from around her waist.

D'Mann watched Desirae walk up to her mother's porch then let herself into the house. Once she waved goodbye to him and disappeared into the house, D'Mann slowly pulled off. Something did not sit well with him. Ever since he'd gotten home last night from being on his way over to his buddy's house on Tibbs, something seemed to have changed with Desirae. It was as if she'd been warm when he left the house then cold when he returned. To make matters worse, D'Mann had a strange suspicion that Desirae had seen more than she was supposed to see when she went exploring down into the basement. He looked back at her mother's house in the rearview as he slowly rolled down the street. *Maybe I need to stay in the neighborhood for a little while*, he thought to himself. No matter how much he enjoyed smashing Desirae

186

twice last night, he still felt as if she was holding something back from him. And he wanted to find out what it was, and if she could be trusted as he had hoped.

When Desirae got into her mother's house and sat her shopping bags down on the floor behind the door, it was as if a heavy weight had been lifted off of her shoulder. In the silence of her mother's living room, she pushed the door closed then stepped over to the curtains covering the large picture window. Barely opening the curtains a couple of inches, she watched as D'Mann's SUV slowly rolled down the street. Even though she'd gotten out of his house safely, she still felt as if he knew something was up. Not only had his line of questioning when he'd discovered her coming up from the basement frightened her, she was also alarmed with how quickly he'd rushed downstairs in the middle of the night only minutes after she'd crawled out of the bed and made her way down to the living room. There was just something about D'Mann's actions that told Desirae he was suspicious of her. This made her hate herself even more because she knew she shouldn't have rushed home with some man she'd just met.

"How could I be so stupid?" Desirae asked herself as she headed toward the dining room. When she stepped into the kitchen, it was clear her mother had been in the house. She'd left a coffee cup and some empty tea packets sitting on the middle of the table. Desirae pulled a chair out and sat down, thinking about the current situation of her life.

Was I overreacting? Was whatever that was hanging from the ceiling really something I need to be worried about? C'mon, Desirae. You know somethin' is up with that nigga. Why else would there clearly be two places where blood had been cleaned up? Why else would there be some sort of rope thing hangin' down from the ceiling like that? On top of that, it was inside of a room that clearly isn't used for anything remotely social. The look on his face when he saw you comin' from downstairs…. The way he looked at you when he came downstairs last night. It was almost like he was watchin' you, maybe makin' you the next victim.

Desirae shuddered a little. She imagined the many true crime episodes she'd seen on television about various serial killers around the country. While it was rare that serial killers were anything other than white men, she didn't want to overlook any major signs and wind up being the victim of a serial killer that had yet to be discovered.

Desirae went upstairs and showered, changing her clothes. She felt refreshed to have taken a shower and wiped all of D'Mann's sweat off of her body. After sitting down in the dining room for a moment to get herself together, she heard her cell phone vibrating from inside of her purse. She dug it out and answered. It was Tron calling.

"Hello?" Desirae answered, calmly."

"Hello," Tron said, the radio playing in the background. "You home and shit. My mama bout to get back on the road and head back to Louisville. The weather is gonna get bad. I can already tell from the way these clouds is out here lookin' that it's gon' be bad as shit. If you don't mind, I can drop James and Titan off in about thirty minutes. Is that coo?"

"Yeah," Desirae said, her nerves finally calming down. "That's coo. I'll be here."

The two of them ended the phone call. Desirae stood up and looked at her face in the mirror. While some of the bruises and scratches were slowly fading away, there were still others that seemed a little more persistent. She'd been proud of herself for doing her makeup just right yesterday when Tron had brought his mother Brenda up to meet her.

Fifteen minutes passed with Desirae checking out of the front window every so-many seconds. Soon enough, Tron's SUV pulled into a parking spot outside. He made his way up to the door, carrying Titan and James. Desirae opened the door and helped Tron inside.

"Wassup?" Tron asked, stepping into the living room. "I ain't mean to rush you and stuff, but I got some business I gotta handle later on that gotta do with the club."

"No, you're fine," Desirae said, not really trying to start any sort of argument. "Did you feed them any of the baby food that I packed in the bag yesterday or what?"

"Yeah," Tron said, nodding his head. "Well, actually, my mama and auntie did. We actually went out and got some more last night at Target." He set the bag on the floor after setting Titan then James down into separate basinets. "They in there."

"Okay," Desirae said, very casually.

Tron noticed the change in Desirae's demeanor, as if she had a lot on her mind. He looked through the living room, squinting through the somewhat see-through curtains. When he'd pulled up into the parking spot out on the street, he didn't see any truck that looked like D'Mann's. He stepped back into the dining room and approached the table.

"Look, I know we've had some rocky shit over the last year, Desirae," Tron said, trying to come across as diplomatic as he could, "but I need to know if you fuckin' round with that nigga D'Mann."

Desirae looked at Tron and rolled her eyes. "And if I am?" she asked. "What is it to you if I am messin' around with him? Why do you care?"

Tron stepped closer to Desirae. His body language was telling her that she needed to listen, and that he wasn't really trying to start anything with her. Tron chose his words carefully. "Desirae," he said, "that ain't the kinda nigga you need to be messin' with. I'm tellin' you, Desirae."

"Why you say that, Tron?" Desirae asked, knowing that she needed to play her cards close to her chest, figuratively speaking. "Why you tellin' me that I don't need to mess around with him?"

"Desirae, look," Tron said, "I used to know that nigga back when I was out in the streets. Back before me and Tyrese had saved up our money and was even thinkin' bout try'na open the club. That nigga is nothin' but bad news, I promise you, Desirae. He is nothin' but bad news."

"Why?" Desirae asked, wanting to hear Tron out for once. "You gotta give me some reasons. Maybe he's changed. I mean, what make you say that he a bad dude?"

Tron looked up toward the ceiling. "Your mama ain't here, is she?" he asked.

Desirae shook her head. "Naw," she answered. "I got here like a hour or so ago, and she wasn't here when I got here. So, no, she ain't here."

"That nigga be killin' niggas," Tron said, sounding very concerned for Desirae. "I swear to God, that nigga be killin' niggas and gettin' away with the shit because everybody is too scared to come forward and say anythin' because he might kill them too."

Desirae heart jumped. She thought about what had happened down in the basement with Makim. Then, she thought about her own adventure down into the basement and what she'd found. "Killin' people?" she asked, wanting to know more. "What you talkin' about, Tron?"

Tron gently grabbed Desirae's arm to show his concern for the mother of his sons. "I know what you think or me, and yeah, I have fucked up some," he admitted, "but everybody in the hood, especially from back then, know that he be killin' niggas that he feel like either gon' tell on him or fuck with his money or business or whatever. I remember it was goin' around that D'Mann had killed three dudes. They ain't never been seen again. Don't nobody know what he doin' with the bodies. From what I remembered, he always lived in weird places where he ain't have a lot of company and shit. I'm tellin' you, Desirae, that nigga is a fuckin' killer."

Just as Desirae was opening her mouth to tell him about her experience spending the night with D'Mann, there was knock at that door. Tron looked back at the front door. "You expectin' company?" he asked, his voice low but rather loud because of how quiet the house was.

Desirae zoned out for a moment, hearing only the clock above the China cabinet. It ticked behind her, almost in the same rhythm as her heart. She shook her head. "Hell naw," she said. "I ain't expectin' no company. I don't know who that could be."

"Did you spend the night with that nigga last night when I saw him waitin' outside when I was here with my mama to get the twins?" Tron asked. "When he drop you off?"

"Like an hour ago," Desirae answered.

There was another knock at the door, this time harder than the first.

"How you even meet this nigga?" Tron asked.

"I met him out south," she said. "You don't think this is him do you? He dropped me off like a hour ago. Why would he even still be in the neighborhood?"

"I don't know," Tron said. "Maybe it ain't him." He turned and walked toward the door. "I can answer it for you just to be safe if you want me to. Just wait right there."

"No," Desirae said. "You don't even live here. What if it's one of my mama's neighbors or one of her friends or somethin'? She would be shitty as fuck if I let some nigga that don't even live here answer the door."

Tron stepped back into the dining room and stood over to the side as Desirae crossed the living room and opened the front door. As she pulled the door open, her eyes met with D'Mann. Deep down, she was startled, but she managed to be strong and not show it. Not even waiting to be invited in, D'Mann stepped inside.

"I ain't interuptin' nothin', am I?" D'Mann asked, looking around the living room. "I was still in the area, about to head back out my way, and thought that I'd just pop back by and make sure that you was coo."

Yet again, Desirae felt very vulnerable. D'Mann towered over her, dominating the room with his muscular physique. "Naw," she said. "Just gettin' my babies back."

"Hmm, hmm," D'Mann said, seeming to not believe what Desirae had said to him. "I see the nigga's car is still sittin' outside. He ain't in here givin' you no problems is he? Remember what I told you, right?"

"No," Desirae said, shaking her head. "We just in there talkin' bout the twins and stuff. That's all."

"Where he at? Why the nigga hidin' and shit? He scared or something?"

Before Desirae could open her mouth to respond to D'Mann's inquiry, Tron had stepped out from behind the dining room wall. "Why the fuck you askin'?" he asked, boldly.

D'Mann chuckled when he looked up at Tron. "Long time no see, huh?" he said. "I ain't think I would still see you here."

"My kids live here," Tron said. "So, yeah, you gon' see me here. There ain't no problem with that, is there?"

191

As D'Mann moved closer to the dining room entrance, Desirae feared what was about to happen. Just thinking about how D'Mann had shot Makim in the basement was enough to make her fear for the life of her sons' father. More than anything, she wished that she could go back in time and not have answered the door.

"And if there was a problem, what you gon' do about it?" D'Mann asked. "Long time no see. But I know you ain't forgot what you heard about me from back in the day."

"I ain't forgot," Tron said, shaking his head as he looked dead into D'Mann's eyes. "I remember real good how you was killin' niggas left and right and gettin' away with that shit."

D'Mann held his hands up and smiled. "Look, we all do stupid things when we young like that," he said. "Plus, if niggas don't fuck with me then we don't have no problem."

Tron nodded. "That's good to know," he said.

There was a long pause in the conversation where the two men simply looked at one another. Desirae tried to come up with something to say that would make D'Mann leave. D'Mann then looked back at her. "This chick is a sneaky little bitch, I will say that," he said. "I leave her at the house for five minutes and come back to find that she done been explorin' and shit."

Tron looked at Desirae, concerned over how angry D'Mann might be at her. "Yeah, well," he said. "She prolly won't be back over there at this point."

"Why?" D'Mann asked, reaching into his inside jacket pocket. "She think I might kill her or somethin'?"

As Desirae felt her heart race inside of her chest, she knew she had to jump out of the way. While D'Mann reached into his jacket pocket, Tron leapt across the room. The tension in the room had finally snapped. Within the blink of an eye, the two men were scuffling in the middle of her mother's living room floor. First, Tron was on top. He punched D'Mann in the head a few times before D'Mann was able to push him off of him and get a few licks in himself. The two men eventually got back on their feet and were deep into a full-blown fist fight. Desirae screamed, wanting more than anything to somehow get D'Mann's gun away from him.

Tron scuffled with D'Mann as hard as he could, but D'Mann's size was simply too much for him. Obviously growing tired, he pulled at D'Mann's jacket, causing it to partially come off of his body. When it did, D'Mann pushed Tron forward, sending him into a wall where crushed pictures lay on the floor below. Desirae heard a loud thump then what sounded like metal scooting across the floor as she watched the brawl from the other side of the living room.

"Get it, Desirae!" Tron yelled, trying to hold D'Mann as long as he could. "Get the gun, Desirae! Kill this nigga before he kill us!" He pointed at D'Mann's black handgun, lying on the floor. "Get that shit!"

D'Mann looked back, realizing that he was now vulnerable as the one piece of absolute power he'd come into the house with was on the floor. Just as he was about to reach for it, to save his own life, Tron had pulled him back and began to throw punches at him. In retaliation, D'Mann fought back, with his ultimate goal to get across the room to his gun before Desirae had a chance to grab it.

Desirae moved a couch out of the way and swiped the gun up off of the floor. D'Mann froze in his place as Desirae pointed the gun at him. "You ain't gon' kill me over this sorry ass nigga, is you?" he asked, breathing heavily. "Remember what you told me about his ass. C'mon, Desirae. Don't be stupid. Just give it to me and everything gon' be cool."

Desirae cocked the gun, purely going off of what she'd seen in the movies. "You be killin' people, don't you?" she said. "Nigga, don't lie to me. I saw the rope hanging from the ceiling in the basement in that one small room. The blood on the floor. You are a fuckin' serial killer or somethin'."

D'Mann chuckled, stepping closer to Desirae. "Look, you trippin'," he said, opening his eyes wide to let Desirae know that she didn't need to bring up the Makim thing. "I'm tellin' you, that ain't what you think it is. I took you shoppin' and shit and showed you some of the finer things in life, and here you go try'na side with some nigga that don't even want your ass."

"Then what is it?" Desirae asked. "Why you ain't want me to go down into the basement?"

"Bitch, you was even lucky to be up in my house for real though," D'Mann said. "I just wanted some pussy, not some nosey ass bitch with a busted up face that gon' take it upon herself to go lookin' around my shit and shit. Don't be stupid. You not gon' kill me. Look at the way that gun's shaking."

Desirae kept the gun pointed at D'Mann as she glanced at Tron. The look in Tron's eyes said it all. Just then, D'Mann lunged for her. Out of fear for her own life, and the life of her children, Desirae pulled the trigger. She fired the gun three times, all three bullets making impact with D'Mann's body. The first bullet went into his shoulder while the other two went into his chest.

Desirae shook uncontrollably, not believing that she'd just actually shot somebody. D'Mann stumbled forward slightly and lost his bodily functions. He looked down at his chest then up at Desirae. His eyes looked as if he were seeing the light and trying to turn around. A few seconds passed, then Desirae and Tron watched him collapse, falling into her mother's coffee table. Desirae and Tron breathed heavily as she lowered the gun and pointed it toward the floor. She had learned a valuable lesson with talking to D'Mann: everybody is not what they appear to be.

Afterward

Luckily for Desirae, the prosecutor neglected to file charges in the shooting death of D'Mann Sims. Part of the reason was because she was a young mother to two newborn babies. The other part of the reason benefited the prosecutor, as D'Mann had been under the watchful eye of the law for some time. The system was just looking for the right reason to get him – dead or alive. Desirae didn't care what the system did with her, however. She only cared about being alive for her children.

Desirae and Tron hugged one another after she shot D'Mann. Even in Tron's arms, after their ups and downs, she could feel the love he had for her. This love may not have been in a romantic sense; rather, it was in the way that any man would show love to the mother of his children. From that point on, because of this shared experience, the two were able to patch things up and have some sort of friendship, regardless of what may or may not have been going on with Reese.

A year later, Desirae wound up meeting a great guy who had just moved to Indianapolis from Chicago. At first, she was a little nervous. She didn't think that anyone worth having would want to marry a single mother with twin baby boys. However, this guy, John, proved Desirae wrong. After a year of dating, he put a ring on her finger and asked her to be his wife. At their wedding, which was small and personal, Desirae looked out at the small crowd of close family and friends and smiled. Now that she was a man's wife, she'd never have to be a side chick again.

The end of the Diary of a Side Chick Series! I hope you enjoyed the journey!

CPSIA information can be obtained
at www.ICGtesting.com
Printed in the USA
LVOW13s2008020317
525948LV00013B/1105/P